TWISTED MINDS

JODY VALLEY

Bella
BOOKS

2016

Bella Books, Inc.
P.O. Box 10543
Tallahassee, FL 32302

Printed in the United States of America on acid-free paper.

First Bella Books Edition 2016

Editor: Shelly Rafferty
Cover Designer: Kiaro Creative

ISBN: 978-1-59493-481-0

Other Bella Books by Jody Valley

A Venomous Cocktail

Dedication

To my wife, Elaine Thomason, my partner of 26 plus years and whom I had the honor and pleasure of marrying on March 22, 2014.

Acknowledgments

A special thanks to Ingham County Clerk, Barb Byrum, for having the courage to defy Michigan's Attorney General, by calling in her staff on a Saturday morning and issuing marriage licenses to gay couples before the AG could close it down. And to the Rev. Kathryn A. Bert, our Unitarian Universalist pastor, who showed up at the courthouse on that day and married us.

Acknowledgments in the birth of "Twisted Minds"

To the entire staff of Bella Books.

To my knowledgeable, supportive and patient editors: Shelly Rafferty, PhD and Jacalyn Eddy, PhD of Crossfield Writers.

To Elaine Thomason: beta reader, editing skills, for the title and cover design idea, as well as a patient wife.

To my entire family for understanding my all-to-often absence in family time.

To Penny Gardner, PhD, and Marilyn Bowen for their undying support.

To my daughter-in-law, Carrie Zay: a Wiccan/pagan resource.

To a local women's ritual circle whose practice is mostly Dianic Wiccan.

To Rachel Crandall, Executive Director, Transgender Michigan (Helpline: 855-345-TGMI)

About the Author

Jody Valley lives with her wife, Elaine, in Michigan. Together, they have four adult children and three wonderful granddaughters, Eowyn Zay, Ella and Layla Souza, as well as two dogs, Lucy and Daisy. In the past, Jody has worked as a feature writer and columnist, and has been a social activist since the eighties. As a clinical social worker, she has worked with people with PTSD. This is her second book, a sequel to *A Venomous Cocktail*. She is currently working on the third book in the Kera Van Brocklin series; its working title is *Overboard*.

Author's Note

The action depicted in Twisted Minds takes place in 2012, in the months leading up to the reelection of President Barack Obama. This is a work of fiction. Names, characters, businesses, places, events and incidents are either the products of the author's imagination or used in a fictitious manner. Any resemblance to actual persons (except for Yvonne LeFave of Go Green Trikes), living or dead, or actual events is purely coincidental.

Although I have worked to accurately describe the suffering of a former soldier with PTSD, Kera Van Brocklin's symptoms and treatment (and self-medication) are neither prescriptive nor representative of all who suffer from this traumatic illness. Learn more about PTSD at: http://ptsd.va.gov/public/PTSD-overview/reintegration/overview-mental-health-effects.asp

CHAPTER ONE

He opened the tailgate. With his leather-gloved hands he yanked the woman out, letting her limp body drop to the wet ground.

A sickly groan belched out of her.

The woman had been rolled up in a blanket, cocooned, and then jammed into the rear of his minivan. She had no better standing with him than the rest of the objects that he'd stashed in with her: a small suitcase, computer bag and shovel.

He'd brought with him only what he thought was needed, nothing more, as nonessentials might be accidently left behind, connecting him to his night's work. His plan was to keep it simple, thorough, swift.

The van had been rented under a false name. He'd worn a stick-on mustache, a pair of fake glasses, and had spoken in a deeper pitch. He planned to ditch his clothes and gear when the job was finished, then have the vehicle detailed before its return.

She wasn't dead yet, just drugged and boozed up. But leaving her out in this place with no medical intervention—along with the exposure from the cold spring night—would probably kill her.

But he'd better not chance it. Didn't matter, finishing her off was no problem for him.

It would've been better had he known of a good place to dispose of her somewhere in the Lansing environs. That way he could've quickly gotten rid of her body. But since he didn't know of a good spot, he waited until he got to the Lakeside City area—a familiar place where he knew the territory. The chances of anyone being around this particular place, especially at this time of night, were negligible.

It'd been frustrating. He didn't know his way around Lansing, never had been to the capital. It was his fault, he'd forgotten his damned GPS. Trying to get out of the city, he'd somehow ended up in East Lansing before he found his way back to the western side of the state. He'd driven carefully— he had used his blinkers, come to a standstill at stop signs, and driven several miles per hour under the speed limit, all the while trying not to get stopped for some random traffic violation. That's all he would have needed, to be pulled over by the cops, and for whatever reason they'd get curious and peer into the back of his van…

It would have been all over.

There was another reason to return to Lakeside City. No doubt the capital city of Michigan would have a better-equipped police department with more resources than the Lakeside City Police Department. He didn't expect to make any mistakes or leave evidence that would lead to him, but you never knew. Life didn't come with guarantees, so he had a backup plan, an arrow pointing to someone else, if the body were ever found.

Part of him, actually a big part, wanted her grave to be discovered.

He sat down on a tree stump by the elevated, two-tire track road that ran through the wetlands and put on his boots. Then he got up and grabbed the bottom of the blanket near his victim's legs and dragged her limp body into the marsh. The putrid smell of decay—winter's brew below the ice—floated up from the mostly thawed water. He brought up the bandana around his neck to cover his nose. Thin clouds allowed for a dim light to filter through from the stars, just enough for him to make out the surroundings.

She gave out another groan as the freezing water iced its way into her consciousness and awakened any remaining awareness. The shallow water, five inches, maybe six, splashed into his unfastened boots and up onto his pant legs, sending shivers through him. He'd decided to leave his coat—a favorite hunting jacket—in the vehicle. He didn't want it to get dirty.

Irritated, he dragged her cumbersome, drugged body awkwardly through the mucky water. Scraggly stumps, fallen tree branches, and sharp stick-like plants poked up from the earth and snagged the blanket, hindering his progress, delaying her fate. His back let him know she was no lightweight. Hell, she'd be heavy even if she were cooperating. He stopped, dropped her, placed his hands on the lower part of his spine and arched backward in an attempt to ease the pain. Feeling some relief, he reached down and picked up the blanket that shrouded her.

"Fuck!" The saturated blanket released icy water onto his shirt and pants, soaking him. He wondered why he hadn't thought to wear waterproof clothing but then remembered he hadn't planned on this place for the burial.

From where he stood, he estimated how much further he'd need to go. Her grave had to be out of sight. In time, Mother Nature would rehab the ground and cover his tracks.

He found a suitable site, dropped her, then grabbed the ends of the blanket, unrolled her naked body until it spilled out and splashed into the frigid water of the wetlands.

Her groggy eyes stared up at him.

Reflecting what?

Not anger. She didn't appear angry.

Not distress. Her face didn't register any anguish, as far as he could tell.

More like numb, vacant…

Whatever. He wouldn't dwell on it.

He took out his jackknife, opened it up, then bent over her and carved a design into each breast and one on her belly. He stepped back, assessed his handiwork, and then carefully folded in the bloody blade and stuck it into his pocket.

He wondered why she hadn't seemed to squirm when he'd carved his designs into her—he thought of them as tattoos. Maybe the drugs and icy water had numbed her, kept her from feeling pain, along with his razor-edged blade he'd spent hours sharpening. He wanted his carved symbols to be clear and identifiable. They were a crucial piece for the backup plan, the insurance policy he would be happy to cash in on.

An opportunity.

Two birds; one plan.

A win-win for him.

He flipped her onto her stomach, pushed his knee down on her upper back, then held her face down into the sludge. He felt a minor, lethargic push back, gurgling, then stillness…

Life left quickly.

Easy come, easy go.

Initially he'd intended to dig her a grave. However, here in the wetlands, no shovel work would be required. He snapped off branches and arranged them over her body, then scooped up winter's rot for the covering, blending her grave into the earth.

From muck to muck. He snickered.

He stood back, pleased with his work. Using the obscurity of the wetlands to do the burying worked well. And it wasn't like hikers would be trekking through here at this time of year. Even if someone came by this remote area, the body shouldn't be noticeable, given his rubble camouflage. Of course, spring weather might move shit around and expose the carcass. But surely hungry critters would feast on her and leave only remnants that would sink out of sight well before there'd ever be a full-out search. His imagination rolled on. If there were a hunt, they'd bring in dogs, volunteers, possibly even helicopters. He pictured himself watching the entire spectacle on TV. Undoubtedly the manhunt would be televised…

The event would call for some beer and popcorn.

His stomach growled, but dinner would have to wait, like maybe fifty or so miles from this place. He gathered up the water-soaked covering and made his way back to the van. The blanket would be tossed in some faraway Dumpster along with what he was wearing. A change of clothes couldn't come too soon; he was soaked and freezing from the penetrating night air.

He scanned the backseat of his car to make sure he'd brought his duffel bag. He had. Then he remembered Stacey's computer and suitcase in the back of the vehicle. By taking them, his plan was to make it appear as if she'd taken off somewhere, a last-minute kind of decision. Come to think of it, why not dump the bags right here? After he retrieved them, he slushed back to where she lay under the debris. For sure the heavier computer bag would slip down into the mud. Just to be certain the suitcase would follow, he found a few rocks to weigh it down. When he opened the case he spotted the purse he'd tossed in earlier, and then removed any sources of identification. The police would have to work harder to ascertain who she was, and making more work for the cops appealed to him. He cracked a grin.

On the ground, he found a spindly tree branch and dragged it along from the water's edge to the door of his car, erasing his footprints.

He searched his pockets for his package of cigarettes, plucked one out with his lips, lit it, and sucked the nicotine into his lungs.

Satisfied, he headed for dinner.

CHAPTER TWO

Kera grabbed the remote and clicked off the TV. She wondered why she'd even turned it on. It was only March and she was already subjected to the crazy, no, nasty political ads that came with elections. She guessed the Republicans' ability to spawn such bad candidates couldn't hurt. It'd give Obama a better chance to win a second term, but to listen, once again, to conservatives use the gay community as bait was beyond aggravating.

She pushed a hairbrush through her thick, short hair, and then cased her cue stick. The jingle of keys, as she slipped them off the hook and opened the heavy, creaky wooden door, drew four large canine paws with nails that clicked against the metal staircase as the German/Rottweiler mix flew down and came to a halt at the door.

"Well, sounds like you were up in the lighthouse tower. Hoping to see ships come in?"

When she opened the door, the dog bounded out, took a quick pee, then came back, slurped Kera's hand and stood next to her, ready. Kera scratched the dog behind her pointy, flapped-down ears inherited from the Rottweiler lineage, otherwise, she favored the German shepherd side of her roots.

"How about we go shoot some pool tonight? Vinny will be waiting for us."

It was a cool spring evening and a chilly breeze blew off Lake Michigan. The lighthouse's residence offered her a first shot at penetrating cold winds. This year's past winter had been mild, and, except for this cool evening, spring had shown up early.

The residential quarters of the old—now automated—lighthouse suited her fine, actually better than fine. It was peaceful and as close to perfect as it could get. The red brick house had a great view of the Turtle River as it tumbled into the harbor of Lake Michigan. The place offered her an ideal refuge, even though Deidre, Kera's identical twin sister, thought she'd become a hermit and called it a *hideout*.

Kera knew that Dee, the name most people called Deidre, understood Kera's need for retreat, as much as anyone could who hadn't personally experienced combat in the Iraq war. But Dee didn't understand the intensity of her need for a getaway. Outside the safety zone of her sanctuary, the noise, bright lights, and people flitting from one place to another unnerved her. Kera obsessed about most everyone in her environment, where they were going and their motivations, and who, she frequently wondered, might be concealing a bomb. Commotion made her nervous, edgy, ready to pounce. Like a stalker, the nightmare of Iraq had followed her back to the States.

Kera whistled to Lakota to get in her Jeep—ragtop down—on their way to town.

* * *

The Out-and-About was a gay bar, the place where Kera had spent the majority of her time since coming home from Iraq almost three years ago. It was her second home and the only public place where her vigilance could stand down. The stone castle-like bar served up most of her lunches and dinners, as well as providing a place to be with her friends, hone her pool skills, and meet with her clients.

"Hey Ker, thought you two might not make it tonight." Vinny Belsito sauntered over and held his arms open to the tail-wagging dog who jumped up and gave him a wet slurp.

Vinny had trained Lakota to be Kera's service dog to help her deal with her post-traumatic stress disorder. Without Lakota, Kera's quality of life wouldn't be worth shit. Trained to check out Kera's environment, the dog lessened her hyper-vigilant, knee-jerk reaction to life. Running her fingers through Lakota's fur had a calming effect on her.

Kera set her cue case on a chair next to the pool table. "I wouldn't miss our Thursday night pool tournament, Vinny. Hell, it's one of the highlights of my week, and it's one of the few events you're on time for."

"I function mostly on gay time, Ker, you know that."

"Yup," Kera laughed, "but I can count on you being here in a timely fashion for pool night."

"Sometimes, not showing up is a good thing, at least for some people." Vinny winked.

"True enough." Kera winced. Last week her game had been a disaster—she'd missed easy shots. She thought it might have to do with the fact that she'd put too much time in at work and didn't get enough alone time. But to be honest, her bad game was a result of a lack of concentration, brought about by that night's imprudent mix—and amount—of alcohol and weed. When she was on a job, she used marijuana judiciously, just enough to keep functioning. Her weed usage was something she didn't bring up to her therapist, who thought she took prescription meds. Kera preferred home remedies, like Lakota, Bell's Ale and marijuana to prevent or diminish the nightmares, flashbacks, and panic attacks that snuck up on her and threatened to take her out of commission, and embarrass her.

"Shit, I was about ready to feed you to the fish last week," Vinny said scornfully, while he pretended to box Lakota's ears as she bounced against his chest with her front paws.

Vinny, a burly guy with tattoos plastered up one arm and down the other, had taken in Lakota as a stray. In the past he'd learned dog training under the tutelage of a well-known dog trainer.

Kera was surprised to see the manager behind the bar. "Hey Marcy," she called, "Isn't Ally working tonight?"

"Ally couldn't make it in. Not sure why." Marcy was dressed as a peasant—the entire staff dressed in medieval period garb of one sort or another.

"Okay, just wondering if she's all right." Kera opened her cue case.

"Couldn't say, Kera. Darin took the call, but he would've told me if there was anything major." Marcy went back to her mug-filling task.

"I know I'm overly superstitious, but I like Ally at the bar when we're competing." Vinny combed back his hair to get it out of his eyes. "Remember last week when we lost our second game? She'd taken the night off."

Ever since Vinny had let his hair grow longer, halfway down to his shoulders, Kera had had an urge to grab a pair of scissors and chop it off. When she talked to people, it was important for her to see their eyes, even with people she knew and trusted. She didn't think it was as big a deal to her before Iraq, but it was now. Anyway, she couldn't figure out why he'd want to cover his face. He was a handsome guy, in a rugged sort of way.

Her thoughts returned to Ally. Kera had run into her just that morning, at the coffee shop, where Ally had mentioned that she'd see her tonight.

"By the way," Vinny said, breaking her train of thought, "On my trip to the Detroit Gun and Knife Show I picked up a few pieces that might be of interest to you. You said you were looking."

"I'm always looking, Vinny, but I'm broke right now, though I suppose I could come and window-shop. In fact, I'll be getting paid next week for my last job." She made a mental note to stop over at Vinny's Gun and Knife Shop some morning on her way in to town.

Since she had earned her Private Investigator's license last year, Kera had been pretty busy—busier than she wanted to be, and with crazy shit. Her latest weird case could have cost her license. She'd filed it away as the case of the purloined feline. She'd driven to Detroit to try and convince her client's sister to give back the cat she'd taken. Kera's retrieval had been successful, but dealing with the crazy cat burglar had been an over-the-top life experience. The thieving sister claimed the animal was hers—not because it'd been abused, but because God told her to take the cat when she'd been visiting Kera's client. It wasn't like Kera could have proven to the local cops that the cat snatcher didn't own the mouser—nor did she think they'd care or get involved. So she had climbed in a window and repossessed the kidnapped tabby after the woman left the house. She'd located the cat in a bedroom designed for a newborn, decked out in baby clothes, as it snoozed in a crib under a musical mobile of dancing mice. On her way back home she ruminated over how life had taken her from the war in Iraq, searching for bombs and bad guys, to breaking into a house for a damned cat dressed like a baby. She'd derived a modicum of comfort from the knowledge that there weren't any of her fellow soldiers around to witness her two-bit escapade.

"Hey, Ker, I see you ditched the old-folks car in favor of your hot dyke wheels tonight." Vinny's eyes teased.

"Yup, couldn't be seen in that, not here." Kera laughed. Until she had gotten her Jeep, she'd only owned a 2006 silver-gray Buick Le Sabre she'd inherited from her father. She kept it because of its usefulness for surveillance; it was comfortable and nondescript. But she wanted a vehicle for her personal use, for off-the-road fun, something cool. She had promised herself she would wait until she had the money to buy it. But the problem was, she wasn't good at delaying gratification, not anymore. Actually, she'd never been good at it, but she was even worse now. With PTSD came *impulsivity*, though she liked to refer to it as *spontaneity*—a perk for dealing with an otherwise miserable condition. In other words, she got stuff—like her Jeep—faster than more mentally stable and financially responsible folks.

"Did you get those hot wheels from the dealership here, or in Grand Rapids?"

"Here. I wasn't shopping for one; I just happened on it." Her downfall had occurred when she had driven past the Jeep dealership. She should never have gone by there, never have glanced in the showroom window where the vehicle of her dreams perched on a raised platform, rotating slowly, dancing light bouncing off her shiny curves—an irresistible temptress, a Jeep Wrangler Rubicon, dressed in mouth-watering black forest green. That baby was sweet, that baby had to be hers, and now it was—and so was the bill.

No medicine for impulsive—spontaneous—shopping.

She heard a familiar voice behind her. "I thought I'd find you here."

Kera twisted around to catch Mandy as she came in the door. She was gorgeous, with long blond hair, luscious green eyes, and a confident stride.

Mandy, a lawyer who worked at Lakeside City Legal Aid, was also Kera's friend and girlfriend. Overall, the girlfriend part worked a bit like oil and vinegar, Kera thought, not easily blended. Though so much was good and worked for them, they had different ideas about how they wanted to be together, or, more accurately, how they could be together. Mandy craved the live-together, formal commitment with rings and a ceremony, but Kera couldn't handle that sort of an arrangement. More than anything, she wished she could handle, as Mandy put it, "a real relationship." She loved the woman but couldn't picture it, couldn't go there, couldn't be the other half of a normal everyday couple, plan a future, play house. If she'd ever had the emotional skills for all that, she'd lost them somewhere in Iraq.

Mandy put her purse on the bar, then directed her attention, momentarily, to Lakota. "Hi there, sweet pooch." She bent over and rubbed the dog's ears. Though Lakota only interacted with people with Kera's permission, Vinny and Mandy were the exceptions.

"What brings you here tonight? I'm pretty certain it's not to play pool." Kera grinned and kissed Mandy's cheek.

"No, you're right. I thought I'd bring this over to you. You left it at my place Tuesday night. I ran out to give it to you, but you'd already rounded the bend." Mandy handed her the small black notebook where Kera kept her case notes.

Vinny's eyebrows arched. Kera had told him last week she'd been trying to stay away from the intimate side of her relationship with Mandy, stick to the friendship and working ends of their connection—private investigative work for Mandy's legal practice. Kera felt guilty about her inability to give Mandy all she wanted, and needed, in a partner. She didn't want Mandy to feel like a booty-call girlfriend—not that they didn't do other things together, they did. But Kera decided she should step back a bit, give Mandy a chance to find someone else who could give her more. She didn't really want that; it would kill her, which was probably why she wasn't being successful.

Mandy's voice interrupted her thoughts. "I need to go, honey. I have a meeting tonight with LEAP over at the Pink Door. I don't think I told you we're reorganizing and ready to get active again. I can't believe what a funk our community has been in ever since losing the battle over the inclusion of LGBT people in the city's civil rights ordinance. But there is good news." A smile broke out on her face. "We've made the decision to give it another go. Can you believe it, Kera, it's been three years since we were rejected by this city?" Mandy picked up her purse and blew Kera a kiss. "I love you, sweetheart."

"Love you too." Kera believed Mandy was at her best when she fought for something, whether for her clients at Legal Aid or for the LGBT community. She was a fighter and Kera loved her spunk. But she worried about Mandy, once more putting her neck out there, especially when it came to fighting for gay rights, given what had happened the last time she'd been involved with LEAP. Kera cringed.

Vinny rolled his eyes. "At Mandy's Tuesday night, huh? I get the impression you're losing ground on the stay-away-from-girlfriend front." He hailed the bartender and ordered a Bud draft. "And bring a Bell's Ale for my fickle partner," he added.

"Shut up, Vinny." Kera poked him in the chest with the end of her cue stick. "I'm doing my best…but a girl needs comfort and has needs."

Vinny tilted his head with a you're-so-full-of-shit expression. "*Needs* is it?"

"Yeah, Vinny, like that's a concept you're not familiar with, like you don't—"

"Okay, okay," Vinny held up his hands, "but I don't make any sweeping declarations about giving it up, or declaring my love to anyone. You, on the other hand, have."

"I only made a declaration to *try*. *Try* does not predict success!"

"I'll say not." Vinny took a swig of his beer and wiped his mouth on his sleeve. "Enough of this. Let's knock around a few balls before everyone shows up for the tournament."

Relieved that Vinny was done making fun of her and knowing she had no real defense, Kera grabbed her cue stick and followed Vinny to a pool table. "I can tell it's going to be my night to run the table."

Halfway through the tournament, Kera's smartphone chirped. The text message was from Ally, the bartender who'd not shown up.

Need you to stop by my place after tournament. Important!

* * *

Kera knocked on Ally's door. It was late and she was tired and didn't really want to be anywhere but home in bed, but she knew Ally wouldn't throw out the word "important" carelessly.

Ally, in gray sweats that were a bit snug for her padded hips and thighs and a white T-shirt with a big green frog on it, opened the door. Her chestnut brown hair was spiked up, like the bony plates on the back of a stegosaurus. "Come on in."

"Sorry I'm so late. The tournament went on longer than usual." Lakota trotted in first, then Kera stepped into the hallway.

"Hey, thanks for coming over tonight. I didn't mean to interfere with your pool night activities. I wouldn't have contacted you but—"

"No problem. What's up?" Kera smelled an aroma of some sort, and then saw a stream of smoke curling up from an incense burner on top of a bookcase.

"Have you heard of Erin Duffy?" Ally pushed her dark-rimmed glasses up to the bridge of her nose.

"No, can't say as I have."

"She's an old friend of mine, lives out in the country with her partner, Stacey Hendriks. They're not out or involved in the gay community, mostly because Erin's a schoolteacher—a damned good one too, got several teacher-of-the-year awards. She teaches English and literature at the high school and coaches girls' basketball...oh yeah, and the girls' soccer team in the spring, and softball in the summer."

"Yeah, now that you mention it, I've heard her name, but never met her." Kera understood not being out in a town with only eleven traffic lights, and known for its conservative, Dutch Reformed roots and attitudes. Lakeside City wasn't a town to value a lesbian teacher and coach, even if Erin were the best teacher this side of Lake Michigan, a winning coach, and able to leap tall buildings in a single bound.

"Erin's upset because Stacey didn't come home Tuesday night," Ally continued. "According to Erin, Stacey said she'd be home sometime in the evening but never showed." Ally motioned with her hand. "Come on, I'll let Erin tell you about it. She's been with me all evening. In fact, that's why I didn't come in to work tonight...she's one hot mess."

Kera had never been in Ally's apartment and was immediately struck by the Halloween color scheme. The stone gray walls provided a backdrop for predominantly black furnishings and accessories in splashes of dark gray and orange. A circle of glow-in-the-dark stars tumbled from a mobile in the corner. The furniture screamed "handed down"—several times. Not surprising, Kera thought, Ally was a college student and part-time bartender.

In the living room, Erin sat in an upholstered chair, bent forward with her head hung down, wringing her hands.

"Erin, this is the woman I told you about, Kera Van Brocklin."

Erin stood up, teary-eyed and sniffling, and extended her hand to Kera. The woman wasn't exactly pretty. All her features came together in a nice way, and she might best have been described as handsome. Kera judged her to be close to her own height, maybe a little shorter, around five foot nine. She was big-boned, sturdy.

Erin jerked her head back when she caught a glimpse of Lakota standing beside Kera.

"Don't worry, my dog won't hurt you." Kera motioned Lakota to move back and sit down. The dog could certainly intimidate. In some situations, Kera valued Lakota's ability to threaten, but in cases like this, it hindered her ability to connect with a client.

Erin's hunched shoulders visibly sank with the dog's retreat.

"Ally tells me you're concerned about your partner. You don't know where she is. Is that right?"

Erin sat down and resumed her hand-wringing. "When Stacey was gone for over twenty-four hours, I called the police and talked to an officer. He asked who Stacey was to me, you know, my relationship to her. I wasn't sure what I should say." She shrugged. "I didn't know how he'd respond to a lesbian couple, so I told him she was my roommate. That's when he made it clear to me he wasn't going do anything. He said that most missing person cases tend to solve themselves, like the person shows up sooner or later, and that I should check back in a week or two if Stacey hadn't returned." Erin rolled her teary blue eyes. "Can you imagine that? How long does a person have to go missing before the police care? Twenty-four hours is a long time in my book."

Kera hated to defend the cops, but in all fairness, Erin had told the officer that Stacey was a roommate, not her partner. Kera could appreciate the difference between a wife or partner versus a roommate, as far as the time appropriateness of a missing person report. Roommates didn't have the same responsibility to check in with each other, like people in committed relationships did. But she also understood Erin's fear of letting the cops know about her real relationship with Stacey.

Kera dragged a footstool over to Erin and sat down. "So where had she gone, and when did you expect her home?"

"She was out of town. Stacey travels around the state, teaching new software programs to people, like in businesses, hospitals, places like that. On Monday and Tuesday she had a two-day class at a hospital in Lansing—she works in Lansing a lot. When I talked to her Monday night, she told me she'd be home probably around eight, Tuesday night. Her arrival would depend on whether or not she had a dinner meeting with her boss. But she never showed up, didn't call, didn't answer my calls, and didn't respond to my texts. Nothing. It doesn't make sense." Erin rubbed her forehead, then ran her hand back over her rusty red hair that was drawn back and fell down behind her in a single long braid.

"How long have you two been together?"

Erin pondered the question. "It's hard to say, exactly." She glanced over at Ally as though she could help her, then rolled her eyes up like she was searching for the answer on the ceiling. "Let just say that we've known each other for ten, twelve years or so, but we've been in relationship, together…uh, exclusively, I'd say about three years or so. We've never had a ceremony, so it's hard to pin a date on it."

"Has Stacey ever done anything like this before, not shown up when she says she will?"

"Oh no, she's very dependable. That's what scares me. I know if she had to change her plans, she'd have let me know. I'm sure of it." Erin's head sank again.

"Kera, would you have time to help her find out what happened to Stacey?" Ally asked.

"Sure, if that's what you want, Erin?"

Erin raised her head and nodded.

"Okay, then, I'll check into it for you but I'll need a picture of Stacey, and I have some more questions." She took out her pocket notebook. "And you'll need to be open and honest with me about your relationship if I'm going to be able to help you."

"I will. I'll do whatever it takes to find Stacey."

CHAPTER THREE

Kera drove along the gently rolling hills lined with fruit trees, headed for Lansing. The temperature was already warm and promised to reach the seventies today, way too early in the year to be this warm, and not good for the fruit crops that lined the western side of the state, especially if a frost happened to be in their future. Still, Kera found it hard not to enjoy the trees that had already sprouted buds, about to blossom, and would soon be in full bloom, carpeting the landscape, flowering from white to all shades of pinks and purples, like the brilliant colors in a children's Disney movie. She made a mental note for her and Mandy to take their annual ride early. Now they'd have the advantage of the open Jeep to fully take in the aromas of spring. They usually stopped and had lunch at one of the local wineries. This year she thought she'd surprise Mandy with one they'd never been to before but had heard good things about.

From the conversation she'd had with Erin, she had learned that Stacey always stayed just outside of town at the Starlight Motel—a mom-and-pop operation with a blond brick, one-story structure built in the forties. As she approached the outskirts of Lansing, Kera slowed down and watched for the motel. Even so, she missed the sign and had to turn back. She pulled into the circle drive and stopped in front of the motel office, jumped out and signaled to Lakota to stay in the Jeep. A quick glance revealed that Stacey's vehicle wasn't there; in fact there were no Hondas—or any other black cars, for that matter—in the parking lot.

Kera entered the office and tapped a bell on the counter. A door opened and a short, gray-haired woman, who appeared to be in her late sixties, ambled in. With her rounded body and wire-rimmed glasses, she could have passed for Santa Claus's wife, but according to her nametag, she was Millie Mason.

"How can I help you?" Before Kera could answer, Millie glimpsed out the window where Lakota had her head sticking out of the vehicle. "You're in luck. We take animals here. My, oh my, what a handsome dog."

Kera showed the woman her investigator's license. "I'm not here to get a room, Mrs. Mason, but I'll keep you folks in mind if I'm in the area and need a place."

"Just call me Millie. Everybody does." Her eyes skimmed Kera's license. "Oh dear, what can I do for you, officer?"

"I'm not a police officer, I'm a private investigator." People often mistook Kera as a cop when she showed her license. Sometimes, when it was to her advantage to have a person think she was someone with authority, she let it slide. "I want to ask you about a woman who stayed here this last week. It would have been Sunday and Monday nights. I believe you know her? Stacey Hendriks."

"Oh, of course I know Stacey. She stays with us whenever she's in town on business."

Kera took out the picture of Erin and Stacey on a beach, arm in arm, smiling into the camera, taken last summer. She held up the photo for Millie to consider, just to be sure she and Millie were talking about the same Stacey. "She's on the right, the bigger, dark-haired woman."

"Oh yes, that's Stacey, all right. Oh dear, she's not in any trouble, is she? She's such a nice girl. We enjoy having her here. It would be hard for me to believe that she'd committed—"

"No, no, that's not why I'm here. Her partner is worried about her. Stacey was due back home last Tuesday night. But she never showed up."

"Her partner?" Millie's brow furrowed.

"Ah, well, the woman she lives with." Kera wondered if she'd just outed Stacey. Apparently Millie didn't know much about Stacey's personal life. Kera didn't want to be the one to educate her—not in her job description. Luckily, Millie wasn't stuck on it and moved on.

"Oh, let me check in here." Millie began leafing through a large ledger that looked like it could have been from a Charles Dickens novel. Millie ran her finger down the page, studying her entries. "I know Stacey was here, not sure when she came though. I was up visiting my brother and his wife in Traverse City, so my husband signed her in. Oh, here it is." Millie's finger rested on a name in the book. "Yes, you're right, she checked in Sunday night." She slid her hand horizontally along the page. "She stayed with us two nights. So that means she left sometime on Tuesday."

"Do you, or would your husband, have any idea what time she might have left on Tuesday?" Kera tried to follow the line across, upside down. She couldn't determine if there was an entry for the checkout time.

"You know, I don't have any idea. Hmm, there isn't any time recorded here for when she left. And I doubt if Gerald would know either. Anyone who's staying with us pays the night before so Gerald can have coffee with friends in the morning." Millie smiled kindly. "You know how McDonald's attracts retired men in the mornings. They all sit around and chew the fat." She shook her head. "No matter where you go or what McDonald's you're at, you see it. I guess it's good for the men and for their wives—it gets them out of our hair. That's my Gerald, over there." Millie pointed to an eight-by-ten inch picture of a bald-headed man with a great smile on a shelf behind the counter, then resumed her search. "Let's see, on Tuesdays Gerald has his afternoon bowling league. When he leaves he puts up a sign saying when he'll be returning. Like I said, there are so few people this time of year. And with Stacey, we really don't care—she doesn't have to worry about what time she goes. She was a friend of our daughter, you know. They went to college together. We tell her she can pretty much leave whenever she wants. I do know she often goes out to dinner after work, then comes back, packs up and leaves." Millie glanced over to a calendar with a picture of basset hounds that hung on the wall by the counter. "Oh my, this is Friday. Stacey's been missing since when?"

"She was due home on Tuesday night. I'm trying to find out where she might have gone after she left here."

"Oh dear, I hope she's okay." Millie put her hand over her mouth. "She's such a nice young woman, very sweet and—"

"While you have that ledger open, do you happen to have Stacey's license plate number and the year of her car? I know she drives a—"

"Yes indeed, we keep that information on all our guests… here it is." Millie moved the book around for Kera to see.

Kera jotted down the info. "Do you suppose I could take a peek at the room she occupied? I don't know if it'd help, but—"

"Certainly, I'll show you where she stayed. It's the room she always gets—if we have it available. It's farthest from the office. I'm sorry but it might not be cleaned up yet. Like I said, this time of year we don't get that many people, so our maid only comes on Fridays. She might not have gotten to it yet."

"Actually, it's better for me if the room hasn't been disturbed." Kera walked with Millie to a room at the end of the building.

The maid's cart was in front of Stacey's room. She'd hauled out dirty sheets and a small, clear plastic bag of trash.

"Marion," Millie called out, "could you excuse us a minute, maybe work on another unit for a while?"

The woman nodded and pushed her cart to the adjacent room.

"Here, come on in and feel free to poke through it. I need to get back to the office. I'm expecting a call. If I can help out in any way, let me know."

"Before you go, do you know whether anyone ever visited Stacey here at her room?"

Millie seemed to search her memory. "Yes, now that you mention it, there was a woman who came now and then. Stacey told me she was someone she worked with, but other than that, no, she pretty much kept to herself, as far as I know. But my husband and I are in and out so much that we—"

"Could you describe that woman?"

"I'm sorry. I see so many people coming and going in this business, and I have to say, I'm not good at remembering people. Neither is my husband, but I'll be sure to ask him."

"Thanks, Millie, I'd appreciate it."

Kera questioned the maid about Stacey but got nowhere. When she asked her for the trash bag she'd taken from the room, Marion hesitantly handed it over. Kera searched through it but found nothing of importance. The maid had already made up the bed and dusted, leaving no signs of habitation except for bits of paper and dirt on the carpet. A vacuum cleaner stood by, plugged in, but it obviously hadn't been used yet.

In the bathroom, Kera smelled the strong odor of a cleaning agent. She pushed back the shower curtain and found bottles of shampoo and conditioner on the back edge of the tub. These were not the little bottles motels usually provided, but bigger, more expensive stuff. Regardless of the strong cleaning odor, the maid must have done a quick job in here—a lick and a promise, as her mother would have said—otherwise, she'd have found those containers. Kera picked up the bottles. Underneath the bed, she found a pair of blue Crocs—out of casual cleaning reach. She checked the nightstands but saw only the standard Gideon Bible, and the dresser drawers were all empty. The closet contained a pair of pants and a blouse but otherwise, she found nothing. Kera stuffed the pants and blouse, Crocs and hair products into a plastic laundry bag meant for customer use and then something shiny, poking out from under the bed, caught her eye. It was a silver earring with three concentric hoops that spun when the earring moved, catching and tossing light. She dropped to her knees and hunted under the bed for the other earring, but found only a comb, food wrappers, and used tissues. She tossed the comb and earring into the plastic bag with the rest of her haul.

"Find anything?" Millie Mason stood at the door.

"Yes, I have." Kera opened the bag and showed Millie what she'd retrieved. "Would you mind if I take these back with me to Lakeside City to see if they're Stacey's? I can check them out with her, uh, roommate."

"Well, I'm sure they're hers, so it will save me having to package them and a trip to the post office. But that's not like Stacey to leave behind her belongings, not like her at all. She always leaves a clean, neat room. She certainly must have been in a hurry, that's all I can say." Millie shook her head.

* * *

Earlier, Kera had tried to call Linda Blanchard, Stacey's boss. She'd already left two messages on her voice mail but hadn't received a response, so she decided to try to catch the woman at her workplace. Erin had given her the address, so she punched it into her GPS.

She drove up to the office, located in a one-story brick building with a flat roof, situated near the Ninety-six Bypass and Pennsylvania Ave. She located a shady place to park so she could leave Lakota in the Jeep. When the office secretary greeted her, she flashed her PI license at him, insisting that it was urgent that she speak to Ms. Blanchard.

Stacey's boss appeared to be in her late forties, an African-American who was what advertisers of bras tended to refer to as full-figured. She was neatly turned out, dressed in a green business suit and matching heels, with tightly pulled-back hair, and she projected an air of being overworked and under-appreciated. Her desk was peppered with pictures of kids at various stages of growth, and a portrait of her and, presumably, her husband and kids.

"Have a seat." The woman gestured to one of two straight-back chairs across from her desk. "What can I do for you?"

"Thanks for seeing me, Ms. Blanchard—"

"Please just call me Linda." Her face softened as she sat down in her chair and took in a deep breath. "So what do you need, officer? I'm sorry, I didn't get your name."

"My name is Kera Van Brocklin and I'm a private investigator." Kera opened her wallet and showed her license.

"Oh, okay. What can I help you with?"

"It's about your employee, Stacey Hendriks. She was due to get home Tuesday night after work but she never showed up. Do you have any idea where she might have gone or where she might be now?"

Linda's brow wrinkled. "I have no idea. She had the rest of the week off. I mean, she had lots of paperwork to get in, but generally she does that at home. She didn't have more software workshops until..." Linda turned to her computer, clicked on a page, and scrolled down until she found what she was hunting for. "Next Tuesday. She'll be doing a three-day seminar in Detroit, Tuesday through Thursday."

"When was the last time you saw or talked to Stacey?"

"Hmm..." Linda rolled her eyes up to the right and pinched her lips together. "Let's see, I talked to her around noon, last Tuesday," she said. "We'd spoken earlier in the week about possibly having a dinner meeting before she left for home. But sometime in the morning, Stacey said that an old friend had shown up unexpectedly...I think it was a person she'd not seen for a long time. Anyway, she asked if she could beg off our meeting. It was okay with me because we'd had time before her workshop to take care of the important points we needed to discuss."

"Did she say who this old friend was?"

"No, and I didn't ask."

"Do you ever meet with her at the motel she stays at?"

"No...oh, yes, maybe a few times I've dropped materials off there, like the evening before her class."

"Did you have to do that this time?"

"No, that wasn't necessary. Stacey had all the stuff she needed for her class."

"Does Stacey work with anyone on her jobs?"

"Sometimes she has an assistant, but not always. It depends on how many people she has registered."

"How about this time? Did she work with anyone?"

"No, the class was small. No need."

"When someone helps her, is it always the same person?"

"Rarely. We draw from a pool of folks."

Linda's answers weren't giving Kera any clues about Stacey's whereabouts, but they at least eliminated possibilities. Linda gave her the impression that she was eager to help, so Kera continued her questioning.

"Have you received any communication from Stacey since last talking to her, like an email, voice mail, whatever?"

"No, but let me check." Linda scrolled down her email list but didn't find any messages from Stacey. Then she switched to her voice mail. "No…However, that's not unusual since she doesn't have another class until next week."

Kera couldn't think of anything else to ask at the moment, but gave Linda her card. "If you hear from her, would you give me a call? Some people are worried about her." She decided not to say who was worried; if Stacey's boss didn't know she was a lesbian, Kera wasn't about to out Stacey, once again.

* * *

Kera sat behind the wheel with Lakota in the passenger's seat. "Well, Lakota, who do you think Stacey's friend is? And as long as you're pondering it, girl, what did they do and where did they go?"

Lakota didn't seem to have a clue.

"Okay, then, how about we get some grub and take it to the park? Then I'll toss you some balls before we head back home. A little food and exercise will do wonders for our detective skills."

Lakota wagged her tail.

CHAPTER FOUR

Mandy Bakker opened her front door and stepped in. Mr. Moxin, her Maine coon cat, sauntered up to greet her, and slowly rubbed his body against her as he wove in between and around her legs. She ran her fingers over his back, eliciting sounds of contentment. When he'd had enough, he strolled over by his dish, rolled it over to show her it needed to be filled, then moved to his water glass. Even as a kitten, he'd insisted drinking out of a glass, not a cat bowl, not a plastic glass, but a real glass. The water level in Moxin's glass was down, beyond the reach of his tongue, so—as he always did in this situation—he carefully lowered his paw into the glass until it reached the water, and licked the liquid from his wet paw.

Moxin wasn't the only one who needed TLC. It'd been a long hard week at work and Mandy felt depleted. She tossed her suit jacket on a chair, then poured herself a glass of pinot noir and sat down on the sofa. The cat hopped up on her lap.

"What's up today, Mr. Moxin? Keeping the mice away for me, are you?" The cat purred as he lay on her lap and allowed her to stroke his fur while she kicked back and sipped her wine.

Her thoughts drifted to Kera. She'd promised Mandy she would call. Mostly she did, but not always. In those cases, Kera'd say she was sorry, meant to, but mostly it had to do with her need to isolate herself. Last Friday, they'd had a dinner and movie night planned but Kera didn't show up, didn't call, and didn't answer her phone. Then, Saturday she called and said she'd overdosed on people and couldn't even bring herself to call or text, and so had had a couple of beers (and weed, no doubt) and had fallen into bed.

Mandy wondered why she didn't move on and find a healthier woman, someone who didn't have big-time demons to fight. At least Kera had a therapist to deal with her PTSD issues. Mandy thought she should have a therapist too, just to deal with being in love with Kera. The problem was, she knew Kera loved her. And to be honest with herself, the sex was undeniably great, and the friendship—nobody was a better friend. Loyalty was probably Kera's best quality. Unfortunately, Kera couldn't utter or act on the words Mandy longed to hear: "forever and ever."

She refilled her wineglass. She knew she shouldn't. The booze was already shooting straight to her head. But it was Friday night, wasn't it? She stretched out on the sofa and tried to rest her glass on her belly but before she could, Moxin relocated himself there.

"Too bad I can't transfer my love to Dee," she muttered out loud. "What do you think Moxin? Neat trick...but definitely bizarre." Her buzzed mind rambled on. Kera and Dee were identical, physically. It would be almost impossible to tell them apart except for their hairstyles. Dee's hairdo was shoulder length, stylish, whereas Kera's was short, suited for a fast getaway. Mandy guessed she could always ask Dee to cut her hair. Mandy giggled as she visualized Dee in a barber's chair, horrified as she watched her hair being chopped off and falling to the floor. But if Mandy could switch Dee from her friend to her lover, she'd get someone predictable, deliberate, and perched on a solid branch, whereas Kera was erratic and impulsive, taking her places she shouldn't go.

Mandy drained her glass and set it on the coffee table. She chided herself; she seldom could handle two drinks, and so rarely had a second. Now she was hungry but didn't want to move. She closed her eyes and continued her swap-the-twins fantasy, though it was losing momentum because, for so many reasons, it wouldn't work. Being in love with one of them just didn't transfer to the other.

Besides, Dee was a lesbian newbie, though Mandy thought it more accurate to describe her as a lesbian "maybe." In the past few years, Mandy and Dee had become good friends and shared a lot. Lately, Dee confided to Mandy that she was questioning her sexuality, wondering if Kera had been right all these years. Kera never had any doubt that her sister was gay, like her, and that Dee's *heterosexuality* was the result of her need to keep the "good girl" image, because she was unwilling to scrape up against society and the expectations of their deceased parents.

Mandy heard a beep, a text. It wasn't Kera; instead, it was an activist who'd been at the LEAP meeting last night and wanted to know when they were scheduled to meet again.

After she texted him back, her mind flipped to that meeting. There'd been a few people who had argued to wait for a better time, a better political environment. But for her, the question was simple: When would that happen? Was she supposed to hold back until a critical mass in the straight community decided to treat gay people like they were human beings? As far as she could tell, it wouldn't happen, not in her lifetime. Thankfully most people agreed with her and they'd voted to charge ahead. She knew LGBT people listed in a civil rights ordinance wouldn't be a cure-all for discrimination, but she firmly believed it would make a statement and point Lakeside City in a more positive direction.

Hopefully.

Kera wasn't on board with her involvement in this civil rights battle, mostly because of what had happened to her the last time. Mandy had been shot by a crazy man bent on robbing the gay community of its leader to stymie its momentum.

And it'd worked. It had taken her almost a year to get her full strength back and a couple of years for her to even think about carrying on the fight. Kera didn't like the political timing either. She argued that because of the presidential elections and all the right-wing chatter, the "nutcases" would emerge, spew their hatred and act out—just as they had the last time. But Mandy thought that waiting for a good time was like waiting for the Rapture.

Her cell phone sang out.

She fumbled around for it, tracking the sound coming from her briefcase over by the door. It was Kera.

"Hi honey." Mandy felt lightheaded. She went back to the couch and sat down.

"What are you doing?"

"Hanging out with Moxin, hoping you might call."

"Hey, the phone rings both ways."

Mandy realized Kera was right, but she believed she called Kera more than Kera called her. Far more. Besides, this time, Kera had said she'd call. However, to point that out would be no way to start off a conversation.

"How'd you and Vinny do in the pool tournament last night?"

"Have you been drinking?" Kera's voice had a grin in it.

"Yes, dear. I had two glasses on an empty stomach. Dumb, I know." She'd made an effort to speak clearly, realizing she'd started to slur, but apparently she hadn't fooled Kera.

"Yup, two glasses is one too many for you…but back to your question. We came in third but that was a gift. Neither Vinny nor I were on our game. In fact, I prematurely sank the eight ball in the last game, which kept us from second place. It's a talent I display from time to time."

"Well, there's always next time." All Mandy understood about pool was that you didn't want to sink the eight ball until the very end. In reality, Kera was an excellent pool player. She and Vinny, more often than not, won the tournaments.

"Well, last week was bad too. I hope this isn't a trend."

"Say, have you picked up any work this week?" Mandy patted her leg, inviting the cat back to her lap but Moxin decided to leave the room.

"Yup…out there shaking the bushes, trying to find a missing girlfriend. I should say, partner. By the way, do you know Erin Duffy or Stacey Hendriks?"

"No, well, not Stacey Hendriks, but maybe Erin Duffy. Isn't she the girls' high school basketball coach?" Mandy had attended several of their games last season.

"That's right. Her partner Stacey was supposed to have come back from working in Lansing on Tuesday night but never showed. So I've been hired to search for her, and in fact just got back from Lansing."

"That has to be scary for Erin."

"Yup. At this point, it seems like a girlfriend running off, though Erin assures me they had a solid relationship. But still, I'm betting on a runaway situation, so this case might not take very long."

"That reminds me, I may need your skills soon. If you keep going on like this, Kera, you may have to hire someone full time to help you." Mandy had a new private client that would require some investigative work. She'd started seeing private clients on the side because although her work at Legal Aid paid the bills, it didn't provide for much beyond that, like a decent vacation now and then.

"Don't get me wrong," began Kera. "I appreciate all the work but only to a point. I don't think I want to become a boss, take on responsibilities like that. Besides summer's coming up fast and Lakota and I—"

"But you have Vinny working when you need him."

"Yeah, but he's my buddy, and I don't feel like his boss or have to treat him that way. I like it the way it is.

"Yes, yes, I know." Mandy hoped the exasperation in her voice didn't make it over to Kera's ears. Or maybe she did hope Kera had picked it up. *Responsibility* was a dirty word for Kera. Well, more like the idea of *commitment*. But, she asked herself, wasn't *responsibility* tied up in the concept of *commitment*? True, Kera was doing better, in some ways. In the past year she had seen that Kera had become definitely more committed to her job. Before that, she'd done private investigative work sporadically and without a license. After much prodding, Kera finally got a PI license and since then, had taken on more work. As far as Mandy was concerned, if Kera would put her mind to it, she could have all the cases she wanted and even be able to hire a staff. People liked Kera, and she was good at what she did, especially considering her psychological problem.

"Kera, before I forget, last night there was this weird guy at the Pink Door who came to our LEAP meeting. I've not seen him in our community before, not that I know every gay person or straight ally around here, for sure, but he sort of spooked me. Our meetings are listed under the Community Events column in the *Journal* and, of course, on the Internet. So you never know who might show up, but he hasn't been there before. I'm sure of that."

"Did he hassle you?"

"No, but he gave me the creeps." Mandy's neck prickled, remembering.

"What was it about him that spooked you?"

"Well, he stood in the back, didn't speak, didn't do anything, really…I don't know. I think it was more his body language, since I couldn't really see his face. He wore a blue baseball cap with the visor down, pretty much hiding most of his face. I'm sure it was nothing, just a feeling. I asked a few people if they knew him but no one did, and no one had seen him there before. There were so many people in attendance, and he was by himself in the back of the room. Who knows? I just wanted you to be aware, you know, in case he causes any problems in the future. It's probably just my overactive imagination at work." Halfway through telling Kera about the guy, she realized she shouldn't have said anything. It would just add to Kera's fear for her. *Damn, damn, damn*, why had she drunk that second glass?

"Just let me know, I'm concerned, especially given the last time you put yourself out there for the gay community. You need to trust your gut more. You have a tendency to pooh-pooh warning signs, write them off—like you just did."

"Really, honey, I'm making a mountain out of a molehill. Say, I wanted you to know I'm going to be tied up tomorrow night. I have to attend a fundraiser for Legal Aid—which I'm really not looking forward to. But I'll definitely be around on Sunday. How about we take your pooch out on the beach in the afternoon for some Frisbee fun, and after, have dinner?"

"Lakota would like that…so would I."

CHAPTER FIVE

A wet tongue slurped her face. Kera opened her eyes to greet Lakota's intense gaze and moist, warm breath. The big mutt was flopped out on her bed, face to face, with maybe two inches between them.

"Lakota, it's only a quarter after seven." Kera brought the covers up over her head and listened to Lakota sniff and tug at the edges of her blanket tent. When she flung the blanket open, the dog jumped on top of her, like a cat on a mouse.

"Do you have any idea how heavy you are?" She rolled the dog off, rubbed Lakota's belly, and got out of bed. They padded down the creaky wooden stairs that led to the kitchen for breakfast.

Coffee in hand, Kera sat out on a bench that overlooked Lake Michigan. It was a clear morning. The water appeared striped, albeit unevenly, in differing shades of blue. It felt like she was gazing into eternity, so vast, so much to grasp, but the horizon put a stop to it, preventing her entry to the beyond.

Lakota let out a frustrated growl. The dog was plopped down beside her and had found interest in some brown crawly bug, her head tilted in curiosity. The dog pawed at the moving speck, causing the small critter to fly off.

Kera switched her attention to the list of calls she needed to make. Last night she'd reached the proprietor of the Starlight Motel to get the names and phone numbers of the customers who'd been around when Stacey was there. Not anxious to bother her customers, Millie was hesitant to give them up but finally relented when she was convinced it might help find Stacey.

No one on the list had any information, and now she was down to her last name. She had to think about how to approach the "regulars" who might not want to admit they'd stayed at the motel. It could be pretty dicey; illicit love doesn't like exposure. She knew about that only too well, given her army experience. Before the repeal of *Don't Ask, Don't Tell*, she and Kelly had been forced to keep their relationship under wraps, a nerve-wracking nightmare, especially when Kelly was killed right before her eyes by an IED in Iraq. Before she could divert the difficult memories, her senses, bombarded with vivid flashes, forced her back:

One second Kelly stood there, full of life; the next, it was as though she had never existed, eradicated by the explosion. Kera ran toward her but was blinded by the blood-colored dust that splatted in her eyes and stuck to her face. With every breath, she sucked in the stench of death and particles of lost life, while detached body fragments flew by her. In desperation, she reached for a leg on the ground, determined to put Kelly back together again…

Her arm landed on Lakota's back. She ran her hand over the dog, rhythmically, like strumming, while a cool nose nuzzled her neck and a wet tongue licked her face. Kera felt herself suspended in the moment, teetering between the past and present. Lakota's bark brought her back; her heart raced and sweat rolled down into her eyes. She sat for a moment and let the breeze cool her face, then made her way over to the edge of the bluff, zigzagging her way down a path toward the boulders and sandy beach below. Lakota followed close behind at first, but moved ahead of Kera as they picked their way down the steep cliff. The thorny windswept trail was littered with small rocks, loosely lodged in sandy soil. At the shoreline, they ran at full speed along the wet hard-packed sand. The breeze blew through Kera's hair and through her mind. Iraq couldn't catch her, at least for now.

* * *

Kera put in a call to Erin Duffy, but Daniel, Erin's brother, answered her phone. He told her that Erin was out, had gone into town to help with the high school float for the St. Patrick's Day Parade. She'd left her cell phone at home, he said, but he planned to run it over to her after breakfast and a shower.

"How's she doing?" Kera was glad he was there and able to support his sister.

"She's a nervous wreck, so it's probably good she's with her students today. It might help her keep her mind off Stacey. I stayed with her last night but she didn't sleep much. Pretty tough going for her. I can't hang here tonight, so I called Ally. She said she would come over for the night."

"Good idea. Erin needs someone with her as much as possible. I know she appreciates what you're doing for her."

"I just wish I could do more," he sighed. "I hope you can come up with something pretty soon. She's a mess."

"I'm working on it."

* * *

In town, Kera found Erin at the staging area sitting under a partially leafed-out maple tree with her backpack and a bottle of water nearby. She had her hands cupped to her mouth like a bullhorn and was yelling out directions to students who were furiously applying last-minute touches to a green and white carnation-covered float on the back of the flatbed truck. The student leprechauns jumped on and off the structure, playfully pushing each other and laughing.

"Okay, okay folks, we don't have that much time left and there's plenty to finish up before the parade starts." Erin walked over to her crew and pointed out what still needed to be done.

Kera sat down by the tree and watched Erin. She could tell by the interactions between teacher and students that Erin was well liked. After the students were back on task, Erin came over to her.

"Have you heard anything? I've been beside myself, imagining the worst." Erin sat down by Kera, her long red braid off to one side.

"Nothing from Stacey, but before I forget, your brother will bring your phone by in a little while."

"Geez," Erin said as she patted her pocket, "I never realized I didn't have it. My God, Stacey could have tried to get a hold of me." She shook her head. "I don't understand, she would have called me, I know—"

"Maybe you've forgotten. Did Stacey mention anything about an old friend in Lansing? Or maybe a friend showed up there unexpectedly?"

"No, I've gone over and over our conversation after we spoke Monday night, trying to remember everything Stacey and I talked about, but there was absolutely nothing out of the ordinary. And nothing about an old friend. I'm certain I would have remembered that. Why?"

"Her boss said they had intended to have dinner together Tuesday night, but Stacey called and asked if it was okay to cancel, saying something about an old friend who'd shown up— she didn't mention who. Her boss hasn't heard from her since."

"No, I don't know anything about that. Maybe it came up sometime on Tuesday, but she still would have called to let me know."

"Well, not if that person had something to do with why Stacey hasn't come back." Kera grimaced. "I have to be straightforward with you, Erin. Her being gone this long without a word, given that she has a track record of always letting you know—"

A blond girl in a short green dress and matching tights, elfish shoes, and green and white ribbons in her hair ran up to

Erin. "Ms. Duffy, other people in the parade are getting on the their floats now. Can we get on ours too?"

"Is everything done and everyone prepared to go?"

"Yes, we're all ready. A man said the parade will move out in five minutes."

Erin managed to smile through her worry. "Okay, Kristen, I trust your judgment. Tell the kids to hop aboard and I'll join you in a few minutes."

After the girl was out of earshot, Erin responded. "I know you're right. Something's wrong, really wrong. Stacey wouldn't do this. I just know she wouldn't. I hate to think what could have kept her from coming home. It scares the hell out of me."

"Is there anyone in the Lansing area that she knows or is acquainted with, someone she might want to see or stay with… for any reason at all?"

"Not that I know of. Believe me, I've tried to think about that, but I draw a blank every time."

"Is Stacey on Facebook? Twitter? LinkedIn? Or any other social or professional media sites that you can think of?"

"The only one I know for sure is Facebook."

"I have to believe, then, that you are a *friend?*" Kera grinned.

"Well, sure, and I do know her password to get on her page, if that's of any value."

"It is. We need to see if she's posted anything lately, or what her last posts were and see if they lead us anywhere. Give me her password, so I'll be able to get on as well."

"Okay. I'll do that."

"Does she have an email, that is, outside of her work one?"

"I don't think so. She told me her work email was all she could keep up with, and if she wanted to contact a friend, she'd message them through Facebook."

"Okay, I'll have her boss get the IT guys to break into her email. Does she have her own personal computer?"

"No, just her work laptop and she always takes that with her. She really didn't need one of her own. Her boss was okay with her having it for personal use."

"I'll check out her Facebook page and keep an eye on it, but you keep checking too. Let me know if you see anything significant or strange to you."

"Okay."

"Something else: when I searched through the motel room, most of Stacey's belongings were gone, but a few items were left. I brought them so you can tell me if they're Stacey's or not." Kera put her hand in the bag and withdrew a pair of blue Crocs. "There's also an earring, a few hair products, and some clothes in here."

"Yes, those are hers, see the paint specks on them? That's the color of our bedroom walls." She managed a slight smile, then took the bag and peered in. "Yeah, it's her stuff." She held up the lone earring. "I don't think this is hers, though." She tossed it back in the sack. "But maybe, it could be, I don't know. She's got so many."

"Well, there was just one, probably lost by someone else." Kera handed over the bag. "Here, you might as well take her stuff."

Kera thought she probably shouldn't give the items to Erin, especially if there'd been foul play. The police would want them if a crime had been committed, but it was most likely a case of a hurried lover leaving for who knew where, taking the chicken-shit way out of a relationship. Still, some trace evidence might be recoverable; no sense contaminating the items more than they already had been. "Erin, keep it all together in that bag, okay?"

Erin nodded. "I'll put it in her closet when I get home."

"To be honest, Erin, if I can't come up with anything pretty soon, you need to consider talking to the police again, and be up front about your relationship with Stacey so they will start taking her disappearance seriously."

Erin flinched. "I so don't want to have to do that. I'm sure you understand how it is for a high school teacher in this town—" She hesitated, her face drained of color. "Good God, this will get out, and when it does, my job will be in jeopardy, big-time. No, the fact is, I won't have a job. But, I understand what you're saying. I do. I so hoped you'd find her, somehow, before I had to go down that road."

"I'm really sorry. I do appreciate what you'd be facing. But Stacey didn't come home Tuesday night, and this is already Saturday morning. I'm only one person and it's up to you. I'll give it a few more days. I've got some leads I'll check into tomorrow, then Monday morning I'll go back to Lansing—that is, if we haven't heard from Stacey by then. There are a few people I haven't gotten hold of, customers that were staying at the motel at the same time as Stacey. Maybe one of them saw her and can give us a lead."

"I know you asked me if Stacey did anything like this before, and she hasn't, but, well, I hope she didn't decide to leave me, and didn't want to do it face to face. I've been left before, another woman, another time. But you'd think Stacey could at least send me a Dear Jane email." Erin got up and brushed tears away from her eyes. "Still, it'd be hard for me to believe she'd do that to me."

*　*　*

Kera sat in her home office, glued to Stacey's Facebook page, but found nothing helpful other than the fact that Stacey hadn't been on it for five days. Her cell chirped 'The Stars and Stripes Forever,' the ringtone she'd had ever since Iraq.

"Hey Dee, what's up?" Kera closed her laptop.

"I'm knocking at your door and scraping my knuckles raw."

"I didn't hear you. Be right down."

Kera was grateful that Dee hadn't shown up earlier. Dee would've been upset to see how she'd gotten into the residence. After her morning run on the beach, Kera realized she'd forgotten her keys, so'd she had to climb up the tower rope to get into the lighthouse, which allowed access to her residence. The rope entrance was her version of a spare key, and safer than a key under a doormat. The rope solution served another purpose; it helped keep her military conditioning. When Kera had installed it, she'd known her sister would be upset. Dee was a born worrier but had become worse after their mother died, then even more intense after their father's sudden death. She was certain something would happen to Kera too. So to allay Dee's concern—knowing Dee would find out, sooner or later—she'd decided one day to have her sister watch her deftly make the climb, thinking it would ease Dee's mind.

But she should have fucking known better.

Dee all but had had a heart attack, yelling up at her, telling her she was going to kill herself. Kera continued the climb in spite of her sister's pleas to come down. She wanted Dee to see that she could do it quite easily. However, Dee bitched to her about the episode for a week, and then never brought it up again. She'd apparently shelved it in some out-of-the-way place.

Dee's constant concern irritated Kera and made her feel loved—depending on the situation and her mood at the time.

Kera ran downstairs to the door.

"Where's Lakota? She usually hears me and barks," Dee said as she removed her jacket.

"She's out exploring and blowing off energy. I guess her morning run wasn't enough for her. By the way, a few weeks ago, I put in a doggie door for her in the connecting room. She loves it. She can come and go as she pleases. If I want her and I'm upstairs in my office, I can whistle out the window so I don't have to come back down to let her in."

"The connecting room?"

"Yes, the room that connects the tower to the kitchen and has a door to the outside."

"Oh yeah, I forgot that's what you called it."

"That's its function, so that's its name." Kera smiled. "Come on, let me show it to you."

"I'd be worried that someone could come through that." Dee bent over, checking the rubber flap.

"No, only a little kid. I tried it myself, couldn't get in. Lakota's body is more streamlined than mine."

"You've done some more work around here. I love the sage color you used in the kitchen, it fits nicely with the rest of the place. Even though I complain about you living in this place, you've really done a great job fixing it up and decorating it."

Kera had put a lot of work into the house. Even before she'd moved in, she'd spent a month painting, repairing, and buying pieces of furniture that maintained the nautical theme and antique furnishings left by previous caretakers. Just two weeks ago, she'd finally finished the kitchen.

"So, what brings you so far out this way?"

"I miss you. I haven't seen you in a while and thought you might want to see me." Dee kissed Kera on the cheek. "You're smoking that shit, again, aren't you?"

"When I'm not working, it doesn't hurt anything if I kick back and relax. And if I need it while working, I only take enough to calm myself, so I can think." Kera took Dee's jacket and hung it on a hook by the door.

"I wish you wouldn't smoke that stuff at all. That's what your meds are for, and I'm afraid you'll lose your PI license if—"

"Yes, mother, can we talk about something else?"

This conversation about her weed was old and overdone. Dee had taken up mothering her—at the age of twelve—where their mother had left off. Kera knew her sister's heart was in the right place, but—

"Well, Kera, I wouldn't have to keep at you if you'd—"

"Let's not do this. How about we hit the reset button and go back to how nicely you think I've fixed this place up?"

"I'm just saying...oh, okay, you're right."

"Great. So, would you like a beer? I was just about to open one." Kera again saw her mother's expression on her sister's face. "Jesus, Dee, it's five o'clock. Not even just *somewhere*, but right here in Michigan. And it's Saturday, for God's sake. Besides that, I've worked today, and furthermore it's St. Patrick's Day. I ask you, what's more appropriate than a beer on this day—other than a green one?" Kera open the refrigerator.

"You got me there. I guess I'll take one since you made such a case for it," Dee called out to her. "What are you working on now?"

"A missing person," Kera shouted back.

"Someone in town?"

"Yeah." Kera walked back in and sat down next to her sister, who'd already flopped on the sofa and kicked off her shoes.

"I just got off work too." Dee lay down with her head on the armrest, lifted her legs, and placed her feet in Kera's lap. "How about a foot rub? I had to run all over the hospital. I must've walked miles on those hard floors in these horrid shoes."

"Why do you wear those damned things if they're not comfortable?" Kera handed a beer to Dee and began to rub her sister's foot.

"Because I was in a hurry this morning and couldn't find any other shoes to go with my outfit. Oh, that feels so good! Have you ever thought of going into massage therapy?"

Kera ignored the remark. It was just another attempt, she suspected, to get her out of the PI business.

"So who's missing?"

"Do you know Erin Duffy?"

"Well, maybe. Is she the cute thing with red hair, a female version of Tom Sawyer?"

"Yes, that's a good description of her. It's her partner, Stacey Hendriks, who's missing. Stacey travels for her job and was in Lansing. She supposed to be home Tuesday night, but never showed up." She set Dee's foot down, and picked up the other one. "How do you know her?"

"I remember her because Erin visited Stacey when she was in the hospital. Stacey needed a place to do some rehab and I was involved with that. Gosh, it was quite a while ago, several years. At the time they never mentioned they were a couple, but I picked it up, so I guess that's why I remember them." Dee paused. "Isn't Erin the girls' basketball coach at the high school? I think I might have seen her picture on the sports page of the newspaper. Not that I read that section much, but I remember it because I saw it when I searched through the *Journal* for the picture they took of you receiving your third degree black belt—the one that showed you landing a foot in your opponent's chest."

"You've got a good memory, and you're right, Erin's the girls' basketball coach."

"You won the tournament too—I still have the article with the pictures."

"Yeah, you and Mandy took me out to dinner to celebrate. Remember? I got a sore jaw and fat lip in my last fight, and it was killing me to chew."

"But I recall you ate every bit of your dinner." Dee laughed.

"Well, yeah, fighting makes me hungry."

"Anyway, champ, that's all I know about Erin, or can remember. And of course, that's HIPAA information, meant to stay in the files at the hospital, so you didn't hear what I just said."

"Got you." Kera made a zipping motion over her lips. "I went to Lansing to see what I could find out, but no solid leads so far. I'll go back Monday and try again."

"Don't you think the police should be involved?"

"The cops weren't that interested. But it'd only been twenty-four hours when Erin reported Stacey's disappearance, and she was scared to tell them about her and Stacey. But if I don't find something out very soon, I'll insist she go back to the police, as much as I don't have any faith in them."

"Ah, speaking of police, I have a date with a cop tonight, so I need to go home and get ready pretty soon." Dee tried to retract her foot from Kera's lap.

Kera held on, grinning. "Tell me, is this a first date?"

"As a matter of fact, yes, it is." Dee's eyes sparkled.

"What? You're hanging out around cops now?"

"Only when one brings someone to the hospital, is cute and flirts with me."

Kera raised her eyebrows. "Next question and the most important, *dear* sister. Male or female?"

"That's for me to know and you to find out, Kera *dear*."

"I'll find out, don't you worry, sister *dear*." Kera playfully pinched her sister's toe, then let go of her foot. "You can't keep information like that from a top-notch private investigator like me. Not for very long anyway."

* * *

Kera climbed the stairs that led to the observation deck of the lighthouse tower. Lakota had already made the trip up.

She knew the dog would wait for her arrival, tongue hanging out and tail wagging. The St. Patrick's Day celebration would end with fireworks over Lake Michigan and she wanted to be prepared. Fireworks unnerved her, as did all loud noises. When the local baseball team started fireworks displays after home games, she'd tried to stay out on the gallery deck to watch but quickly found that the glass enclosure of the lantern room was needed to muffle the noise. She was especially sensitive to the type of pyrotechnics whose main purpose was to flash a bright light and then explode. It was too much like a bomb going off and often hurled her into the worst moments the war had to offer her.

She remembered the first time she'd experienced fireworks after she'd come home from Iraq. Camped by herself at Sleeping Bear National Dunes, she knew severe thunderstorms could send her into a flashback, and she should have guessed, or known, that fireworks would trigger the same response. But she hadn't put two and two together. That would have taken a certain amount of foresight she didn't possess at the time. She didn't know what all had happened that night—her flashbacks didn't come with a memory stick. But sometime that night she'd fallen asleep. When she woke the next day, she was soaked to the skin, muddy, shaking from the cold with her clothes torn and her body covered with cuts and bruises, a lump on her head, and her nose sucking in the moist earth two feet from the Platte River, with a turtle camped beside her. No one had complained about her to the forest rangers, but then, she'd pitched her tent in a remote area with no one else around. For all she knew, she'd gotten banged up battling phantom soldiers.

At the top of the stairs, Kera stepped to the observation deck, set down her ale, got out her pipe, and plugged in her earbuds to listen to soft classical music. She sat on a stool with Lakota next to her, ready for the fireworks, with their blast of color and forms exploding in the starry night sky without loud booms, without destruction, without her return to Iraq.

CHAPTER SIX

When Mandy slammed the car door, it sounded like two ill-fitting metal pieces clanking together. It didn't take long for her to notice that her old silver VW stood out like a zit among the mostly high-end vehicles in the parking lot. She felt like someone from the poor side of the tracks who'd mistakenly shown up at the elegant Sandbar Restaurant.

The restaurant sat high on a sandy cliff. Three sides of the building—seen from the land—were stucco, the top two-thirds sand-colored and the bottom third decked out in blue waves sculptured in relief, creating the appearance of water lapping at the building. The side that faced the water was entirely glass and offered a panoramic view of Lake Michigan.

The restaurant had been rented out for the affair, a fundraiser for the city's nonprofit agencies that served the poor. Everybody who was somebody in Lakeside City or who wanted to be somebody or who wanted to be seen by all of the somebodies—and was ready to donate a big chunk of money— would be in attendance. And since it was an election year, every elected politician from dogcatcher to senator would be there. Usually her boss, Carolyn Rodgers, represented Lakeside City Legal Aid, but she had a family affair to attend, and Mandy, second in command, shouldered the responsibility.

Sounds of music and chattering voices intensified as she opened the door and stepped into the restaurant. Immediately, she saw that the crowd magnet, State Senator Jeffrey De Graff, was shaking hands, smiling and nodding his head. The senator had it all going for him; he was handsome, tall, and strong-featured. His only drawback that she knew of was that he had a reputation for having a short fuse. He was a moderate Republican and socially liberal, mostly. Jeffrey came from a long line of politicians; he'd been born to it, wrapped in the state flag, and endowed with the gift of gab and a plastic smile.

When Mandy had last seen Jeffrey, they'd been at a board meeting for Lakeside City's Mental Health Services. They'd discussed the problems of veterans and the insufficient support they received from the VA. Jeffrey intended to back a special program to serve vets in the area. Mandy wished her father, a Vietnam vet, had had access to a program like what was being developed. When her father had come back, there were no support systems. Had there been, she believed her family might not have disintegrated. As it was, her dad became a drunk and drug addict and lived on the streets of San Diego. She and her mom would find him, coax him home, but before long, the drugs would call him back to the streets. At some point, her mom gave up, sank into depression, and finally committed suicide when Mandy was in third grade. After the funeral, Aunt Margaret took her to Michigan to raise her. As a child, Mandy believed she'd caused her parents to leave her, and that feeling never let go of her.

A tap on her shoulder brought her out of her reminiscence. She twisted around to see Brian Kline. He was an attractive, well-built man with short brown hair and penetrating dark brown eyes. He had gone through the female-to-male transition and wasn't *out* in Michigan. He'd come to the upper Midwest about seven years ago after his gender transition. His transformation had cost him his friends and family in South Carolina. He'd been a client of hers and that was how she'd learned of his past and knew he worried that what had happened to him in the South would happen in Lakeside City if he came out. At the time, Brian told her he wanted to be in politics and since then, he had held various jobs in that field. Just recently he'd gotten the job as Senator Jeffrey De Graff's campaign manager.

"Hey, Mandy, how's it going?" Brian gave her a smile.

"Great, thanks. I haven't talked to you in a while. How's it working out for you these days, traveling back and forth between here and Lansing?" When Brian first had taken his job with the senator, he'd told her that he found the constant travel between his home and the capital tiresome.

"I ended up renting a room. I'm not there that much, but it sure helps when I've had a long day in Lansing and can't face the drive back."

"Where's the senator's wife?" Mandy had expected Victoria to be there tonight, since she often attended events like this. Having her on Jeffrey's arm didn't hurt his ability to impress. She was a looker, always charming at these events, and came from a wealthy, prominent family as well.

"She's back in Lansing, not feeling well tonight…Say, I heard you've revived LEAP to go for LGBT inclusion in the civil rights ordinance again."

"That's right, back at it. Hopefully we'll be successful this time around."

"Frankly, Jeff is worried about your timing; politically it's not so good, Mandy. He wouldn't be able to support your action."

"I can't believe that Jeff wouldn't support us." Mandy stepped back.

Brian didn't say anything.

"So by your silence, am I to assume you agree with him?"

"He can't support the ordinance. And yes, I have to say I do agree with him. Like I said, the timing is wrong. You know what's happening nationally. Our party is being dragged to the right. Moderate Republicans won't have a chance if they don't move along with the party, at least part of the way."

Damn Jeff, damn Brian. And damn Kera too. This was Kera's argument as well. Mandy was pissed Kera hadn't understood the urgent need regarding the ordinance issue. Didn't any of them realize how backward Lakeside City was? She was tired, dead tired of people—like the senator, Brian, and Kera—who expected gay folks to wait for the sea of opportunity to part so they could walk through and pick up their rights.

"How can you be a 'moderate Republican,'" Mandy's voice rose on those last two words, her fingers making quotation marks in the air, "and allow yourself to follow the crazy Tea Baggers into Wonderland?" Mandy looked at him hard. "Just saying." She knew if her glare could kill, Brian would be dead.

Mandy would have liked to go on and challenge him about how he could possibly be trans—and gay—and a Republican, but she really couldn't do that, given that particular information had come from her professional relationship with him. Maybe, she hoped, her tone of voice had made the point.

Brian cleared his throat. "Not everything is about gender or sexual orientation. There are other considerations and—"

"Mind if I join in?"

A thirty-something woman sauntered up to them. She was tall and slim with dark hair, and a face blessed with beautifully carved features. The woman was dressed in black slacks and a vest that matched, with a white blouse, renaissance style. Her silky dark hair was just long enough to curl gently around her face, like a picture frame. Stunning.

"Hey, Jessica." Brian put his arm over the newcomer's shoulder and brought her into a sideways hug. "It's so good to see you. I would guess you're here tonight on behalf of social services."

"Yes, otherwise I'd be at a local bar with a green beer in my hand, trying to pass myself off as Irish," said Jessica with a laugh. "Well, Brian, are you going to introduce me to this beautiful woman, or will I have to do it myself?"

"Oh, I'm sorry, Jessica, this is Mandy Bakker. She works for Legal Aid and is a local activist for—"

"Actually, I know who Mandy is, though I've not formally met her." She extended her hand. "Hi, I'd have to live in a cave not to know who you are. I'm Jessica Mancini. I work with kids."

"She's the head of the Department for Child and Family Services," Brian added.

"It's nice to meet you, Jessica."

"I have long admired your political work for the gay community. I've had to be, well, as you might imagine, circumspect, working where I do, especially dealing with children. I'm not out at social services and have been hesitant to be involved in our community's activities, political or not. Too worried I could lose my job, but I'm thinking I should get more involved, anyway, you know—"

"I do know, and that's why we need to get LGBT folks included in the civil rights ordinance, so they don't have to be worried they'll lose their job if they come out." Mandy shot Brian a look that said, *see what I'm talking about.*

Brian flipped his attention elsewhere, pretending not to hear.

"You're absolutely right." Jessica smiled.

Jessica's large dark brown eyes had locked onto hers and held there, a little too long. It made her feel uncomfortable, somehow. Mandy finally disconnected and took a deep breath. "Come to think of it, I've heard your name from Dee Van Brocklin. She's a social worker at the hospital and a good friend of mine."

"Oh, yes. I know Dee well. She and I often coordinate services, when child abuse is an issue."

Brian's attention returned. "Dee is Kera's twin sister." He saw someone he knew out of the corner of his eye and waved. "Kera is Mandy's girlfriend," he went on to explain. His eyes met Mandy's. "Right?"

"Of sorts."

As soon as the words had escaped her mouth, Mandy wondered why she'd said that, put their relationship in that way? Perhaps, because it *was* that way. But she'd just blurted it out; she didn't have time to clean it up and make their relationship sound normal, like everybody else's. Their love was without a real commitment, without living together, without putting down roots like real couples did. Her heart ached for that kind of attachment. She'd been waiting for the last three years for Kera to heal from her emotional war wounds. Would she ever heal, ever be ready? Mandy sighed.

Jessica was running her finger gently over her lips, like she wanted Mandy to know how soft they were. She raised her eyebrows. "Of sorts?" Jessica repeated.

"It's a long story. Complicated." Mandy broke eye contact again. She wasn't about to talk about it, not here, not with someone she'd just met, not with these big dark eyes delving into hers. She didn't discuss this issue with anyone but Kera's sister.

The lights in the room suddenly went out. Only a few candles glowed from the banquet table.

A boom sounded.

The room went silent.

Suddenly, the dark room lit up with green and gold colors sprinkling out of the sky and falling into the lake. *Oohs* and *ahs* reverberated from the onlookers. The St. Patrick's Day fireworks had begun.

Brian made his way to the senator. Mandy stopped off at the bar, ordered a glass of pinot noir, and grabbed a handful of bar nuts. She'd had no dinner, in spite of her plan to eat finger foods for her meal. But when she surveyed the offerings, nothing tempted her taste buds, at least nothing she'd allow herself to eat, since everything was loaded with calories and fat.

Jessica came up from behind and moved in next to her at the bar, too close, then placed her foot on the bronze foot rail and ordered herself a glass of chardonnay. She put her arm around Mandy. "So, where is your girlfriend tonight?"

* * *

Sunday morning's bright light streamed through the window and penetrated Mandy's eyelids; she shielded them with her hands. Her head throbbed. She fantasized it being surgically removed from her neck by the swift slice of a knife slamming down on a chopping block. Too much wine. She winced at the realization she'd had three glasses—and on an empty stomach.

Jessica's attention had been flattering, at first. Mandy couldn't deny the woman was beautiful, but soon Jessica's attention had turned into flirting and become inappropriate, especially when she'd put her arm around Mandy at the bar. Just to think about it annoyed her. As far as Mandy was concerned, Jessica's advances were uncalled for, uninvited, and way out of line. She had had to tell her twice to remove her arm. After the second time, she left Jessica at the bar and went to schmooze with colleagues from other agencies. The problem was that Jessica kept showing up and trying to get her attention. Mandy thought she'd made it clear to the woman that she wasn't interested, but apparently her message had not gotten through. Then Mandy worried that her "of sorts" response about her relationship with Kera had cracked open the door for Jessica. So maybe it was partly her fault, maybe all her fault. Besides, the woman had been flattering.

Good God!

She curled up in a fetal position and buried her head with a pillow.

* * *

"Don't do that, Moxin. My head hurts." The cat had pulled off the pillow and now pawed at her head. It was past his breakfast time. Mandy reached up, grabbed the pest and tucked him by her side. For a moment Moxin enjoyed her attention, but soon he remembered what he wanted. He jumped off the bed. Mandy heard him vocalizing his distress as he pawed at the cupboard door that held his food.

"Okay Moxin, I'll—" She stopped. The sound of her voice hurt her head. She crawled out of bed and padded to the kitchen. Her stomach and intestines rumbled. Mandy decided that Moxin would have to settle for dry this morning, since she'd barf if she had to smell the canned food.

She was angry with herself, and frustrated. Why did three glasses of wine do this to her and not to others? And she was totally aware that alcohol had this effect on her—and even worse, she hadn't eaten aside from a few bar nuts—why did she do it? Maybe, she'd call Kera, say she was sick…No, she should have known better than to drink that much. She wouldn't cut herself any slack and she would keep her date with Kera and Lakota. Then a horrible thought flashed through her head. What if someone had seen Jessica's advances? She couldn't let it get back to Kera before she had a chance to tell her about it and assure her she'd had no part in it—other than letting Jessica's flirting go on too long when they were at the bar. *Damn it*, she should have left after the first time Jessica placed her arm around her.

She needed coffee, and a shower to try to scrub off some of last night.

* * *

"Sorry, guess it's not my day." The only thing Mandy wanted was to be at home, in bed.

"To put it mildly, you were a bit—how can I delicately put this? Uh…not your usual agile and speedy self. Sluggish, I'd say," Kera teased as she unlocked the door to the lighthouse residence, then stepped back to let her go through.

Mandy wiped the sweat from her forehead on her sleeve. Running after the Frisbee had felt like rocks bouncing in her head. If God were compassionate, she told herself, He'd have struck her dead, out there on the beach.

"No, I guess I wasn't much fun." Mandy took a deep breath, sat down, put her fingers up to her temples and rubbed.

"Hey, are you okay?" Kera hung the dog's leash on a hook by the door.

"I have a bit of a headache, today, that's all. Could I get something for it?"

"Sure, just a minute." Kera went into the kitchen. "Got your pills," she called. "Do you want a glass of wine to wash it down?"

"Oh God, no."

"What'd you say?" Kera yelled back.

"Just water." Mandy's stomach rumbled and she felt like she might vomit at any moment. "And some antacids please, if you have some."

Kera came back with a bottle of water and a Bell's Ale, and plopped down beside her. The movement of the sofa was unsettling, jarring, not what she needed. There was nothing delicate or subtle about Kera's way of moving through life. Her style, if measured on a scale, was more at the pounce or ricochet end of the spectrum. Kera didn't lower herself to a sitting position, no, she dropped and let the cushion catch her, like a safety net. Ordinarily, Mandy found that amusing, kid-like, but not at this moment, not in her present condition.

Also, her present condition didn't want to deal with telling Kera about Jessica Mancini. She knew what would happen. Kera, teary-eyed, would end up saying she should move on to someone who could give her what she wanted and deserved— that was her usual way of putting it. But, what if someone at the restaurant had seen them at the bar and misinterpreted the situation—at least on Mandy's part?

"What's wrong, honey?" Kera handed her the pain pills and Tums, along with a bottle of water.

"Kera, I need to tell you. Last—"

Kera's cell phone rang. "Just a minute, honey, I need to answer this."

Mandy took a long drink of water. Her belly immediately protested. She ran into the bathroom and heaved. She sat on the bathroom floor, waiting for her stomach to calm down. When she was pretty certain she was done puking, she went back into the living room to find Kera getting ready to leave. "Where are you going?"

"I'm sorry, honey, I have go. My client, the one whose partner is missing, she's upset." Kera grabbed her car keys and snapped Lakota's leash on her. "The woman is really distressed, crying, I could hardly understand her, so I'd better go and see what's up. Why don't you stay here and…" Kera's eyes met hers, "Are you okay, honey? Your face is pale. I'll stay if you need—"

"No, no, don't worry. It's just my headache—"

"Are you sure?"

"It's okay, really. I think I'll go home and take a nap. Besides, who knows how long you'll have to be gone." Mandy was not only relieved to be able to leave, but now, she wouldn't have to tell Kera about last night…

Hopefully no one would say anything to her before she had a chance to explain.

CHAPTER SEVEN

He'd gotten in through an unattended door at the fundraiser last night. He wasn't stalking her, exactly, just keeping a close eye on her.

At the bar, a woman had her arm around Mandy, like a man would do with a woman. It disgusted him and turned him on, gave him a boner. How dare they flaunt themselves? He pushed the button on the coffeemaker.

Mandy Bakker was a problem. Too bad she'd recovered from the assault she'd received the last time she attempted to legitimize gays by trying to get them included in the city's civil rights ordinance. She'd almost died. But the dude who tried to whack her didn't get the job done. Now here she was again, back at the same shit. Last time, she didn't learn, but this time she would. He'd get the job done.

He took some solace in the fact that the political mood of the country was turning to the right, thanks to the Tea Baggers who finally understood what was right. They knew it was necessary to get rid of this country's moochers, barnacles, bloodsuckers, pervs—all special interest creeps begging for their "rights." Pervs were the worst, according to what he'd been reading and hearing.

As far as he was concerned, the Republicans offered some good people in the primaries. A few of them seemed really prepared to get the country back to where the Founding Fathers meant it to be. Moderates would finally come to their senses and move to the right.

He yawned, stretched, and grabbed his smokes. He exhaled tobacco fumes from deep in his lungs, then dangled the cigarette between his lips and dropped two pieces of bread into the toaster. He dragged a frying pan out from under a pile of dirty dishes, slapped six strips of bacon into the pan, and turned the burner on high.

Killing had been easier than he'd expected. In fact, it felt okay. He liked having a say in the universe, a chance to set at least one thing right. That night, afterward, he'd had a couple beers, a rare, juicy steak, and fries. He'd ended his feast with coconut cake, the house special, and gone back home for a good sleep.

As the bacon sizzled, he threw in three eggs and spooned the grease over the yolks. He wondered if he'd gotten an appetite for killing. But he wouldn't kill just for the sake of killing, that's for damned sure. He wasn't one of those serial assassins, like the ones that go off and live in the woods and send bombs to people. He wasn't some demented, psycho nutcase. He killed for principle and cause.

The victim hadn't been a random choice, just something that had to be done.

He licked his lips. Mandy Bakker might have to go.

It wasn't looking good for her. He'd seen the determination in her eyes for himself, heard what she had said. And from what he'd observed, she was hell-bent on her path. Frankly, there wasn't a reason *not* to kill her.

CHAPTER EIGHT

Kera opened the back door at the Out-and-About and let Lakota go in first. Ally met her in the hallway.

"So glad you're here. Erin can't stop crying. She's been like this since she got here. I'm really sorry to bother you on a Sunday night but I didn't know what to do next, so I suggested she call you. I thought you might be able to help her."

Kera was irritated. She'd had to leave Mandy and had wanted to spend the rest of the evening with her. Still, as she thought about it, Mandy hadn't been feeling well and seemed relieved to be going home. Kera concluded that the fundraiser must have done her in; it had probably gone too late.

"I'll do what I can. But why did she end up here? I thought she was too closeted to come to the bar?"

"She called me to find out if I could go over to her place, but since I'm working, I had to tell her I couldn't, so she came here. I told her I could slip her in the back door so no one would see her."

Ally motioned for Kera to follow her through the back hallway. She wouldn't have needed a guide, since the smell of popcorn would have led her to the break room. The room served as a storage area as well, with boxes labeled "bar nuts," and "salsa," as well as other condiments stacked high in one corner. Over a bulletin board, a TV perched on the wall, flashing with dancing images, the volume on low. The place was empty except for Erin who sat in a chair by the boxes, wiping the tears that ran down her cheeks and onto her blue and white sweat suit.

"What's going on, Erin? Did you hear anything about Stacey?" Kera squatted down in front of her.

"No," Erin shook her head, "but I can't take this anymore. Something has happened to her, something bad. I just know it. I haven't heard a word from her, not one word. She's not been on her email or Facebook. No phone calls, texts. Nothing."

"Don't give up hope. I'll be going tomorrow to Lansing to see if—"

"I don't think I can teach tomorrow. I can't hold it together another day. I just can't." Erin started to sob.

Kera took a breath. "Erin, why don't you call in sick tomorrow, and if you would like, you can go with me to Lansing while I track down the rest of the folks who stayed at the motel when Stacey was there." She really didn't want Erin to come along, as it would complicate her efforts and slow her down, but it was the only idea that came to mind, and it might make Erin feel useful.

A male employee walked into the room, got a brown sack out of the refrigerator and sat down at a beat-up red Formica-top table, oblivious as to what was going on. He upped the volume on the TV.

Kera focused back on Erin and waited for her to consider Kera's offer.

Excited, tense sounds from the TV caught Kera's attention.

She saw a reporter and behind him, two police cars, an ambulance, and a crime scene investigation unit vehicle. She scooted over to the television. A ticker tape message ran along the bottom of the screen, *Body found in the wetlands*...

She quickly reached up and brought the volume down, hoping Erin hadn't heard or seen anything, but Erin was not paying any attention to the TV. She was ensconced in her own bubble of misery.

"Hey, what ya doing?" complained the guy at the table. "I can't hear what they're saying, damn it, would you—"

"Just hold on, I'll bring it back up in a minute," Kera shot back in a loud whisper. The fool must be half deaf if he couldn't hear it. Then she noticed the earbuds stuck in his ears, yanked them out, and tossed them on his lap. "There, jerk, does that help?"

"What the fuck? Why'd you do that?" he said. As he spoke, white bread spilled over his lip.

Kera ignored him and walked back to Erin, blocking her view of the TV. Luckily, even if Erin could have seen it, her eyes were probably too watery to view it clearly.

"Get her out of here," Kera mimed to Ally.

* * *

Kera jumped in her Jeep and flipped on the radio scanner to listen to the police channels. She'd seen a blinking tower behind the TV reporter, so she knew the general direction, but there was a lot of land out that way. She picked up a cop talking to the medical examiner on his way out to the crime scene but needed more directions. She whistled for Lakota who'd taken advantage of the delay to relieve her bladder.

After about a fifteen-minute ride toward the wetlands outside Lakeside City, Kera spotted the lights the police had brought in order to work during the night. She parked the Jeep off to the side of the county road behind the local TV van. As she and Lakota walked up toward the crime scene, a female cop approached her.

"Dee, what on earth are you—?" The cop squinted at Lakota, then a flash of understanding registered across her face. "Wow, I'm sorry. At first I thought you were Dee. You have to be her sister, Kera. You certainly are identical." The cop smiled.

"I'm at a disadvantage here." Kera offered her hand. "You are, and you know my sister, how?"

"I'm Casey Simmons. I went out with your sister the other night."

"Oh, really."

"Yeah, we had a great time." Casey's eyes sparkled. "Dee talked about you and your dog." She nodded toward Lakota, who hung in close to Kera's side, watching intently. "If I hadn't seen your pooch there I'd still be confused."

Kera felt her delight push out into a smile; the mystery of the gender of Dee's date was now solved. A female. But a police officer? How would Dee ever deal with a cop as a girlfriend? A girlfriend with a "dangerous" job. Kera knew she was rushing it, but what if this relationship took off? Would Dee let Casey know just how miserable her occupation made her, like she did with her sister being a PI? Kera shook her head. *Poor Casey, she doesn't know what she was in for.*

"Something wrong?" Casey looked confused.

"Ah, no, not at all. Dee said she had a date with a cop, just didn't expect to meet you like this, that's all."

"Same here," Casey chuckled. "Dee told me you're a PI. I'm guessing that's what's brought you out here. Right?"

"What's going on here?" Kera gestured toward all the activity. She'd sidestepped Casey's question because she didn't know how much she wanted to divulge about Erin's case if it had nothing to do with the crime scene.

"A body, female, probably in her early to mid-thirties, been there for a while." Officer Simmons removed her uniform hat and exposed her butchy blond hairdo. She wiped her brow, then put her hat back on.

"How did the body get discovered?"

"Some kids out riding their ATVs on these back paths spotted a hand and a leg. They thought it was a joke until they saw the rest of the body. Must have scared the shit out of them. I doubt they'll be riding back this way any time soon."

"That's for damned sure." Kera shook her head. "They're going to be having nightmares for the rest of their lives. Any identification found on the vic?"

"Not so far, at least. No driver's license or any other ID. They did find a computer in its case but it won't help with IDing the body, especially since the water flooded the case and ruined the computer—though it's amazing what our techs can retrieve. But even if they can get something, it'll be a while. It won't be of any help to us now. Oh yeah, and there's an overnight bag, but still nothing that points to her identity. We have people combing the area for whatever else might be here. My job is to keep the public at bay, not that there are that many people out here, at least so far, but with the media finding us, the crazies will soon follow." Casey's eyes scanned the area.

Casey gave Kera the impression she could take care of herself. She was about her height, maybe a little taller, like possibly five eleven, and she was sturdy, formidable. The woman had enough heft that if she had some decent fighting skills, she could probably take out just about anyone. Kera'd want Casey on her side in a fight.

"I would've thought this would be Sheriff Carter's jurisdiction this far out, not the city's." Kera took a pack of spearmint gum from her pocket, put a stick in her mouth and offered a piece to Casey.

"Thanks." Casey took the gum. "Yeah, that would have been true a couple of months ago before the city limits were extended out…Say, you didn't tell me what's brought you out here?"

Kera hesitated, aware of Erin's problem of being outed, but concluded there was no other way she'd get the information she wanted if she didn't let Casey know why she was there. Besides, she didn't want to be accused of holding back information that might help ID the dead woman. And, if it happened to be Stacey Hendriks's body, then Casey, being a lesbian, might be more sympathetic to Erin being a closeted teacher, so she told her.

"Do you have a picture of her?" Casey asked.

"Yup, right here. She's the one on the left."

"Damn." Casey held her flashlight close to the picture. "It sure could be." Casey studied it some more. "Shit, hair color, body type are right." Casey pointed to Stacey's face on the picture. "What's the mark on her cheek, by her chin, on the left side? See there?"

"Yeah, I asked Erin about that spot too. She told me it's a birthmark."

"I'm thinking the woman we found is Stacey all right." Casey gestured for Kera to follow her. "Come on. Let me show this to the investigator on the case, Detective Brown."

Kera stopped dead in her tracks.

"What's wrong?" Casey caught Kera's grimace.

"Detective Brown and I have a history, that's all. It's okay, really. I can deal with him. But I know he won't be the most sensitive person when it comes to working with this situation, if you know what I mean."

"I do and I agree with you."

"I guess I can't do much when it comes to protecting Erin and her job. It is what it is."

"It'll be tough on her, that's for sure." Casey nodded. "I'll do what I can, but frankly that's not much."

Kera and Casey walked over to where Detective Brown was speaking to several of the crime scene technicians. When the detective saw Kera, he raised his eyebrows and stared at her, obviously annoyed. Then he quickly directed his attention to Casey. "What you got there?"

"I think we may know who the victim is."

* * *

Kera and Detective Brown had been civil to each other; or, more accurately, each had pretended the other one wasn't there. Though they had bumped into each other on several occasions, it was the first time she and Brown had crossed paths—in a major way—since he'd tried to pin a murder on her three years earlier. After the brief greeting—or non-greeting—she, Casey and the detective had all concluded that the woman was Stacey Hendriks.

It had been one hell of a long day, but despite the late hour, Kera resolved to get to Erin's place before the detective so that she could be the one to break the news about Stacey. She'd do it in a more gentle way—if, she thought, the word, "gentle" could ever be applied to a situation where you had to tell a woman her partner had been murdered. She'd also called Ally and Mandy to get them over to Erin's as soon as possible. Ally for support and Mandy to keep Erin from Brown's inquisition.

At the crime scene, she had steeled herself to be able to view the body, a body that had died without respect, without dignity, without goodbyes. She'd seen too much of that kind of death.

Way too much.

As she drove along, her mind couldn't shut out the sight of Stacey's face and of her body, tossed like garbage into the mucky wetlands. It was like a branding iron had burned the image into her. The stench of decay hung over her. She tried to focus elsewhere, anywhere, but it was as though her life's camera had become stuck on that scene. Her mental armor began melting away, causing her to slide through the threadbare curtain that separated her present from her past, and the sounds and sights she'd endured.

She fought back at the flashback takeover that stalked her everywhere, ready to pounce.

She reached out to grab the *now* of her life. But the overthrow was out of control, fast tracking her into the Iraqi nightmare. She searched in vain for an exit, an off-ramp from her past…

Her eyes on Kelly, so beautiful, standing a few yards away.

Kelly knows she's looking at her and smiles and moves her lips in a kiss.

Then, the blast…

Kelly's gone, scattered in bits and pieces flying through the air.

Guns firing, people screaming, running, blood everywhere.

Life gone, bodies strewn, here and there.

Smells of death, dry hot death, Iraqi deaths.

Sand scraping her face, burning, flying into her eyes, against her teeth, in her nostrils. She dives to the ground, puts her arms over her head, trying to protect herself from gunshots and flying debris…She peers through her arms at the melee…

Then…Wolf appears, in front of her, tilting its head, slowly moving in closer…

She reaches out, touches its fur—

A loud bark, followed by a screaming horn that pierced the night.

She'd drifted into the oncoming lane. Truck lights bore down on her, fast. She swerved and barely missed it as it screamed by.

Total silence, but not in her head—the screaming horn lingered as she looked out at the blackness of the night.

She pulled over and shut down the engine. Her heart pounded and sweat poured down her forehead. She mopped it with the sleeve of her shirt.

Lakota whimpered.

She looked over and saw her power animal, Wolf… Or was it Lakota? She closed her eyes, opened them, blinking, struggling to get all the way back to her present, her now.

Lakota watched her, her head cocked to one side.

"Thanks, Lakota. That was a close one, wasn't it?"

* * *

It took everything Kera had to keep from doing something violent or stupid to Detective Brown that would have landed her in jail. As soon as he'd arrived at Erin's, he started grilling her. It hadn't been easy—and not completely successful—to keep Erin from spilling her guts to the bastard. Kera wanted to stuff a rag in Erin's mouth. So when the doorbell sounded, she rushed to the front door, grateful to see Mandy.

"Hi honey." Mandy smiled through a yawn, then gave Kera a kiss on the cheek. "So, where's Erin?"

"She's in the den with Brown and Ally."

Mandy started for the den, then stopped. "What's that aroma…sandalwood?"

"Uh-huh, it's incense, over on the altar." Kera pointed to a coffee table-sized altar with a light green cloth covering, set in a corner of the living room. On the table were candles, a bouquet of cut spring flowers, a statue of three women and miniature black caldron-like pot, and on either end, a silver chalice…

Mandy stopped. "Is that a, a dagger on the…what do you call it? An altar?"

"Yup, but not to worry, it's not for killing people or carving on bodies." Kera tossed Mandy a sick smile.

Mandy didn't seem to be amused, but rather horrified as she took in the altar. "Really strange—"

"Not if you understand it. Erin is Wiccan. Now is the time of the Spring Equinox…Ostara, it's called."

Detective Brown's loud questioning voice rang out, then a female voice responded with something Kera couldn't make out. She and Mandy glanced at each other, knowingly, and quickly hurried to the den.

* * *

"Whew, long night." Kera followed Mandy into her townhouse.

"How do you think it went tonight?" Mandy tossed her suit jacket over a chair.

"I love it when Brown has met his match. It pleases me to see him so frustrated," Kera smirked. "But I hope Erin didn't say anything she shouldn't have when I went to the door to let you in. At least when we were there, I think it went okay." Kera started pacing. She could feel herself getting agitated, hyper. Her thoughts were flying around like frantic bees.

"That was my concern too. It doesn't take long to say the wrong thing to the police, especially him. Say, do you want a beer?" Mandy asked.

"Sure do, thanks." In her head, Kera saw Brown's pompous face. Every time she encountered him, she'd had all she could do not to kick that arrogance out of him with a swift foot to his groin. Her anger at him went way back and gained intensity every time she had to deal with him. Right now, it felt out of control. A drink couldn't come too fast, but what she thought she really needed was a hit or two. "Honey, I'm going to take a trip out to the Jeep, relax a little. I'll be right back for that beer."

* * *

"You better now?" Mandy asked when Kera returned. She had changed into flowered pajamas and slippers while Kera was out.

"Yeah, mellowed out. Say, I'm sorry I didn't pick up that you weren't feeling well this morning and teased you about the Frisbee game. I just thought you were tired from the late night *schmoozing* at the fundraiser...By the way, how did it go?"

"It was fine, you know, the usual stuff. Nothing much to say about it, really." Mandy handed her a mug of beer.

"Is something wrong, did anything happen there, honey?" Kera wondered if Mandy had seen that weird guy again because her face was tense, more than just fatigued.

"No, no, just the usual bullshit stuff." Mandy replied, quickly. "You said Daniel Duffy was at Erin's tonight, before I got there. What did you think of him?"

"He seems like a nice guy. He and Erin certainly looked like brother and sister—couldn't mistake that one—and he's behind her all the way." She sat back down on the sofa.

"Sounds good, but I hope she has some others to support her. Ally will do what she can, but she works and goes to school. She can do just so much." Mandy yawned.

"I asked Daniel about their parents, hoping they might be able to be there for her." Kera sipped the foam off the beer. "He said they were retired and now live in Florida. Just as well, I guess, since he mentioned they don't know that Erin is a lesbian."

"Do you think her brother will continue to be supportive? She's sure going to need it. Especially given that her parents won't be there for her." Mandy sat down in a chair across from the sofa.

"He told me he wanted to help in any way he could."

"The question is, how much free time will he have for it?" Mandy flipped off the slippers and curled her feet under her.

"I guess the good news—for Erin anyway—is that he was just recently laid off, so he's got time on his hands."

"What's he do?"

"A sales rep for a propane company." Kera put her feet up on the coffee table. "Interestingly, he told me that he had been a cop at one time, somewhere in the Upper Peninsula. Munising, I think he said, but he gave it up because, 'it ruined his marriage.' He didn't go into that, but—"

"That's a stroke of luck for us, Kera. He's got a skill set we could use. I'm going to need your help, and it's pretty clear you'll have to dig up some other suspects, since Detective Brown is homing in on Erin."

"Well, maybe I could use him, but only in a pinch, say, if Vinny's not available. Vinny really likes working for me—when he can—and he's good at it, got a real knack for snooping. But one way or another, I'm sure we will be able to use Daniel, if only to keep Erin calm and from doing or saying something stupid." Kera set her mug down. "By the way, is there a reason, honey, why you're not sitting over here next to me? I know you said you're okay, but you seem tense to me. Maybe I could help relax you—since you're not into weed. " Kera smiled and patted the empty space next to her on the sofa.

Lakota jumped up next to her.

"Lakota, get down. I didn't mean you."

Mandy giggled, got up, and settled next to Kera.

"Now, isn't that better?" Kera took Mandy's hand, kissed it, and then rubbed it gently.

"It's really late, honey, you know we both have to work—"

Kera wrapped her arms around Mandy and brought her in close. Her lips floated over her lover's silky face and down her neck.

Mandy let out a soft, purring moan, leaning into Kera's touch. "I'm too tired to resist."

Kera gently brought Mandy down and in, entwining their bodies. Her hands moved automatically, caressing, lingering…

Unwrapping…releasing…

Seeking and opening more territory…

CHAPTER NINE

In the office of the Starlight Motel in Lansing, Kera rang the bell for service. Millie Mason emerged from the backroom with a friendly smile and a nod.

"Sorry to bother you, Mrs. Mason, but I—"

"No, no, it's no bother. In fact, I was just about to call you." Millie leaned over the counter toward Kera and lowered her voice. "You know those 'regulars' I told you about?" Her eyebrows raised. "The ones who I suspect aren't married but pretend to be?"

"Yes ma'am."

"Well, lo and behold, they checked in early this afternoon— twice in a week's time, mind you—I didn't expect them for another month." Millie pursed her lips. "I thought you might want to talk to them, so I'm glad you showed up. Saved me a call." Millie ended her report with a hard nod of her head.

"I'm glad I did too. What room are they in?" Kera had hoped to get back to the Starlight a day earlier but needed to wrap up a previous case. Now she was grateful for the delay.

"The Smiths," Millie said with a wink, "are in room nineteen, but I don't want them to think I put you onto this, so I'd appreciate your discretion. Know what I mean?" Millie stepped out from behind the counter and peeked through the window. "Yes indeed, the lovebirds are still in there all right, no slam-bam-thank-you-ma'am stuff with him. No sirree, once they get here, they usually spend two or three hours in there. I tell you what, you've sure got to give the old fart credit for that." Millie suppressed a grin.

"How long ago did they check in?" Kera was quite certain they wouldn't be in any mood to talk if she interrupted.

"Hmm, I'd say they've been in there for maybe one or two hours. Can't say for sure because my husband checked them in while I was at the grocery store."

Back in her Jeep, Kera searched her bag for a biscuit for Lakota when she detected movement, out of the corner of her eye, in the window of room nineteen. Curiously, the heavier curtains hadn't been drawn; the daytime sheers revealed two people, silhouetted by a light behind them.

As she waited for something more to happen, her mind was free to wander, a danger she faced during stakeouts, and one that could take her back to the nightmare of war. So, she forced her thoughts to something pleasant, like her late dinner date with Mandy tonight, after the LEAP meeting. That led her to think about the weird guy that had made Mandy uncomfortable at an earlier meeting. She wished she could get back early to see if he was there tonight. But she didn't know how long it would take her, here at the motel. By the time she got back, the meeting could be over. She texted Vinny, *need u to get to LEAP meeting tonite, check for the creepy dude, keep eye on Mandy.*

More movement by the window and flashes of red.

The two figures, entwined, moved. Were they dancing? Kera squinted. No, she realized, they were stripping. The entangled, shadowy couple rolled on the bed, with legs and arms vigorously engaged. Wow, Kera thought. A porn movie at the Mom and Pop Motel. Snooping could be boring but it had its better moments.

Observing the Smiths through transparent curtains was like watching a sex show through hazy gauze. When it came right down to it, she decided it was a scene she didn't—or shouldn't—want to watch, although she found it hard to pull her eyes away.

A text came from Vinny: *Will keep eye out for creep.*

It was becoming clear that she would need more of Vinny's help on this case, thanks to Brown's involvement. Given her experience with the detective, she knew only too well what would happen. He solved cases by pointing his finger at the first possible suspect to cross his path, then gathered pieces of evidence mixed with a liberal amount of speculation. After that, he adjusted his notions and "facts"—or lack of them—until they appeared to fit his foregone conclusion, and *voila*! He'd cracked the case. And this time Brown had Erin in his crosshairs. When he was done with her, he would hand her over to the legal system and count on a jury of Lakeside City's crazed citizens to finish the job. He'd feel justified in ridding the community of a killer, and a homosexual—conflicting facts and missing pieces wouldn't stand in the way.

Her mind returned to Vinny. She'd been pleasantly surprised with his skills. When she'd first asked him if he could help her on a case—mostly out of desperation, not able to find anyone else on a part-time basis—he'd come through like a star. It amazed her because when she'd first met him, he was insecure, sort of awkward, and a little shady—actually that part of him often came in handy. But he took to detective work like a dog to a steak bone. He could bend rules as needed. In her business, if you were an avid rule follower, you'd never get the job done. Vinny had a good touch and knew how to walk the line. If he stepped over, he could walk it back and cover his tracks.

She heard voices. It was Millie's husband, Gerald, walking with a man by room nineteen, where the lively activity caught Gerald's eye. He quickly looked away, but the potential customer had stopped to peer in at the Smith's performance. Gerald steered him away.

Kera wondered how long the Masons had been married. No doubt a long time since Stacey had gone to college with their daughter. Would she and Mandy last long enough to be an old couple? She couldn't imagine it. Every time she tried to conjure up the image, it moved, like shifting forms of clouds on a breezy day. Maybe someday she'd have it together and be the kind of partner Mandy deserved, but no guarantees. She knew vets who'd been away from war much longer than she, and they still hadn't gotten their shit together.

A light close to the window snapped on in the couple's room, a hopeful sign they were finished. As far as she could tell, they'd been in that love nest for almost three hours. Long enough.

"Come Lakota, we're going in."

She tapped on the couple's door. When there was no response, she put her ear to it but heard nothing. Then Kera heard murmuring and rustling. The door opened, slightly, to the full extent of the interior chain lock. Two sets of eyes—one high and one low—peered out of the narrow space.

"I'm sorry to bother you but I'm searching for a missing person and I'd like to know if either of you might have seen her here." She held up the picture. "I promise, it will only take a minute of your time."

The four wide eyes remained glued on her.

"Have either of you seen this woman?" She shoved the photo up close to the crack for them to see. "Her family is very concerned." The concept of a distressed family, she hoped, might soften any anxiety they might have about her being at their door, but the strategy didn't seem to be working. So, she decided to normalize her inquiry by making it nonspecific. "I'm asking everyone in the motel if they've seen her, I'm hoping that someone can help me."

The door closed and the chain slid off.

Kera's chin dropped, but she quickly closed her mouth. If ever there were a time for a poker face, it was now. Before her stood a man and a woman who looked to be in their late eighties. The man was over six feet tall. He'd thrown a blanket over his shoulders and held it with his hand, but the substitute bathrobe allowed for an opening exposing black boxers with red hearts. Red lipstick spotted his face, especially around his lips. His hand momentarily lost its grip, exposing the gray hairs that poked out from his chest, not unlike what was happening on the top of his head. His muscles were still intact, mostly, and no potbelly. He could be a poster elder for how to stay in shape at eighty. The only sign of his age was his somewhat sagging, rippled skin and craggy face.

Beside him stood a woman that Kera gauged to be several inches south of five feet high. She was senior-citizen adorable, in a hussy sort of a way. She wore a sheer, red kimono-style robe, allowing a fuzzy view of her silky black teddy with its red flowery bodice. Her filmy covering extended to her hips where black lace stockings hooked from a red garter belt took over. Her tousled gray hair hung down almost to her shoulders. She held her robe closed, tight to her chest.

Kera had never considered such a scene. Having grown up on the conservative side of the state, she was stunned, but also, delighted. She'd never thought old people were interested in sex, let alone burlesque.

The woman spoke. "I'm sorry but we're both a little hard of hearing. What can we do for you, dear?" She and her lover stood there, unembarrassed, in their rendezvous outfits.

"First, let me explain. My name is Kera Van Brocklin and I'm a private investigator." She showed them her license. "I'm searching for—"

"Oh, Harold, this woman is a private investigator. Can you imagine?"

"Well, I'll be, Lizzy." Harold gently shook his head. "I didn't know girls went into that kind of business. I guess they can do just about whatever they want these days."

"They always could, Harold, they just weren't given the chance," Lizzy scolded.

"I have a picture here of a woman who's missing. I'm showing it to all the patrons here to find out if anyone has seen her around." Kera handed the picture to Lizzy.

"Pretty girls. Which one you looking for?"

"The one on the left. There." Kera pointed to Stacey.

"Hmm…" She put her finger to her lips. "Maybe—"

"She was here last Sunday and Monday nights and was supposed to have gone home on Tuesday, but never showed up."

"Harold, what do you think?" Lizzy held the picture up. "Was that the young woman in the office getting some coffee that one day? You remember, the one who poured a cup for each of us after she saw us waiting."

"Could have been, let me see that closer." Harold studied the photograph, straining to see. "I don't know. I need my glasses." He searched the pockets of his shirt and pants, draped on the back of a chair, without success.

"My husband never can find his reading glasses," the woman laughed. "Sometimes they're right on his face. Been like that for sixty-five years. Maybe sixty-six."

"So you two are married?" The words spilled out of Kera before she could stop them.

"Oh, so you're wondering why we come to a motel, aren't you, dear?"

"But really it's none of my business," Kera said. "I shouldn't have asked, but it just sort of slipped out."

"Oh, I bet that Mrs. Mason told you we're not married." Lizzy put her hand up to her mouth and giggled like a naughty schoolgirl. "We always sign in as the Smiths because it makes us feel like young kids. You know, sweetie, it's more fun that way. We've been sneaking away regularly now for, let me think, probably the last fifty years, give or take, usually every month or so. Though," she tittered, "we thought it was our anniversary last week, so we came here to celebrate. But then we realized we were a week early. Well, we just splurged on another trip this week. It's been wonderful." Lizzy glowed.

"I can see that." Kera couldn't believe she'd allowed another uncensored comment to slip out of her mouth. But Lizzy didn't react to her second faux pas.

"Are you married, dear?"

"No ma'am."

"Well, when you do get married," Lizzy said, as she shook her finger like a schoolteacher, "just remember a little zing in the sex life keeps your man at home or," she giggled, "at the motel with his wife."

"I'll certainly keep that in mind, ma'am." Kera couldn't hold back a smile.

"Come on in, dear." The woman stepped back. "Let's close this door. I'm not exactly in my street clothes."

"I have my dog here with me." Kera nodded toward Lakota who'd been positioned at the side of the door, out of sight. "I can put her back into—"

"Oh?" Lizzy peeked out around the doorframe. "Now isn't that a beautiful specimen of a dog. You can bring it in with you. You know, we once had a dog, when the kids—"

"Ah, here they are." Harold came out of the bathroom with his reading glasses and studied the picture. "Lizzy, I think you're right. I do believe this was the young woman."

"Do either of you remember when you saw her in the office?"

"It had to have been Tuesday morning." Lizzy's eyes sparkled and she lowered her voice. "We'd decided to make it a two-nighter, instead of our usual one-night stay." She slapped a hand over her mouth. "I almost said, one-night stand. Anyway, I came into the office with Harold that morning to get my coffee. We planned on an early start, and I'm no good without my coffee," she said with an impish smile.

Harold's face reddened and he put his head down. Kera didn't know what to do with her eyes, so she stared up in the air. Lizzy finally came to the rescue, filling in the awkward silence she'd triggered. "We saw her in the morning. Isn't that right Harold?"

"That's right." Harold seemed to have recuperated. "It was around seven in the morning, maybe even a little earlier than that. The girl said she had to hurry to get to work, but she still poured us our coffee, even put my cream in it. Nice girl, very respectful."

He put a hand to his hip and fiddled with the elastic waistband of his jockey shorts. Apparently realizing that much of his underwear was exposed, he grabbed his pants and sat down on the chair as Kera and Lizzy watched.

For Kera, the scene became increasingly disturbing. Harold was trying to get his pants on but had a difficulty with one pant leg that had been turned inside out. In his struggle to correct the problem, the slit in his shorts threatened to expose what lay within. Kera held her breath. After a moment, she realized Harold's likely exposure was something she didn't want to witness and turned her eyes away, searching for something to look at. Finally, she dropped her gaze onto Lizzy.

"We've sure had great weather, haven't we?"

"Yes, dear, it's been wonderful. I've been outside, battling my weeds."

She and Lizzy talked about garden problems—something Kera knew little about—for what felt like hours until Harold finished.

"Now, where were we?" He buckled his belt.

"I was wondering if either of you happened to know what room Stacey was in? Or did you see her at her room?" She wanted to validate any further observations they might have.

"I don't know what room number it was, but it's the one down at the end of the building." Harold pointed. "The very last one, over there. I saw her take her coffee and go into that room. Shortly after, she drove off in a black car."

"Did you see anyone else around her room, or observe anyone going into or out of there, either in the morning or later that day?"

"Come to think of it," Harold scratched his head, "I did. That's when I went out to our car to find my book—Lizzy was getting all dolled up for our anniversary dinner, so I thought I'd read while I waited. That's when I saw a man go into her room."

"Can you describe him?"

"Well, let me think about that one. He was a ways off, but I'd say he was about, oh, six feet tall or thereabouts, medium-build. That's about all I can tell you."

"Did you see what he was wearing or his hair color?"

"Couldn't tell you about the color of his hair. He had on one of those baseball caps with the brim pushed down—couldn't see much of his face."

"Color of his hat?"

"Dark, but I couldn't tell you the color. Oh, come to think of it, he wore a green and brown camouflage jacket, like the ones they wear for hunting. I remember thinking it was a little warm for it, but then I realized that it was starting to get a little chilly. It reminded me to get my jacket and Lizzy's wrap."

"Did the man have a vehicle?"

"Hmm," said Harold. He rubbed his chin. "It was a minivan. My oldest grandson has one of those vehicles. A Dodge Caravan, I believe it is."

"Do you remember the color or anything about it that would be distinguishing?" Kera took out her small notebook.

"Not really, other than it was dark. Maybe blue. Yes, probably blue, but I couldn't be one hundred percent sure of it."

"Any dents? Was it dirty or clean? License plate number?"

"Well, I don't remember any dents, but it was a late model. No idea what year, but it wasn't dirty or muddy—I'd remember that, 'cause I don't like my car dirty. I wash mine regularly. I wouldn't bring Lizzy here in a dirty car. It wouldn't be respectful to her."

"Speaking of vehicles, do you remember if the black car— the one you'd seen Stacey drive earlier that morning—was still at the motel?"

"Yes, I do believe it was."

"Thank you, Harold. This has been very helpful." She put the notebook back in her pocket.

"He has a great memory. Always been known for it." Lizzy peered up at Harold, as though he'd just been accepted into Mensa.

Kera smiled. "He sure does."

* * *

After she'd finished speaking to the old couple, she'd returned to the office and found Millie, but wasn't able to glean any more useful information. Millie and her husband had been out of the office all that day, and none of her customers had mentioned or complained about anything. So all Kera had to go on was the man Harold had seen. He could have been the old friend Stacey had planned to see that night, or not. If he was the old friend, who was he?

Kera was en route to Lakeside City to meet up with Mandy for their dinner date at the bar. She estimated she'd arrive just about when the meeting ended, or maybe a little earlier.

CHAPTER TEN

Mandy felt energy zipping through the community center as excited voices tossed out ideas and made plans. The right-wing Republicans' scapegoating efforts had revved up the engines of activist gays and their allies. They were pissed, tired of it. Mandy was taking advantage of that energy to guide their resentment into action. Before they'd gotten started, she'd given her usual pep talk to everyone, then divided the group into committees to work on different elements of their attack.

The door opened and Jessica Mancini sashayed in.

What in hell is she doing here? Mandy took a deep breath and let it out. She remembered that Jessica had mentioned that it was time she came out and got involved. Mandy hadn't believed she'd really follow through, or take a chance on getting fired from her job.

Jessica spotted her and ambled over.

"Hi Mandy, I thought it was about time I got out of my closet and there's no better time or place for it than here and now. Don't you think?" She didn't wait for an answer. "Besides,

I just found out that my new boss is gay, though not that many people know. I talked to him about working on this campaign and he assured me it wouldn't be a problem for him." Jessica smiled.

Mandy felt like slapping her, knowing there really wasn't anything she could do about Jessica's sudden need to be out and political. The bitch didn't fool her.

"Well, it looks like you got everyone in task groups, like little worker bees." Jessica rubbed her hands together. "So, point me in a direction and I'll get right to work." Her eyes stuck onto Mandy's like barnacles.

Mandy snapped the sight line, fast. She would have liked to point Jessica in a direction all right: out the damned door. But this was a public meeting for gays and their allies. She had no control over who could be a part of it, so she would just have to deal with it, somehow. Luckily Kera wouldn't be here because she didn't want to be part of LEAP. Mandy had been disappointed by Kera's refusal to become part of the group, but now that Jessica had joined in, she was thankful for Kera's skepticism and disinterest.

"I don't care, Jessica, find whatever group suits you." On further thought, since the woman insisted on joining the campaign, she might be helpful on the committee that contacted political leaders. Jessica was articulate, well-connected, and had standing in the community. The added bonus would be she'd be a busy woman, between her job and running around chasing after politicians—and out of Mandy's hair.

"Jessica," she called out, "why don't you check out the committee over in the corner by the television?" Mandy gestured toward the group. "They're working on strategies to influence local political leaders to get them to endorse our efforts. I think you could put your talents to work there."

Jessica nodded and smiled, obviously pleased with her suggestion. She winked at Mandy and strolled over to the group.

Mandy took a deep breath. Had she just encouraged Jessica? Good God, well, too late.

She saw Vinny come in and head for her. By his expression, she knew he'd caught Jessica's wink.

"Hi Vinny. What's up?" Maybe if she ignored Jessica's wink, Vinny might too.

"Kera texted me and asked me to come over until she can get here. She's concerned about that creep who was here before."

"Haven't seen him tonight." Mandy'd been so busy trying to stay on top of things, she'd forgotten about him. The only person making her uncomfortable, at this moment, was Jessica, and she wasn't about to talk to Vinny about her.

He sat down in a chair near her, took out a package of m&m's and offered her some.

"Thanks, Vinny, I'm hungry. I hope it's not too late before Kera gets here." *Not too late, but more importantly, not too early, either.*

"Okay, I'll hang with you until she arrives. If it gets real late, we'll go over to the bar and wait for her there. Okay with you?"

"Sounds good, but I'll need a lift. I don't have my car. I caught a ride with George tonight, since Kera will be picking me up." Mandy took the bag of candy, shook a few out and tossed them in her mouth. She glanced over at Jessica. She was counting on her being gone by the time Kera showed up but decided not to chance it. She'd facilitate her desired outcome by cutting the meeting short.

The door flew open and Marc hurried in, an intense expression on his face. Mandy had expected him, earlier tonight, to arrange for a room for next Tuesday night's meeting, but he clearly had something else on his mind. He hustled over to the television.

"Sorry to interrupt, Mandy, but I thought you'd want to hear this." Marc flicked the remote until it came to a local channel that showed a male reporter at the site where Stacey's body had been discovered. The young reporter stood in water that covered his shoes and several inches of trouser leg. A strong breeze ruffled his fine blond hair and his yellow tie flew off to his side. He spoke into his mic: "…word is, the murder victim, Stacey Hendriks, who was found a few days ago here in the wetlands, was killed by a Satanist or Satanists. Though it's not been confirmed by the LCPD or the coroner's office, sources are telling us that Hendriks' body was carved with satanic symbols, but we have no information on what the symbols were, or their location or how many there are."

The television screen flashed back to a woman in the newsroom.

"As we know," the newswoman said, "the Hendriks murder has stunned this town. These further findings—alleged findings—will surely fuel the fire of terror in our community. We'll keep you informed to—"

Mandy signaled Marc to shut off the TV. The meeting room fell dead quiet, shocked, then whispers intensified to a nervous buzz.

The word *satanic* sent a shiver through Mandy's body. The expressions on people's faces indicated she wasn't the only one who felt freaked out by what had just been reported. And bringing the devil into this murder would no doubt scare the shit out of the citizens of Lakeside City. Any community would be upset and terrified. But to this knee-jerk, ultraconservative community, she knew it would electrify their fears and propel them to conclusions. It wouldn't be pretty.

It was an hour earlier than their usual stopping time, but after hearing about the killing, there'd be no way anyone in the room could be productive. Besides, Mandy had wanted to stop it early, anyway, and this was a good excuse. She got everyone's attention and suggested that they quit for the evening and meet back next week. With that, people got up and left, still obviously stupefied by the news. She knew they'd be even more upset if it'd been reported that Stacey Hendriks was a lesbian. It wouldn't be long before that got out. Secrets had a short shelf life in Lakeside City.

"Wow! That was a shocker!" Vinny said.

"My God. Let's get out of here and go to the bar." Mandy grabbed her purse. "I could use a drink."

"I think I'm going to like working with LEAP," a silky voice said. "Thanks for telling me about it." A hand from behind touched Mandy's shoulder, startling her, then it moved down slowly to the small of her back. Jessica's hand lingered there as she gave Mandy a sideways hug, but didn't drop her arm.

Just as Mandy twisted out of Jessica's embrace, she spotted Kera coming through the door. Kera's eyes glared at them as she stopped and signaled Vinny to join her. Mandy watched as they talked to each other. She saw Kera's body tighten, her face flushed.

Mandy glowered at Jessica. "You need to leave. Now," she demanded through clenched teeth.

Jessica didn't budge.

Kera left Vinny and was on her way toward them.

Kera and Jessica locked onto each other with their eyes. Mandy wondered how long they were going to stand there, sizing each other up, like gunslingers.

"Have a long day, honey?" That was lame, Mandy knew, but it was the only thing she could think to say. She wiped the moisture from her forehead. Her heart pounded.

"Yes, I got back sooner than expected. I don't know your... uh, friend, Mandy." Kera neither took her eyes off Jessica, nor extended her hand.

Mandy felt like she'd been frozen in ice, unable to move her mouth to speak.

"I'm Jessica Mancini. Mandy and I met at the fundraiser Saturday night. She told me about LEAP, so I decided to give it a try...Well, I guess I'd better get going. I've really enjoyed the meeting, Mandy, and look forward to working with you."

Mandy saw the flirt in Jessica's smile and knew Kera had too. Kera didn't respond but her glare followed Jessica, pushing her toward the door. If Mandy could magically make someone disappear from the face of the earth, she would've done it right there, right then. Poof. Gone. Evaporated. But Jessica took her sweet time, her hips swaying to the rhythm of her intent, and dropping breadcrumbs along her path.

Mandy sighed, thankful, but she knew that bitch had left something for Kera to gnaw on. She had to tell Kera about Jessica tonight, knowing full well how Kera would interpret what she'd just witnessed, or thought she'd witnessed. She took a deep breath, and let it out.

She'd truly rather be attacked by a pack of rabid dogs.

* * *

Mandy and Kera sat at a table at the Out-and-About. The music of the Zac Brown Band blasted throughout the bar. Mandy liked the band but wished the music wasn't so loud. She didn't want to have to shout and be overheard. She asked the waiter, when he brought them their drinks, to lower the volume.

"You haven't eaten yet, have you?" She grabbed two menus and offered one to Kera.

"No, I haven't. I was waiting to eat here with you."

On the way to the bar, Mandy had avoided the topic of Jessica. Instead, she filled Kera in on the latest news on the Stacey Hendriks case. Just before they'd gotten out of the Jeep, the radio reported that the chief of police had made a public statement, giving other facts—including the lesbian issue, as well as confirming the presence of satanic symbols. The chief refused to say how many, where they were located, or what the symbols were. He called for calm and assured the community the police had good leads and would find the killer soon.

"Their special tonight is chicken nachos," Mandy said as she peeked over her menu. "I know you love them. Would you like to share an order?" She really wasn't hungry anymore, since the bitch had ruined her appetite.

"Sounds okay." Kera placed her menu back in its holder.

Kera's terseness wasn't lost on her, but she just couldn't bring herself to say anything; she'd wait until after dinner.

"So," Mandy began, her voice breaking. She cleared her throat and took a sip of water. "What'd you think about the latest we just heard on the radio about Stacey being lesbian, Erin being her partner and the satanic symbols carved on her body?"

"It was bound to come out." Kera's expression was flat, detached. "It won't play well for Erin."

"Why not? Shouldn't it put the police on another path, start them looking elsewhere for Stacey's killer?"

"Not so sure of that. People freak out when they think the devil is involved. Think about it, Wiccan, witches. Shit, they even refer to themselves as witches, not evil or into devil worship, not their bag, but—"

"But what do Wiccans or witches have to do with the devil?"

"Nothing. Absolutely nothing." Kera threw up her arms in exasperation. "But, to give you an example of what I'm talking about: I went to this concert, when I was in college, where the singer was dressed in red, wore a witch's hat and black cape. She danced around the stage with a broomstick as she sang, enticing the backup dancers who were dressed like demons in red outfits and devil ears, all the while fire shot up around her as though she were in Hell. That, in a nutshell, epitomizes the confusion."

"Now that you mention it, I had a woman client at Legal Aid, a couple years back, who wanted to sue someone because that person was a witch who'd cast a spell causing her to get cancer. When I let her know there wasn't anything I could do about it, she decided to have an exorcism, since the spell must have made her possessed by the devil."

"Yeah, and it won't take long for this community to confuse Wicca with devil worship. We don't exactly live in a city of enlightenment," she scoffed. "It will be known, before you know it, that Erin is Wiccan, then add lesbianism into the mix. She'll be treated to the equivalent of a burning at the stake."

Mandy swallowed hard.

"Did you see Detective Brown when he left Erin's house?" Kera didn't wait for an answer. "He stopped and stared at the altar, the dagger. I'm sure he'll put his own interpretation to it. You know he's not going to bother to listen to anyone who might foolishly attempt to set him straight—and neither will the citizens of this *fine* city." Kera rolled her eyes.

"Oh God, it will get out. I had forgotten about her altar." Mandy had to admit that, until a few days earlier, she hadn't known much about Wicca, and the little she did know—or thought she knew—wasn't exactly positive. The only reason she knew differently now was because Kera had educated her the other night.

They sat there for a while, not talking. Kera had turned inward, staring down at nothing in particular. Mandy dealt with the uncomfortable silence that churned between them by rearranging the condiment caddie.

Then Kera blurted out the obvious. "So, what's going on between you and Jessica?"

Oh God! Mandy hadn't been expecting that. Well, she'd expected it, but not right then, and not the bluntness.

Kera's eyes dug into hers, waiting.

She wondered how she could be so innocent yet feel so guilty. Maybe, she reasoned, she felt responsible because she should have left the bar the first time Jessica put her arm around her. She'd sat there and listened to Jessica blab on, all the while, trying not to be rude, not to offend, yet feeling irritated and uncomfortable. In retrospect, she should have left the fundraiser earlier. But at the time, she'd felt obligated to mingle and talk to others since she was representing Legal Aid and was supposed to make professional connections, not the kind of connection Jessica had tried to make with her.

Mandy worked to hold a matter-of-fact tone. "It's not complicated, honey. I met Jessica at the fundraiser. She flirted with me, for sure, but I assure you I didn't reciprocate, in fact, I tried to avoid her. And, when I first met her that night, I talked about LEAP, but I didn't invite her to join or have any idea she'd show up—"

"Really, when I asked Vinny tonight if he knew anything about you and Jessica, he told me—after I all but threatened him—that a friend of his who'd been there that night saw you two together, and told him, 'something was going on, there.' Vinny heard it from another source too." Kera's eyes were watery.

"I can see how it might look to others, but, I didn't encourage her and I didn't flirt back. I tried to get away by leaving her and talking to other people, but she kept following me—"

"Like to the meeting tonight."

Mandy heard the sarcasm in her voice, loud and clear. It was just what she feared, Jessica's behavior Saturday night had gotten back to Kera before she had a chance to explain. But it was even worse now because Kera and Vinny had seen Jessica in action, and Vinny's friends had misunderstood what had really happened. So now Kera was convinced that Mandy was trying to deny and cover it up.

"Whoever saw us misinterpreted, at least on my part, what was going on that night. I was irritated with Jessica's unwanted attention and I kept trying to ditch her. She showed up tonight, uninvited and unwanted."

Kera set her mug back down on the table. "Yeah, right!"

Mandy saw the pain and sadness in Kera's eyes that had quickly switched to anger. Then, it was as though a curtain had dropped and the scene had ended for Kera. She didn't say anymore. Her face appeared empty of any emotion at all.

"Kera, I'm so sorry, I didn't tell you about her before you heard. I really meant to but—"

"It's time for me to go." Kera got up from the table, lifted her mug and drained it. She patted her leg for Lakota to come with her and left the bar.

Mandy's stomach felt like she'd swallowed a rock. She followed Kera with her eyes, hoping she would turn around and come back, listen to her, believe her.

She sat there for a half hour and watched the door…

Then she called a cab.

CHAPTER ELEVEN

A piece of Kera wanted to go back in the bar and try to believe Mandy, and if she couldn't believe her, forgive her. But her hurt, her pain, and her pride pushed the key into the ignition. She drove around, aimlessly, until it suddenly occurred to her where she needed to go.

Kera made a right onto Turtle River Drive and drove along until she came to the house where she'd grown up—and where her sister now lived. Even in daytime she wouldn't have been able to see the house, because it was tucked back into the wooded land, close to the river. Still, traveling down this road brought back another time, a time when she was carefree and still enjoyed the comfort of her parents' love, a time when she still had her innocence. She pushed on and followed along the road until it crossed over into the countryside where folks who found no ease in huddling together lived. She pulled into Moran Brady's driveway and cut the engine.

From the front, the old Victorian house looked dark. Moran wasn't an early-to-bed person, but still, Kera realized she should've called instead of operating on instinct. That rapid-fire decision-making was part of her pathology, reacting from the gut, not considering consequences. She had to work on that, but not tonight, not as she felt herself unraveling, coming undone.

Tonight she'd had had a knee-jerk reaction, as if a switch had been tripped when she saw Jessica with her arm around Mandy, and Mandy breaking it off when she'd seen her coming in. How long had it been going on, she wondered. No matter, she had to face it; Mandy was moving on, just as Kera had feared, and had even suggested, on occasion. Well, Mandy had taken her up on it, and this was the day. But, it felt like the last piece of something, something essential, was being wrenched out of her, something that had been patched over—fragilely— by Mandy's love. A scab broken, exposing all her loss. Some goddamned force kept sneaking up behind her and pushing the delete button on people she loved. *Poof!*

The real bitch of it was, unlike with her parents and Kelly, she'd be seeing Mandy around, alive, with someone else. When she'd first realized what was going on between Mandy and Jessica, she'd felt numb, but now it felt as though she dangled in emptiness on a fraying rope. She reached over and put her hand on Lakota, needing to be stabilized, steadied, moored. Still, swirling emotions churned inside of her, screaming silently, ready to take her under. That's why she'd come to Moran Brady.

Moran was more than a shaman to her. She was the woman who'd stepped in when her mom died when Kera was twelve. Her father had worried about Kera's fascination with the "old hippie" woman with "strange practices and ideas." According to both her parents, Kera had been the difficult child—an assertion Kera couldn't deny. But when her father realized that Moran's influence was generally a good one, he stepped back and pretended not to notice, and she'd been aware of his *pretending not to notice*, and loved him for it.

Lakota jumped out of the Jeep, perking her ears to the beat of a drum, staccato, that came from the riverside behind the house. Kera and Lakota followed the sound.

The old woman was perched on a rock on the bank of the river, next to a small bonfire. Her well-worn hiking boots stuck out from under the blanket snugged around her. She was drumming and calling in her spirit world. It was the shaman's way of propelling one's consciousness to another world, a world that held teachers, power animals and understandings, a spiritual journey interconnected to all of creation on the wings of a trance. It was a world she had shared with Kera.

In the filmy, dark gray atmosphere, objects appeared as solid black to Kera, except where the star and moonlight sparkled off the wet rocks and rippling water. Moran's baseball-capped head tilted up to the evening sky. Except for her tapping fingers on the drum, the old woman was as still and solid as the stately trees. Kera walked softly, and sat down on a nearby rock across from Moran. Lakota took the cue and lay down on the other side of Kera, keeping vigil.

Kera gazed out into the glittering water as it flowed, murmured and tumbled over the rocky falls on the far side of the river. She drew in the moist night air, repeatedly filling her lungs to capacity, and slowly let it out in preparation to join Moran in a journey. She felt her spirit opening up as she swayed gently, calmly, to the melody of the whispering breeze that stroked her face, and made connection to something bigger, something not of her, but of the ages. The rhythmic drumbeat and flickering firelight danced in her head, blurring together until she felt herself setting off, taking her pain along, as she soared off to another world on the back of something feathery...

Her guide and transporter, Owl.

She lay—wounded—on the bird in flight, separated from connecting thread.

Her gut split open; entrails spilling out, a geyser of red liquid spewing into nothingness, depleting her, sapping a reason for being.

From somewhere, floating to her, a lacy ribbon of gauze, twisting in a puff of air as in dance. It moved toward her and entered her gaping wound, sopping up the pooling blood, pressing to coagulate.

A stopgap measure, keeping the patient alive till emptiness could be filled and connection restored.

Owl came to rest on a rock, waiting.

She felt a soft moistness lapping her belly.

Wolf had come, her guardian and power, tending her wound, mending the cavity, closing the gap into a jagged scar.

The drumbeat intensified, faster and faster, bringing Kera's consciousness back to the riverbank, back to her resident world, then ceased, leaving only the sounds of the tumbling water and crackling fire. She opened her eyes to notice her fingers buried in the dog's fur, and Moran regarding her.

"It was nice of you to join me. What brings you out so late, my dear?" The old woman bent forward attentively.

Kera's lips wouldn't move.

"What's wrong?" Moran's eyes filled with concern.

"Mandy is with another woman." Saying the words out loud startled her and made it more real.

The flames from the fire illuminated the pained expression that crossed Moran's weathered face. "I'm so sorry, dear…I'm glad you came here."

"I didn't know where else to go."

"This is always the right place for you."

Moran's words warmed her, brought comfort. It was her coming home place, the safe place.

"Not doing so well, huh?" Moran took her stick, stirred the fire, kicking up the flames and the smell of burning wood.

"I'm a little better now."

"Tell me about your journey?"

"I rode on the back of Owl. My body was split open; my guts flew out, splattering all over. There was so much blood whooshing out of me, like a geyser, red everywhere, until a ribbon of gauze came to keep the blood from gushing. Then my power animal, Wolf, licked my wound, stopping the bleeding, and then my body closed up."

"Ah." The shaman leaned forward. "So, Wolf and Owl are there to help you in your new pain. Stay here." The old woman went into the house. When she came back, she had two small marble fetishes—one of a wolf and the other an owl—and handed them to her. "These are to remind you that your Wolf protects you and your Owl offers wisdom and healing. They'll give you the strength you'll need to get through this."

Kera took the fetishes and rubbed them with her fingers, feeling the cool smoothness of the marble against her skin. She knew what she needed to do. She would get out of town, way out of town, somewhere she could heal, to a place where, at least, she could stop the bleeding. She knew where to go.

CHAPTER TWELVE

Kera camped out at Sleeping Bear Dunes National Lakeshore, hiking the trails and sandy bluffs until physically exhausted, her spirit elevated from the connection she felt being with nature. Leaving felt like a huge scab being ripped off.

When she returned home late Wednesday night, she couldn't bear the thought of being around people, so the next morning she finished her case charting, then spent the rest of the day on the beach, promising herself she'd get back to business bright and early Friday.

Bright and early hadn't worked out. So here she was, late afternoon, wandering around the two acres of city park that surrounded Lakeside City Hall. She was trying to find the man she'd followed and lost. His brown shirt had disappeared into the crowd before she could get out of her vehicle.

The rally or protest, or whatever they called it, was in full bloom. Some local clergy were in the process of uniting the citizens of Lakeside City to put pressure on the authorities to find the satanic killer.

Kera was disgusted with the whole damned event. Citizens were scared enough when the official announcement was made about the satanic symbols carved into Stacey's—a lesbian, no less—flesh. To add to the alarm, several prominent right-wing ministers were advancing their brand of trepidation and fear. It didn't take long for the news media to join in and focus on little else. The talk shows and editorialists were having a field day. State and national news organizations had shown up and thrown their fuel on the fire kindled by the already sizzled nerves of local citizens… The city had lost its moorings.

Kera made her way through the mass of people, looking for the brown-shirted guy, Ralph Clark. Erin had told her about him when Kera had gone over to her place to apologize for being out of touch the last few days.

According to Erin, Clark's daughter had been on her fall soccer team, and Stacey had acted as the assistant coach. This father was, as Erin put it, a real asshole. He thought he knew how to coach the game better than either Erin or Stacey. For some reason, he'd mostly taken on Stacey with his attacks.

One day, Clark had come to the game early, mad as a hornet. He told Erin that his daughter had declared herself a lesbian, and he blamed Stacey for it, and yanked his kid from the team. Erin and Stacey felt they'd been very circumspect around Tiffany, and around all the girls, for that matter. Erin had found it strange that he'd pegged Stacey as a lesbian but not her, but wrote it off as having more to do with their adversarial relationship than anything else. Erin believed he hadn't told anyone else about his daughter's supposed conversion to lesbianism, probably out of his own sense of shame for her, and what people might think of his parenting skills.

In February, shopping at the grocery store, Stacey had had her last encounter with Clark. She'd told Erin that he'd sneered at her. But since they'd heard nothing more, they concluded he'd dropped the issue. Kera had a picture of Clark taken at one of the soccer games. He was in the background but the image of him was good, and he appeared to be about the right build and height as the man Harold had described. It was a promising lead.

Just walking into a situation like this took all the determination Kera could muster. The protest was packed with people carrying signs that bobbed up and down, many with Bible verses. Her body was locking up, becoming tenser and threatened with every footstep. She thought she might hyperventilate and fly full-speed into a panic attack, maybe more. She took a deep breath and put her hand in her pocket and more rubbed her marble fetishes. She stopped a moment, leaned up against an oak tree to steady herself, then put her hand on Lakota while she concentrated on her breathing. She called to mind what her therapist had told her to do when she felt herself getting overwhelmed: "Distance yourself, view what's happening as though it were a movie."

Okay. It's movie time.

She glanced around the area and noticed a young mother with two kids in a wagon. One held a sign that read: "Save Us From Satan"; an elderly woman, wearing a church-going hat dating back to the fifties, held a sign that proclaimed: "God Is Punishing Us for Our Sins"; a man dressed like Jesus walked, stooped, dragging a cross. Written on the cross was the message: "Homosexuality Has Brought Down God's Wrath." The Jesus impersonator was a community staple. He sniffed out and showed up for just about every supposed sin on display in Lakeside City. Only last week she'd watched him as he tugged his cross in front of a teen center that had recently purchased two pool tables. So now he had a new gig.

After her light-headedness had passed, Kera left the support of the tree and pursued her quarry. First she heard, then spotted a man behind a microphone on the steps of City Hall, announcing the upcoming speakers. However, he was being drowned out by another loud male voice emanating from the crowd, blasting out from a megaphone.

"What do we want?"

"The Satanist," the crowd shouted back.

"When do we want him?"

"Now!"

The man with the megaphone appeared oblivious to the speaker behind the mic, and continued his refrain, energizing the crowd and bringing them along with other, equally obnoxious chants.

On one side of City Hall, the Right to Life group had set up their display, and next to them, a couple booths represented several churches. Further down in the very back, she spotted the Republican tent with its red, white and blue elephant flag flying above it.

She sighed. It seemed to her she'd moved around in circles and still hadn't caught a glimpse of Clark. Maybe a better strategy would be to grab a bench and wait for him to come her way. As she sat there, her thoughts floated back to Tuesday night after she'd left Moran's.

She'd gone home and collected her camping gear and left for Sleeping Bear, not wanting to see or talk to anyone, or to be found. She'd arrived in the early hours of the next morning and pitched her tent in the dark in the most remote spot possible. Taking her flashlight and backpack, she had wandered the trails until dawn when she returned to her campsite. But she wasn't tired. She made her breakfast and sat there staring into the campfire, debating if she should leave Lakeside City and start new somewhere else.

Apparently she hadn't gotten far enough away. Dee came walking into her campsite sometime around six o'clock, when she was making her dinner. Kera hadn't told anyone, not even Dee, where she'd be, and had turned off her cell phone just in case a call made its way into the remote campsite. She should have gone somewhere else; Kera hadn't thought it through. Dee was aware that this place was her getaway safe place, especially since coming home from Iraq.

Actually, it really didn't matter, Kera realized. Dee could have simply raised her internal antenna to find her. It was as though they were connected by an invisible thread. Not only did they possess identical physical features, but they felt each other, physically and emotionally. When Kera was wounded in Iraq, Dee told her she'd felt pain in the very same place where Kera had been shot, and on the same day. Her sister had even gone to the doctor, only to find out that nothing was wrong.

That exchange of energy worked for them on the emotional level as well. Still, since Kera had been diagnosed with PTSD, she wasn't nearly as adept at sensing Dee's distress as she used to be, though her anguish continued to make it over to Dee, loud and clear.

According to Dee, Mandy had called to tell her about the Jessica thing. She was worried and had been frantically trying to get a hold of Kera, calling, texting, and finally she'd gone out to the lighthouse. That's why Dee had come looking for her and ended up staying that night, holding Kera as she slept. The next morning, Dee tried to convince her that Mandy wasn't involved with Jessica, and gave her the same story that Mandy had. Kera figured Dee had bought Mandy's story, not having seen Mandy and Jessica together or heard others who'd seen them at the fundraiser.

Kera finally decided to come back after Dee convinced her that Erin needed her. She knew Dee was right, and if she was going to keep Erin out of Brown's clutches, Kera knew she needed to be there for her—whether or not she was ready.

A mosquito landed on her arm, bit her, snapping her out of her ruminations. Sitting and waiting for Clark to come to her wasn't working, so she nudged Lakota and they started out again.

It was almost six thirty p.m. and cooling off quickly. Her stomach was beginning to tell her she hadn't eaten dinner. At a vendor, she bought a single slice of pizza. Suddenly, over by a clump of aspen trees, the brown shirt she'd been searching for popped into view. Clark stood by three other men, all wearing gray T-shirts emblazoned with "Militia" overlaid on an outline of the state. They were handing out written materials.

She wondered if Clark was part of the Michigan Militia too. It was apparent he knew the T-shirted fellows pretty well. Why had the Militia members shown up? Did they think they could find the Satanist and take care of him, not trusting law enforcement to get the job done? Actually, she could sympathize with that sentiment, since that was why she was here. But obviously, no governmental officials would want the Militia's help. So maybe they were just seizing the opportunity to spread fear and further their cause.

Thinking about Mr. Clark possibly being part of the militia gave Kera the creeps. And maybe, she considered, it said something about the way he dealt with things he didn't like, and how he might have gone after and killed a lesbian coach who, in his warped mind, had turned his daughter gay.

She'd intended to question Clark when she found him, but now she wasn't sure it would be the smartest move, given his militia buddies' presence. Instead, she'd keep an eye on him for a while, watch what he might do. She found a tree to sit under where she could watch the soccer dad, but appear to others as if she were merely resting, eating her pizza, and taking in the speakers at the event.

She heard a choir singing. As she twisted around, she noticed a commotion at the Republican tent, caused by the arrival of Senator De Graff, his wife, Victoria, and his campaign manager, Brian. It made sense that Jeff would show up, a pretty wife on his arm. In politics, there was no bad place to ask for a vote. People were trying to get the senator's attention. Kera squinted her eyes, thinking she saw Mandy talking to him. She stood up to get a better view…Damn, it was Mandy, and Jessica too. Well now, weren't they a tight twosome, she thought. Maybe that's what Mandy had wanted all this time, someone to be political with her and help fight the battles. That wasn't Kera's bag. She'd had enough of politics, having been the daughter of the late mayor of Lakeside City. So, if that's what Mandy really needed, Kera wasn't her girl.

It was one of those moments when she didn't really feel angry, but instead, numb, and her eyes flooded with tears. According to her therapist, her watery eyes had something to do with her sadness trying to push through the blocks of anger or detachment, both of which kept her out of touch with other feelings. Well, something was bubbling up. She wiped her eyes with her sleeve, determined not to let it out, not here. Not anywhere.

She alternated her attention between Clark on one side of the building and Mandy, Jessica and the senator on the other.

Mandy and Jessica appeared to be in a hot debate with the senator. He kept looking around, probably trying to find a way out. Kera guessed he didn't want to hear what Mandy and Jessica had to say to him. He wasn't stupid.

Brian left the conversation with Victoria to go over to Mandy and Jessica. He diverted them away from Jeff and was now talking to them. Kera focused in on Jessica, and threw darts at her with her eyes.

She dreaded Stacey's memorial service tomorrow, because she'd see Mandy there, and maybe Jessica. She couldn't bear to watch them any longer. It hurt too much, so she directed her attention to Clark, who now wore a Militia shirt and was passing out materials.

Holy shit!

CHAPTER THIRTEEN

The memorial service for Stacey was held in a clearing next to Turtle River Park. Kera stood just outside the gathering but in a place where she could easily see who was there and what was going on. Aware of a mildly sweet fragrance, Kera noticed some wildflowers in bloom nearby; the same kind filled a vase on the altar situated by the river. A bug landed on her cheek. She slapped at it, annoyed that it had accompanied the early spring weather. The pesky insect flew by Lakota, who snapped at it, but missed too.

Kera knew about half of the people who'd shown up and assumed that the other half of the fifteen or so gathered were members of the coven. Erin's brother, Daniel, and Stacey's sister stood on either side of Erin like bookends. Stacey didn't have a parent to grieve for her since her mother was dead and she'd never known her father. Dee stood behind Erin, while Casey walked the perimeter of the gathering. She'd volunteered her time as a civilian to keep an eye out for intruders who might get wind of the event and show up to make trouble.

Kera couldn't help but notice Mandy. The woman she loved stood next to Dee, dressed in a silky, sage-green blouse and matching pants. A slight breeze caused her clothing to cling to her legs, arms and breasts. Her blond hair, held back from her face by two flowered hair clasps, flowed down her back; crystal earrings, caught in the sun, dangled and sparkled.

Mandy caught Kera staring at her. Kera turned her eyes away and focused on Lakota. When she glanced up, a woman in a dark blue dress emerged from the woods into the clearing, but didn't move in to join the others. She wore large-framed sunglasses and a wide, brimmed hat that covered much of her face—probably by design. Kera understood that many people wouldn't want to be recognized at a Wiccan ceremony, especially in a town where "Wiccan" seemed synonymous with devil worship. Still, Kera wanted to know who she was and why had she shown up.

Ally had informed Kera that the service would be simple, earth-based, and brief, before gawkers and harassers had a chance to show up. Ally and a guy were leading the Wiccan funeral ritual. According to Ally, they were the priestess and priest of that coven. The urn holding Stacey's ashes had been placed on the small altar along with the flowers, candles, and objects Kera couldn't make out.

The service began with both the priestess and priest chanting. As it progressed, Kera sized up the crowd, but tried not to allow Mandy to come into her field of vision.

Suddenly, a low-flying helicopter with the logo of a local TV station came into view. It drew closer until it hovered over the gathering. A photographer's camera hung over the side. The sound of rotating blades all but drowned out the speakers, compounded by the arrival of a second 'copter. Kera imagined the footage on the nightly news and front-page photos in the morning paper.

Though Ally invited people to share memories of Stacey's life as a way for her spirit to be able to cross over, the overwhelming noise prevented the ritual.

People hurried back to the parking lot. The woman with the wide-brimmed hat disappeared back into the wooded area.

Kera hustled over to the spot but the woman was already out of sight. Kera ran into the woods just in time to see her get into the passenger side of a black car. The vehicle tore out on a dirt road—before her door had completely closed—kicking up a shield of dust and dirt that prevented Kera from getting the make of the car or its license plate number.

When Kera got back to the service, Ally and others were clearing off the altar. As she moved closer, she overheard Daniel tell his sister that he'd take her to his house where the press wouldn't be able to get to her. Erin's face was pale and she seemed barely able to move. Ally told Kera she had to get back to the bar but invited her to stop by later for a drink, with the warning that she'd also asked Mandy and Dee. At first, Kera thought she wouldn't go; why torture herself? But she didn't want to spend the rest of her life sidestepping Mandy. Some weed would help her get through it.

* * *

When she arrived at the bar, Kera picked out Dee and Mandy at a table in the corner. Ally—behind the bar—noticed her. "One pint of Bell's Two-Hearted coming right up," she hollered out.

Dee waved her over.

"Come on and sit down." Her sister gave her a quick hug, kissed her cheek and pulled out a chair.

Kera's eyes met Mandy's, just for a second, but Mandy quickly dropped her head. Kera was sure Mandy had looked down because she was embarrassed and guilty about how she had handled the changing-of-the-girlfriends. Mandy's eyes were moist. What was her problem? Kera was clearly the injured party—the one thrown over, dumped.

"Hey Mandy, how's it going?" Unwilling to let Mandy know how bad she felt, Kera managed a slight smile, then sat down next to Dee.

"Okay, I guess, but Kera, I wish you'd hear me out and—"

"Look, Mandy," Kera cut her off. "We have a work relationship going on here, so let's keep it professional and leave it at that." Kera felt halfway decent. The medicinal herb had mellowed her out and almost made her think she didn't care.

"You're right," Mandy said, nodding. "That's probably the wise thing to do for now. But if you'd only listen—"

"Is anyone else ready for lunch? I'm starved," Dee interjected, passing the menus around like a dealer at a casino.

Ally arrived with Kera's drink and a bowl of nuts for the table, and then took everyone's order and handed it to a passing waiter. She didn't need to get to work for a while, she said, so she'd be able to join them for lunch. Kera was grateful for Ally's presence; it helped to dilute the tension between her and Mandy.

"So, Wicca is pretty much just one form of paganism but with witches, is that what you're saying?" Dee sipped her wine.

"Yeah," Ally laughed, "but there's more to it. There's lots of variation within covens, but that's about right." The conversation paused until the waiter who'd brought their lunch had left. "We witches are into spells, amongst other of our traditional ceremonies. But what people don't understand about Wicca, or care to understand, is that we only practice good spells—for instance, someone might need healing. Our coven never gets into negative stuff. Some groups do, but it's never about a devil, just what they call black spells. And as for Satanism, it hasn't anything to do with Wiccan or our practices. But try to tell others that. You can't, because the minute you bring up Wiccan ears close and preconceived ideas take over." Ally regarded Kera. "At least with Shamanism, you have better press."

Kera swallowed a mouthful of food. "Well, maybe. But unless you're Christian around here, you—"

Dee glared at her sister. "Kera, not all Christians are like that. Don't be so—"

"I know, Dee. I'm not talking about you or people from the enlightened branches of Christianity, but there aren't many of your kind around here. And even so, most Christians don't really know jack shit about the various forms of paganism, nor have I found them very interested. And it's not like we're all out there trying to convert people to our way of thinking—like some religions I know. Why do you always get so damned defensive about your Christianity, anyway?"

Kera wondered why she and her sister were snapping at each other, or rather why she had started picking on Dee. She didn't need to belittle Christians, nor was she upset with most of them. And she wasn't irritated with her sister. Not really. The person she was mad at was Mandy. Then it came to her—or the voice of her therapist—that she was dumping her anger at Mandy onto Dee, a safe place, because her sister would never leave her—unlike Mandy.

"Now, now, sisters, settle down." Ally raised her hands. "I want to tell you a few things that might be helpful to Erin's case before I have get back to work. It didn't occur to me until this morning that it might be important. I'm not sure what all Erin has told you, but I am pretty certain she didn't tell you about this."

Kera leaned in. "We're all ears."

"Well, I got a call last night from Tori De Graff."

Mandy interrupted. "Any relationship to Senator De Graff?"

"His wife."

"What? Tori? Oh, I get it, short for Victoria. I didn't know she went by 'Tori.' I've never heard anyone call her that."

"Well," Ally continued, "when she was with Stacey and Erin, she called herself 'Tori,' so everyone else did too."

"What do you mean? Are you saying she was 'with Stacey and Erin'?" Mandy made air quotes with her fingers.

Ally lowered her voice and leaned forward. "Tori, Stacey, and Erin were a threesome."

"A ménage a trois!" Mandy's chin dropped.

"I prefer the less fancy word since I come from a blue-collar background." Ally smiled. "I'll stick with 'threesome.' Anyway, they all lived together, oh, I'd say, for two or three years, maybe longer."

"My God, how did they get away with that around here?" Dee asked. "If people had gotten a hold of that arrangement, they'd have been run out of town on a rail."

Kera feared what would happen if that little tidbit got out to the public. On second thought, *when* it got out.

Ally shook her head. "You're right, but they probably got by because they were so isolated, living out in the boonies with no snoopy neighbors around. I've known Erin for years and was sworn to secrecy by her, but now—"

"What happened? Like, why did they split up?" Kera scooted her chair in closer to the table to hear better.

"I can only tell you what Erin told me at the time, and it wasn't a great deal." Ally took a breath. "You see, Tori—or Victoria—comes from a well-to-do and political family from Grand Rapids. When I met her, she was pretty much in rebellion against all that her family stood for—the money as well as the conservative politics. Later, when Tori left, Erin told me that she thought Tori was feeling the pressure from her family to come back into the fold—not that they ever knew she was a lesbian, let alone involved in a threesome. I don't know, maybe she had moved out of her rebellious phase. Maybe she just wanted to go mainstream or needed the acceptance. Who knows for sure? Anyway, Tori just up and left one day, regained her family's status, and married well."

"She didn't tell anyone?" Mandy patted her lips with her napkin.

"Nope, she didn't tell either Erin or Stacey. She just left a note saying her leaving had nothing to do with them and that she still cared for them both. She asked them to respect her decision and privacy. And as far as I know, they did. That's pretty much it in a nutshell."

"Wow. Erin and Victoria sure have some secrets." Dee took a bite of her sandwich.

"Why didn't you tell me this before, Ally?" Kera asked.

"I didn't think it had anything to do with anything. But yesterday, Tori called me and asked when the service would be, because she wanted to come but didn't want to be seen there—for obvious reasons. She told me Brian would bring her if she could get in and out without being noticed. I gave her the when and where of it all, and that it'd be a small gathering, not publicly announced. So, I let her know about the back wooded area, on the DNR access road, and—"

"Oh, so that was Victoria who stood in the back with the big hat and sunglasses," Kera said, "and Brian was the driver of the getaway car."

"I guess I never thought of it as a getaway car." Ally laughed. "But yeah, Brian was the driver."

"When I noticed her coming in from the woods," Kera remarked, "I thought she walked with an air of self-importance—I guess she didn't know how to disguise that." Kera laughed.

"That's Tori all right, even when she was with Erin and Stacey, she pretty much got her way; 'entitled' Erin once called her when she was mad at her. But she brings to Jeffrey the wifely qualities needed for his position—or at least he thinks he needs—as well as a beautiful woman at his side. He makes no secret that he aspires to higher office."

"I know who Brian is, but have I personally met him?" Kera glanced at Mandy.

Mandy nodded.

"Oh, yeah," Kera remembered, "at that political event you took me to last year, right?"

"Well, more like dragged you to."

"Damn it, Mandy, I went willingly. Don't make it sound like I didn't." A surge of anger rushed through Kera.

"I didn't mean anything by that, just that you don't like—"

"Hey, you two." Dee held her hand up. "Let's get back on topic. Remember, you agreed to stay out of the personal."

At least she'd expressed her anger to the right person this time, Kera thought, even if she shouldn't have let it out at all. She took a breath, leveled out her voice, and got herself back under control. She wanted to hear what else Ally might know.

"So, can you tell me any more about Brian? I mean, would Jeff want his wife at this pagan ceremony for her ex-lover? I would think he'd want that swept under the rug and kept there. But then, does Jeff even know about Victoria's past?" Kera signaled a waiter for another drink.

"No, I'm quite certain he doesn't, at least not to my knowledge. Tori was determined to keep it from him, even though Brian knows."

"You don't think Brian would tell Jeffrey?" Dee asked Ally.

"No. Brian and Tori—Victoria—get on well. And I really do understand why Victoria went to the funeral. I would have, too, if I were her. You have to remember, Tori didn't leave Stacey or Erin out of anger. I'm sure it had more to do with her not being able to deal with her sexuality and being separated from her family. But aside from Tori's past relationship with Stacey, it was very risky for Brian to take Victoria to the funeral—risky for both of them."

"Well, yeah, if they'd been seen by the wrong person... Jesus." Kera could only imagine the field day the press would have had with that one, another three-ring event at the Stacey Hendriks' circus.

"I wonder," Mandy chimed in, "why Brian would agree to bring her? Why he'd be so involved in Victoria's efforts to get to Stacey's service. It doesn't make much sense to me, politically speaking."

Ally shrugged. "I don't know. I can only guess it had to do with the fact that Brian had a personal connection with both Erin and Stacey. Maybe he wanted to be there because he needed closure too...Though he actually didn't attend, did he? Well, maybe he cared enough for Tori to risk helping her say goodbye to Stacey."

"How did he know them?" Kera accepted a mug of beer from the waiter.

"Actually, he used to be part of our coven, along with Erin and Stacey." Ally paused. "I don't know if he's still Wiccan, but probably not, given his position with the senator. He most likely has gone mainstream or, at least, is not a practicing Wiccan."

"Was Victoria Wiccan too?" Kera asked.

"She said she was 'vaguely Christian.' I remember those were her exact words because I was curious as to what it meant." Ally laughed. "When I asked her, she said she wasn't very religious but observed major holidays like Christmas and Easter. But to answer your question, she definitely wasn't interested in Wicca. But I also know she wasn't bothered that Stacey and Erin were."

"Who knew about Stacey, Erin, and Victoria's relationship?" Kera asked.

"As far as I know, no one knew other than Brian and me. Stacey told me that she'd told Brian." Ally shook her head. "I can't remember why she'd let him in on it, but I do recall her saying that he promised to keep it quiet. And I'm sure he did, since that relationship really never got out to the rest of the group—if it had, I would have known." Ally grinned. "I imagine it was quite a shock to Brian, later, when he found out that Jeffrey's Victoria was the 'Tori' of the threesome." Ally checked her watch, then drained the last few drops of her beer. "Geez, I need to start my shift. But if you have any more questions, let me know. I'll be behind the bar all night." She got up, collected a couple of empty glasses and left.

Jesus! Kera ran her fingers through her hair. *So many secrets.*

* * *

Kera sat at the bar and ordered another draft to help wash down her misery. She knew Dee needed to get to work, but suspected that Mandy's quick departure had to do with Jessica, even though she'd claimed it was work. Her knuckles were getting sore from rapping on the bar; she could only stop for short intervals.

She struggled to focus on Erin's case and the information Ally had revealed at lunch. But she obsessed over Mandy. She knew she had given others the impression that she'd become emotionless because of what she'd gone through, but that wasn't true. To survive, she'd learned to smash her emotions into unidentifiable parts and hide them, deep down, out of sight. It was the only way she could survive what she had gone through in Iraq, and now with Mandy. Her pain gnawed at her. It had been pure torture being so close to Mandy, close enough to smell her fragrance, a scent, all her own. Kera wondered if she'd really smelled it—they hadn't been sitting that close— or whether Mandy's presence brought the scent to memory. It didn't matter, really. Mandy's fragrance lingered with her, prompting memories and creating yearnings that needed to be shaken off. Buried.

Damn it. She needed to focus.

She juggled the pieces of information Ally had revealed and attempted to create a picture that would make sense of it all. The threesome was certainly a new piece, but was it germane to Stacey's murder? The most obvious possible implication was that Senator De Graff wouldn't want all that information about his wife to become public. She knew Brian was devoted to De Graff, but would he have gotten involved? But, why kill Stacey and not Erin? Either one of them could've spilled the beans…

"Want another?" Ally startled her.

"Sounds good. Say, can you tell me any more about Brian?"

"Well, let me think. He came from the East Coast a few years back. He joined our coven and was pretty active, at least for a while. I—"

"Why do you think Brian would take such a risk? I get why Victoria went, sort of, but just because Brian was once part of the coven, it doesn't make sense to me that he'd take a chance like that."

"I agree." Ally looked thoughtful. "I don't see why this would have any bearing on the case, but, well, did you know he's transgender, and gay?"

"No."

"Not many people know, he's always been closeted about it, and it makes even more sense, now, with the job he has. And most people—gays and straights alike—have a harder time with people who are transgender and live as gay people than those who transition and live a straight lifestyle. At least that's my observation.

"Yeah." Kera wrinkled her forehead. "I have to admit, that's true for me. It's hard to wrap my mind around why a woman—who's sexually attracted to men—feels an overwhelming need to become a man, a man who's attracted to men. Like why go to all the bother?"

"But Kera, gender and sexuality are two different issues… Think about it. If you feel as though your true gender was male, but you were trapped in a female body—how uncomfortable would that be? And, the fact that Brian has always been attracted to men is just about his sexual orientation, not his gender. Like I said, two different issues."

"Yeah, I guess…but I'm not sure that has anything to do with this case." Kera considered. "Except for the fact that hiding something like that must be really hard on him. I wonder if he found a kinship with Victoria, her being bisexual—something she'd most likely not want known, and even more detrimental, having been a part of a lesbian threesome. They both have big-time secrets. Maybe that's overthinking it, but it could be a reason Brian would have felt sympathy for her and risked doing what he did. They'd become friends."

"Just a minute," Ally leaned in, "I don't know why I didn't think of this earlier. It could be important."

"What's that?"

"Well, back in the day—the early days of the coven—we were trying to educate ourselves on other forms of paganism. So members took turns researching and giving reports on various pagan traditions, especially in other cultures. It was all very interesting and gave us a sense of our Wiccan roots. People could choose whatever they wanted to investigate. Well, one week, Brian said that he had a report he wanted to give that week—he hadn't told anyone what the topic was, so no one had any idea about it. The report ended up being on Satanism."

"Really."

"Yup, and that pissed off many members of the coven. Most people left that night before he ever got very far into it. They didn't want to hear about it. As you well know, lots of people think we're all devil worshippers. Frankly, I think Brian spooked people when he wanted to talk about it in the coven, as though it were part of our tradition. After that, he only came once, maybe twice. I'm sure it was because our members were cool toward him."

"That's interesting…Do you think he had a personal interest in Satanism or just made a bad choice of subject?"

"To be honest, I couldn't tell you. I know he knew devil worship had nothing to do with paganism. At the time I'd thought he'd just made a stupid mistake presenting that when we were exploring our roots, like maybe he didn't understand our focus. Anyway, he became defensive and got all up in arms, telling people they were narrow-minded because they wouldn't listen to another kind of belief…There were people in the coven that claimed he was into Satanism. How they knew, or thought they knew, I don't know. Maybe they were like little kids who like to tell ghost stories to scare others."

"Hmm, maybe," Kera muttered.

Ally was called back to her bar duties, which left Kera to think about Brian. If he'd gotten into Satanism, and if the senator had decided to have Stacey killed, perhaps Brian had volunteered to take care of it, adding a satanic touch. That would certainly steer any suspicion away from his boss.

Since Erin could be in danger, if she happened to be next on the list to be silenced, Kera decided she'd better check and make sure Daniel was keeping an eye on her, because tomorrow she planned to shut off all communication with the outside world, at least for a day. She needed to back off, recover. To be alone.

CHAPTER FOURTEEN

Pedaling uphill, Mandy calculated that she lagged about an eighth of a mile behind Dee. Dee had been begging her to start biking with her for over a year. Mandy kept promising she would but never got around to it. However, today she was there because Dee said she wanted to talk to her but wasn't going to do it on the phone. She'd suggested they go someplace where they wouldn't be disturbed or overheard. So now Mandy found herself out on the path, huffing and puffing, her legs screaming for mercy as she tried in vain to keep up.

The trailhead for the bicycle path started at the mouth of the Turtle River at Lake Michigan, followed the river through the Old Fisherman's Village, and then continued through Lakeside City and on to Turtle River Park. From there it cut through five miles of wooded countryside before it reached the train bridge and looped back. She'd told Dee that before she could even think of joining her riding club, The Pedal-Pushers, she'd need to be in better shape. The ride today confirmed it. She kept pushing herself to get up the hill, albeit more and more slowly.

"You can do it! Just a little farther." Dee's words barely made it through her heavy panting. She knew they were meant to encourage her, but she imagined Dee up there, watching her struggle and giggling to herself.

"That last hill did me in." Mandy finally made it to the top, out of breath. "I should have stopped earlier," she panted. "Good grief, are you trying to kill me?"

"Trying to get you in shape, that's all, but you're right, it's quite a trip up to the top. I don't know the grade, but it's steep. But just wait. It's crazy fun going down." Dee laughed.

"What do you mean, 'crazy fun going down'? All downhill is easy." Mandy grabbed her water out of its holder and took a swig.

"Well, you certainly don't have to pedal hard, but you'll want to lean on your brakes all the way, just to keep in control and not take flight."

"I was trying so hard to get up here, I didn't think about the going down part. You know, I haven't ridden a bike since I was a kid."

"That long ago?" Dee got a small towel from her bike bag and rubbed the sweat from her face. "You didn't tell me that."

"I didn't think it would matter." Mandy put her hand out for Dee's towel.

"Well, it'll be easier from this point on. There's a great place up here for us to stop so we can talk." Dee tossed her the towel. "Let's get going. It's only about another mile to go."

"I'm so out of shape. I don't think I can make it...I'm not kidding. My legs are killing me and I'm still out of breath." Mandy slipped off her bike. When her feet hit the ground, it felt like needles were poking through her feet and rushing up into her calves. She moved her bike off the trail.

"No, no, don't put it down. It's not that much farther, really."

"Too late." Mandy let her bike fall to the ground. She grabbed her water bottle and hobbled to sit down under an old oak tree. As far as she was concerned, she was going no further. Period. She tipped her bottle up to her lips and guzzled it dry, then took off her helmet.

"Don't get discouraged." Dee parked her bike and sat down next to her. "It takes a while—and granted, that last hill was a real bitch. By the end of summer, you'll make it up with no problem. I promise."

"Really?" Mandy rolled her eyes.

"I'm sorry, I hope you're not mad at me. I shouldn't have tried to push—"

"I'm not mad at you. I'm angry for not being in better shape." She rolled back until she lay on the ground and stared up at the sky.

"Believe me, Mandy, I was sucking air too."

"So, what was so important you wanted to tell me that you had to bring me way up here for?"

"Well, I found out at the hospital—overheard the coroner talking to…well, I won't get into it. Let me just say, I know what the satanic symbols on Stacey's body were. I thought I'd tell you, just in case it would be of any help to you in defending Erin. But under no circumstances can you tell anyone else. It's not supposed to get out to the public. I don't have to tell you what would happen if it ever got out that I told you. That's really why I didn't want to tell you on the phone or any other kind of device that could be hacked."

"Okay, but did you tell Kera?"

"No, I tried to call her but she's not answering her phone. Must be one of her hermit days. Sunday often is. You can give her the info, if you think it's important for her to know."

"Okay, so what were they?"

"Inverted pentagrams, symbols used by Satanists."

"I'm trying to picture it, but not sure I know what that looks like."

"First, let me tell you that most everything I tell you in regard to Wicca and Satanism I found out on the Internet, after I heard what they were. From what I understand, the problem is, Wicca uses a pentagram too. It's a five-pointed star, like on the US flag, but it's encircled. Each point on the star represents factors needed to sustain life: fire, earth, water, air and the spirit. But in Satanism, the star is upside down." Dee took a stick and drew in the dirt. "Like this, the one point of the star that was straight up, is now pointed down, representing the dark side. But it's not always one way or another. It all gets pretty muddled because witches have used the inverted pentagram, too, representing the dark side, uh, when they do black spells. But, like Ally said, Wiccans don't believe in doing that, yet they call themselves witches. Good witches, I guess." Dee laughed. "However, in Satanism, the two upright points in the inverted pentagram imply the horns of the satanic goat. Sometimes, this goat is drawn into the image. I don't know the extent of the carvings on Stacey's body, but they're being interpreted as satanic…There were three, one on each breast, and one on her stomach."

"Oh my God." Mandy felt like she was about to vomit. She closed her eyes and willed herself to keep her lunch from coming up.

Dee was watching her. "I know, it's sickening, Mandy. Like I said, I'm not sure it would help you with your case, but—"

"At this point, I don't see how, but you never know. I'm glad you told me—it's not good as a defense lawyer to get surprises, and who knows when I would find out…but probably the most important part is that it explains why Wicca and witches get thrown into the same bag as Satanists. And why so many people in this city are going nuts…"

"I know this case is wearing on you, along with what's going on between you and Kera. You've got dark circles under your eyes."

"Frankly, my dark circles have more to do with your sister." Mandy took a deep breath. "As I told you, I did nothing wrong that night. I didn't reciprocate—other than being initially flattered by her adoration." She felt her face grow hot, having to admit her susceptibility to adulation was embarrassing. "Anyway, my ego-takeover didn't last long and I tried to get rid of her. You believe that, don't you?"

"Of course I do, and I tried my best with Kera but—"

"She can be so exasperating, so quick to believe the worst—it's like she's programmed that way." Mandy picked up her water bottle, peered into the empty container, then tossed it back down on the grass.

"Here, have a drink of mine. She didn't used to be that way, not before Iraq and Kelly's death."

"So, how's it going with you and Casey?" Mandy decided it was time to get off her problem with Kera. She needed to think about something else.

"Pretty good." Dee set her helmet on the grass, then combed through her hair with her fingers.

"Pretty good?"

"Okay, it's going well, but it is early on. I don't have a lot of confidence in relationships, male or female, having been through a few since Don's death."

"Uh-huh, and you've been driving your sister nuts, swinging back and forth in your gender selections, not that it bothers me. But when you told Kera you're bisexual, she didn't take to that either."

Mandy knew how distressed Kera had been when Dee dated a male, and then how relieved she felt when Dee swung back to a woman. She figured Dee must get some joy out of making Kera crazy, since for so long Kera had tormented her for being with a man. According to Kera, identical twins should have the same sexual orientation, lesbian in their case, and any other claimed orientation on her sister's part was a lie, a self-deception.

"So, tell me about Casey, I don't know her and you haven't said much." Mandy retied a shoelace that had come loose.

A smile popped on Dee's face. "Let me see, she's cute… comes off a little like she's tough but she's really very sweet down inside. Maybe she got the tough side from being a cop, having to prove to the men on the force that women can do the job as well as they do. You know how that goes, she's kind of like Kera that way."

"Uh-huh," Mandy nodded, "that describes Kera all right, but back to you and Casey. What do you two like to do?"

Dee's smile morphed into giggles.

"Okay, moving on." Mandy laughed.

"Really, pretty much all we've done so far that's social is to go to the movies and out to eat. Oh yeah, we went to one of Casey's cousin's wedding."

"I think Kera likes her." Dee thought for a moment, "But, I guess, guarded would be the best way of putting it. She has seen my choices—in a husband and other miscellaneous attachments—so, knowing my track record, she's not going to make any snap decisions. They seem to get along fine, so far anyway. But I'll tell you this, any potential partner—whoever she or he may be—is going to have to have Kera's stamp of approval. I won't get into a committed relationship with someone she doesn't like. I've been down that road and it's not pleasant."

"Really? I mean, I know what you're saying. I've been around to see it, for sure, but you need Kera's approval?"

"Not exactly approval. I'm sure we all like to have family approval. But there's an added layer, being identical twins, at least in our case. My being with someone Kera doesn't connect with—I think that's a better way of describing it—is like having a stone in my shoe and trying to run a marathon."

"That certainly adds an extra burden on anyone trying to date you." Mandy picked up a stick and snapped it in half.

"Frankly, I'm surprised Kera is getting along with Casey. As you well know, my sister isn't overly fond of cops."

"I'm not big on them either, but I'll stay open. Since Casey is a woman, I'll put some extra effort into it," said Mandy, grinning.

"Well, thank you, Mandy Bakker," Dee said in mock appreciation. "I sure want it to work out between Casey and me—at least I think I do. As you know, it's a lot easier, living in this world—especially Lakeside City—having a boyfriend than it is having a girlfriend."

"Yeah, for sure, but you're bisexual. I would think you could make the choice to be with a man if you wanted to."

"It's not that clear-cut," Dee said with a frown. "At least not to me. I'm not saying I couldn't do that—I suppose I could. But if I did, it would be like I'd be letting the world tell me who I am and whom I can love."

"Speaking of being with a woman, I know you've been worried about coming out at work, so how's that going for you? Have you told anyone at the hospital yet?"

"No, and I'm not sure I will…at least, not anytime soon. I really think that it might be harder coming out as bisexual than as a lesbian."

"Really, I don't get that."

"Well, just listen to yourself. You know, what you just said to me. You thought—since I'm bi—that I could simply choose to be with men, and not women. You're not the only one who thinks of it that way."

"Well, Dee, if you get that shit from anyone, come see me. I'll balance that attitude out for you by letting you know you'd be a fool to be with a man when you can choose to be with a woman."

They both laughed.

"I'll do that…You know about how I felt guilty having sex with a woman?"

"I seem to remember a conversation or two about that." Mandy smirked.

"No more. It's been good and feels so right with Casey. I'm starting to get over it. Way over it." Dee grinned.

Mandy offered her fist. Dee reciprocated, sealing the deal with a fist bump.

Mandy noticed a man and woman riding along the trail. They stopped just before they'd have to make the descent down the hill. The man initially smiled at her, then his face contorted, angry. He steered his bike toward where they sat. His female companion came up behind him. The man's eyes locked onto Mandy.

"Hey, bitch, haven't I seen your picture in the paper?" He didn't wait for an answer. "Yeah, I know who you are. You're the woman lawyer who's defending the devil-worshipping lesbian, aren't you?" He stopped about a yard from her and straddled his bike.

The woman gawked at Mandy. Her eyes bugged out as though Mandy were some kind of evil creature. "Come on Jake. Let's get the hell out of here. This woman could be one of them devil people."

Mandy couldn't believe what she was seeing, hearing. Was this really happening to her? She'd received hate mail and emails along with nasty phone calls ever since taking on Erin's case. But now this? Those threats had frightened her, but she hadn't envisioned a scenario like this. And besides, she'd felt some comfort, some shield from danger, because Kera had asked Daniel to keep tabs on her—which he'd been doing, checking in at least twice a day. But the problem was, Daniel had two people he needed to keep an eye on, both her and Erin. And even though Daniel was aware she and Dee were out on the trail today, he'd told her that he had to take Erin grocery shopping in a nearby town because she feared being recognized locally. He didn't know how long he'd be, but if he got back in time, he'd join them, or meet up with them along the trail. But that didn't seem likely. Besides, it was a long trail. Actually, when they'd talked about, it hadn't been that important to her. She wouldn't be in her office or in court, places where some crazy person might show up.

She would have to handle this on her own. But now, Dee was in danger as well.

"It's none of your business whom I defend," Mandy snapped back. "Everyone is entitled to a defense, and—"

The guy sneered. "Devil worshippers deserve a stake through their hearts, like vampires."

"You are jumping to conclusions about someone who hasn't even been charged yet with a crime or—"

"Oh, is that right, lawyer lady?"

"That's right, and you—"

Dee twisted her head slightly toward Mandy, covered her mouth like she was about to cough, but instead, whispered. "You're not in court, stop arguing. It won't—"

"Lady, everyone in this community knows that woman is a witch and worships the devil."

"The community is wrong. They need to wait and let the court—"

Dee kept her eyes down. "Come on, let's leave," she whispered. "This man is a nutcase, and he's not going to let this go. He's dangerous."

"Not so fast, lady." He frowned at Dee. "Did I hear you call me a nutcase?" The guy's face had become distorted with rage.

"Who are you, anyway? Oh, I get it, you're her queer lover." His icy blue eyes bore down on Dee.

Seeing him glare at Dee like that made Mandy shudder.

Dee didn't respond to him, as if she were suffering from a mind freeze. Mandy scanned the area, but saw no one. Nobody to come to their aid, nobody to call the cops.

"Answer me, bitch!" he snarled.

Dee was right, he didn't want to be reasonable, he wanted a fight, and he was out for bear. What the hell, Mandy decided, it probably wouldn't do any good, but she had to try to defend Dee.

"It's none of your business who she is, but she's not my lover."

The guy rolled his bike closer to Mandy until the front wheel rolled onto her left tennis shoe. He bent forward, bringing the weight of his body onto the front of his bike, and crushed down on her foot, sending excruciating pain through it. He laughed when she cried out.

Dee jumped up and started to push at the bike and the rider. The guy tried to hold Dee off, but she kept at it. Finally, she lost her balance and fell over the guy, which took them both down, along with the bike, freeing Mandy's foot. Mandy managed to get up and limpted over and to help Dee up. Having fought his way out from under the bike, the guy pushed her down as Dee rose up. He twisted around and smacked Dee, who fell on top of her. He kicked both of them, repeatedly. One blow struck Dee's thigh, hard, making her scream out. Mandy couldn't defend herself with Dee on top of her. All she could see were arms and legs, kicking and hitting. She thrashed around until she was able to roll out from under Dee. Dee, on her back, screamed and kicked at the man. Unfortunately, she wasn't doing any damage to him. In fact, he was more amused than anything. Before Mandy could get her bearings or strike out at him, he spun around and kicked her in the midsection. She doubled over and fell to the ground, groaning in pain, barely able to breathe. She watched, helplessly, as the guy went back to Dee, picked her up, held her close with one arm around her neck, and squeezed. He cocked his fist, preparing to punch her when Mandy heard a voice behind her—

"Get the fuck away from them!"

Mandy looked in the direction of the voice and saw a man running toward them.

It was Daniel Duffy, his gun pointed at their assailant.

CHAPTER FIFTEEN

So far this morning, Kera had put off dealing with any calls she'd received yesterday, when she'd holed up at home, brain in neutral, phone off, window shades drawn as she watched old movies.

The timing of her unexpected visit to see Erin in the morning had worked out for her. She sat in Erin's living room and waited for Daniel to fetch his sister, who, at nine fifteen, hadn't gotten up yet.

Daniel came back in the room. "Can I get you some coffee?"

"No thanks, I'm good." Erin padded in behind him, still in her pajamas.

"I'm sorry Erin, I meant to call but—"

"That's okay, I had a hard time getting to sleep last night." Erin sat down across from her. "I'm glad you're here. I wanted you to know that my principal thought it best I be given an indefinite leave of absence." She sighed. "I guess I'm okay with that since I don't think I could stand up in front of a classroom anyway."

"I get how difficult that would be for you. You need to get past this before you can go back." Kera didn't want to step on Erin's hope to return to her teaching position, but she didn't like the word "indefinite." For her, the word meant *it's all over. Done.*

Kera asked Daniel to give them some privacy. It was important to impress upon Erin the need to keep her mouth shut, especially around the police, and she didn't need Erin's protective brother around to coddle her.

"I'm going out of town today and I wanted to stop by this morning so I could discuss a few things with you." Kera waited until Daniel was out of earshot, then continued. "It's vitally important for you to understand that Detective Brown is not on your side. He has an agenda. And that agenda is not in your best interest. So, don't talk to him—or any other cop, for that matter—without Mandy. And don't—under any circumstances—offer up any information. Brown will figure a way to use whatever you say against you. I can promise you that. He sees you as easy pickings."

Erin didn't have an alibi. The night Brown had questioned her, before Mandy had arrived, he'd asked her what she had been doing all day Tuesday and over the next several days. Erin told him that she'd woken Tuesday morning, sick with the flu, and had stayed in bed for two days, except for a brief trip—she couldn't remember which day—to a convenience store, where she'd picked up some kind of roller food, maybe a corn dog. All that time, with no one to corroborate her story, unfortunately, left her vulnerable. Theoretically, she would have had the time and opportunity to kill Stacey; no one could verify her whereabouts.

"Okay, it's just that I grew up thinking that the police were my friends. I'm not inclined to be on guard around—"

"It's naïve. You have to remember Brown will try to pin Stacey's death on you because he's too goddamned lazy to look elsewhere. Don't forget that fact for one moment." Kera realized she'd become too intense and took it down a notch. "I'm not saying all cops are bad, but Brown, well, I've had dealings with him in the past and I know how he operates. Letting him know you had a quarrel with Stacey before she left was like waving a chicken in front of a fox."

"I know, I know. I was being stupid, not thinking, but I didn't set out to tell him that, he sort of tricked it out of me." Erin grimaced.

"That's why you don't say word one, answer anything, unless Mandy is there with you, and specifically says that it's okay."

"Mandy told me the same thing last night when she called me. I got it now, I really do…Uh, has Mandy told you about the insurance policies? Erin said with a hesitation in her voice.

"Insurance policies?"

"She said she was going to…Well, I don't know how, but Detective Brown found out that Stacey and I both had life insurance policies with each other as beneficiaries. Mandy thought he'd gotten a tip from someone."

"Who would know?"

"I suppose just about anyone who knew us. It wasn't a big secret. I know Stacey told people at her work, and some friends of ours who helped us move. We got the policies because we bought a house together that's not paid off, and we depend on each other's salaries to make the payments.

"Is it just enough to pay off the house, or substantially more?"

"…I guess it's a fair amount more…It's not easy on a teacher's salary…and I have other bills—"

"Erin, how's your credit? I mean, are you in debt far more than you should be, like in over your head?"

Erin grimaced. "I spend too much…it's not good."

Jesus, Jesus, Jesus! Kera shook her head.

Now Brown had the motive.

* * *

Lakota stuck her head out the window while Kera drove the Jeep toward Lansing. She couldn't stop wondering who would have told Brown about the insurance policies. It was one thing that it was no secret, another to have someone tip off Brown. She made a mental note to get Erin to tell her everyone she knew who might have that information. Definitely something to check out.

She planned to visit Victoria to find out if she'd told her husband about her former life. But first, she'd decided to visit Lizzy and Harold, the elderly couple from the motel. Lizzy hadn't called her with anything new, but in Kera's experience, it oftentimes took a personal visit to get people thinking and remembering things. Lizzy and Harold lived in the small town of Potterville, close to Lansing. She'd called Millie Mason at the motel before she'd left Lakeside City, and after some convincing, Millie gave her Lizzy's address. Millie did seem a bit disappointed when Kera let her know that the elderly couple was actually married.

Kera's GPS took her to a white bungalow in a well-kept working-class neighborhood.

Lizzy opened the door. A big smile spread across her face when she saw Kera. "Hello, oh I'm sorry, I've forgotten your name. But I remember that you're that detective woman."

"Right, and it's Kera. I hope I'm not interrupting—"

"No, no, you come on in." Lizzy glanced past Kera, out at the Jeep. "Now you go get that dog of yours and bring her in with you."

When Kera whistled, Lakota jumped through the window and bounded up to the porch and through the open door.

"I'm baking cookies for my great-grandchildren, and two great-great-grandchildren."

Lizzy wore a granny-type housedress covered by a yellow and white checked baker's apron; instead of lace stockings, she wore regular hose and support shoes. Her hair was pulled back up into a bun, no makeup, no adornments. Kera tried to reconcile the two images, Lizzy the motel siren and Lizzy the great-granny in an apron, home in the kitchen baking cookies. Holding those two contrasting pictures in her mind at the same moment was like watching two different genre movies that had been accidently combined and poorly spliced.

"Thank you, Lizzy, this won't take long. I just have a few questions for you."

"Oh, that's no problem. I enjoy company and I just got done putting in my second pan of oatmeal cookies. My first batch is cooling. They'll be ready to sample very soon. Would you and your dog like to have some tea and cookies with me? Well," Lizzy reconsidered, "the dog would probably prefer a dish of water to a cup of tea." She chuckled as she led them back toward the kitchen.

"That sounds great, Lizzy." Kera's mouth watered as she followed the old woman.

"I hope you don't mind if we sit in here to take our tea. I need to keep an eye on my cookies. If I don't, I'll forget them and they'll burn on me."

"No problem." Kera sat down at the white metal kitchen table adorned with squiggly black designs.

Lizzy put on the teakettle and offered Kera a cookie.

"Yum." Kera licked her lips. "These are great." It was obvious to Kera that keeping her husband happy in the sack all these years wasn't Lizzy's only talent.

"Thank you, dear. My family loves them, so I try to keep my container full." She gestured toward a green roasting pan on the counter. "I keep them in there." Her face took on a serious expression. "I don't want to see disappointment on the faces of those little ones if they were to lift the lid off that pan and didn't find my homemade cookies."

"I bet they head for it the minute they come in."

"Oh, you bet they do." Lizzy's eyes twinkled.

"Lizzy, I wanted to come and see you because I was wondering if you or Harold happened to remember anything else. Like, if either of you might have seen anyone else at Stacey's room besides that man your husband told me about?"

"Now that's funny you should mention it, because Harold said something, just this morning, before he left. He thought there might have been a woman there, but then he decided that it was probably the maid—so I guess that's not important. However, he also said that he remembered that the man had a mustache…Harold used to have one years ago, I thought it was pretty sexy, like a movie star."

Lizzy's cougar-ish smile caused Kera, once again, to flash on Lizzy's femme fatale motel attire. She shook it off and forced herself back to the cookie-baking granny.

"Did he happen to remember the color of the beard?"

"Well now, I asked him that. He decided that it was not real dark, sort of medium-shade, but he couldn't say what color, exactly, but maybe a brown or dark blond. You know men, they don't pay good attention to things like that, so I wouldn't put my money on it, if I were you."

The man probably didn't have blond hair, Kera concluded, because Lizzy's husband most likely wouldn't be able to make out blond facial hair, even if it were a dark blond, not from where Harold had shown her he'd been standing. So, she could probably eliminate blond hair. Then again, she considered, many men sport muchaches that differ in color from the hair on their heads, so the color of it wouldn't be that helpful.

"Anything else?"

"No, he only had a quick glimpse of his face and from a distance."

The teakettle whistled, Lizzy got up and poured their tea and brought more cookies. She looked over at Lakota—who was eyeing her movements—and tossed one to the dog.

Lakota leapt up and caught it, midair.

* * *

Kera drove north to Lansing with a small sack of cookies that Lizzy had insisted on sending with her. She'd spent a couple of hours with the elderly woman, even though she had been unable to glean any new information. Lizzy had shown her pictures of her family, and with pictures came stories.

Her cell phone rang. She grabbed it.

"I hear you took off with the clothes that were found in Stacey Hendriks's room at that motel in Lansing," a male voice growled. "Is that right?"

"Would you do me the courtesy of telling me who's calling, please?" Kera knew it was Brown, but he was being a rude bastard by not introducing himself.

"Detective Brown, and you knew it was me, Van Brocklin. No doubt my number identified me, if not my voice."

"You assume too much, Detective." He was right, on both counts, but she wasn't about to give him the pleasure of knowing it.

"Van Brocklin, I was at the Starlight Motel, there in Lansing," he barked, "and the woman who runs the place said you found some of Stacey Hendriks's clothes and took them with you."

"That's right."

"You should have turned them over to us immediately, or better yet, called the police to let them come in and handle the situation. You know better than that. I can have your license for tampering with a crime scene. As it stands now, you've contaminated all the evidence you took—and I don't suppose you wore gloves. Like I said, I could…"

Goddamned fucking asshole, trying to threaten her. Kera felt like throwing her phone out the window to let his voice dissipate into the nothingness of the roadside ditch. But she restrained herself, only because she needed her phone, but she was in no mood to control her response.

"Bullshit, Brown," she barked back. "When I went to the motel, it wasn't a missing-person case, and your department— your own guys—didn't want anything to do with it. Your boys made it very clear to Erin Duffy that Stacey Hendriks couldn't even be considered a missing person. That's why Erin asked me to help find her. And for all anyone knew, she'd taken off for a few days. The fact of the matter is, I thought I was merely returning a few items Hendriks had left behind—as Mrs. Mason requested of me. At the time, there was no body, no hint of foul play."

"Well, I picked up her sack of clothes from Erin Duffy, but now they're contaminated, all because of you. One of these days, Van Brocklin, I'm going to—"

"Sorry, Brown, maybe your department should be more on top of it."

"You've got no right to—"

Kera punched the End button on her phone.

If she'd stayed on with him any longer, she'd have said something she probably shouldn't. For herself, she didn't care, in fact, she would have enjoyed it, but she didn't want to hurt Erin's case—not that it probably mattered.

Kera hadn't intended to stay so long with Lizzy in Potterville. Plus, she'd gotten a late start because of her stop at Erin's. She felt tired, edgy and needed to hibernate. Her state of mind wasn't conducive to meeting with anyone else, or making good decisions for that matter. Brown's phone call had contributed greatly to her crappy mood. It'd be best for her to pick up a sandwich, chips and beer, and go to the Starlight Motel for the night. Mellow out. She'd get a fresh start tomorrow.

* * *

Settled in her motel room, Kera's thoughts turned to Mandy. She wondered about the upcoming LEAP meeting tomorrow night. Hopefully, someone in the activist group would get the big picture and realize the timing for their political agenda was all wrong, but she wouldn't hold her breath. Mandy was a strong and persuasive leader; people liked and respected her opinions. They'd probably hang in there with her, bad idea or not.

Her anxiety from being out in the world all day increased when she thought about Stacey's killer still loose and all the crazy shit going on back home. Then she remembered Mandy telling her about the strange guy who'd come to the LEAP meeting. Vinny wouldn't be available to check things out for her at the meeting tomorrow night, since she'd put him on the trail of Ralph Clark. She decided to text Daniel to have him escort Mandy home. She'd add Mandy on Daniel's message so she'd know he was coming and wait for him.

She missed Mandy far more than she would ever have guessed. Even though she'd told Mandy—over and over—she should find someone else, that had been a message from her head, not her heart. The heaviness felt like trudging through life while her heart reached out for threads of something no longer there.

Maybe she'd call Mandy on the pretense of giving her information on Erin's case, just to hear her voice. She dialed, no answer. Maybe she'd try later. No, not a good idea. The sound of Mandy's voice would taste good but would sour in her stomach. She reevaluated and decided to stick with only necessary calls, and to take care not to drink the entire six-pack, which could lead to calling Mandy. What'd they call that? Drunk calling? Or was it drunk dialing? She couldn't remember, but she didn't want Mandy to know how bad she felt about losing her.

Kera was exhausted, too much dealing with people, too little coping ability left. Her scrambled thoughts swirled around in her head like fall leaves on a windy day, not able to land on anything for more than a few seconds. She grabbed the TV remote, popped a beer, and got out her pipe.

CHAPTER SIXTEEN

Kera had avoided drunk-calling Mandy; however, she'd forgotten to let Dee know that she was spending the night in Lansing. What the hell, Casey was occupying her sister these days, so Dee probably wouldn't miss her.

When she'd woken up, she'd gone on the Internet and found De Graff's Lansing home phone number and address from a site known to disregard people's privacy. De Graff's maid answered and told her that Victoria was out. Kera pretended she was a friend who'd planned on having lunch with Victoria but forgotten their meet-up place. The woman revealed that Mrs. De Graff always ate lunch at the Eighteenth Hole Grill at the Spruce Forest Country Club after her golf game.

The country club was aptly named, as the private road leading up to the main building was lined with spruce. The red brick structure reminded Kera of a modern southern plantation. She pulled into the parking lot, trying to decide if she should she go in and search for Victoria or wait for her to come out. This place didn't appear to be the kind that allowed the public—

the riffraff—through their doors. So she'd need to figure a way in, and without Lakota. Getting in there unquestioned would be hard enough, but a service dog would bring her unwanted attention.

She walked around the exterior of the facility toward the back, figuring the grill would most likely be located close to the 18th hole, so golfers could enter right after playing a round. Hopefully Victoria was close to finishing her game or already in the grill. People were going in and out; no one seemed to be monitoring the entrance. Kera didn't exactly have on a cute little golf outfit like the rest of the women, but her blue polo shirt and khaki pants didn't raise anyone's eyebrows as she entered.

The grill's motif was done in murals of golf course hills, water holes and sand traps. Each table flew a flag with a tee number on it, making it appear as if the tables were placed in the middle of the course. She spotted Victoria sitting at table nine with two other women, all in golf outfits. She didn't have the patience to wait around for them to finish, so she came up with an idea to get Victoria away from her friends.

At the bar, Kera sat on a stool and ordered a local micro-brew beer from the menu. Most exclusive country clubs required their members to pay by signing a tab with their membership number. She counted on that being the case here. When the bartender asked her to sign for her drink, she pointed over at Victoria and told him Mrs. De Graff was buying her the drink, so she would sign for it. He studied her, skeptical, but went over to table nine and whispered in Victoria's ear. When Victoria glanced over at her, Kera signaled her to come over. At first Victoria looked puzzled, then annoyed; however, she got up, said something to her friends, and came to the bar.

A politician's wife needed to be gracious, Kera had learned. Her mother had been a political spouse, the wife of the former mayor, and had put up with all kinds of shit from people, yet took care not to offend voters, all with a put-on smile and unending patience.

"I'm sorry, I don't believe I know you, do I?" Victoria stood there, wearing a mask of diplomacy.

"No, Tori, we've never met but we need to talk." Kera patted the barstool next to her. "Have a seat."

"I'm sorry, my name is Victoria, I don't go by Tori." The color had drained from Victoria's face, and her singsong voice lowered, became tight.

"But you used to go by Tori, back in the day. I believe it was in the days of Erin and Stacey."

"I don't know you," Victoria snapped back, "or what you're talking about. I'm going back to my table." She started to say something to the bartender, but Kera quickly butted in before she could get the words out of her mouth.

"Really, Tori, I'd rather talk to you about Stacey than to the cops, but it certainly is your choice." She thought it was best to keep referring to her as "Tori," figuring by doing that, she'd keep the woman off-balance.

Victoria's eyes widened, her jaw dropped.

"We can talk here or we can go out to my vehicle. Again, it's your decision." Kera patted the barstool again.

"Well, I guess I can go outside, but I'll have to excuse myself first." She returned to the table where her friends were eating.

Out in the parking lot, Kera opened the Jeep door and told Lakota to get in the back. She made a half-hearted effort to brush the dog hair off the front passenger seat.

"Before I get into your vehicle," Victoria had her hands on her hips, her jaw set, "I'd like to know, at least, who I'm talking to."

"Kera Van Brocklin, private investigator." Kera handed her PI license to Victoria. "I'm investigating the death of Stacey Hendriks. I believe you knew her. In fact, you were at her funeral service, weren't you?" Kera gestured for Victoria to get in, then went around to the driver's side.

"Okay, so I knew Stacey and Erin. So what?" Victoria handed the license back. "What's that got to do with any—?"

"Get off it, Tori, you more than knew them, now didn't you?" Kera's eyes burrowed into Victoria's—intending to intimidate. She'd learned that tactic from Detective Brown—the fucker had been good for something.

"I don't know what you mean."

"I'm not in the mood to play games with you, Tori. Just so we can have a starting point, let's agree that you, Stacey and Erin were lovers, a threesome. But then you left Erin and Stacey, and sometime after that you married Jeffrey De Graff. Since then, you've been playing the role of the devoted wife to the senator. Have I got that right so far?"

"What's your name again?"

"Kera."

"Kera, you need to understand, I don't know anything about Stacey's horrible death, and my past with Stacey and Erin is irrelevant to what happened to her." Victoria's voice intensified with each word. She caught herself, turned down the volume, as her eyes darted around the parking lot. "As you can imagine, I can't let this get out to the public, it would ruin my husband's career. Is that what you're out to do? Is that why you're here?"

"No. I'm aware of that, Tori, I'm not here to expose you. Not my goal at all. But I do need some information from you and if you cooperate with me. I'll do all I can to keep this from…"

* * *

Kera turned out of the country club parking lot, on her way to find Senator De Graff. As she drove along, she mulled over her conversation with Victoria. The woman had finally told Kera that her husband knew about her past with Stacey and Erin. According to her, he'd found out about a year before when he'd come across an old love letter that had been stashed away. They'd fought about it at the time, but they'd eventually called a truce when she'd learned that he'd had a fling with one of his employees.

Kera yawned. She hadn't slept well last night because she'd watched the news on television and had become agitated. Stacey's murder and the ordinance issues were getting big play in Lansing—probably all over the state. She did catch a representative of LEAP—a man she didn't know—being interviewed, instead of Mandy who'd always dealt with the press. The temporary spokesperson had said she couldn't be found. She didn't like the sound of that, but finally decided she was with Jessica, and not answering her phone.

Kera's first stop had been the senator's office in the Farnum Building, but he wasn't in. His secretary told her that he had meetings scheduled all afternoon and wouldn't be able to see any of his constituents. Not having his schedule for the rest of the week, she'd advised Kera to call back tomorrow or the next day and she'd try to find a time for her to meet with him.

Try to find a time! That was bullshit, unacceptable. Well, she didn't have the time, or more to the point, the inclination or patience to wait until next week. Patience wasn't her strong suit. It had never had been a virtue of hers, but since Iraq, it was pretty much nonexistent. She was hardly capable of standing in line, anytime, anywhere. When she went to a store, any store, she'd grab what she needed, then find an empty checkout to go through, if there was one. If not, she'd drop the merchandise on the nearest shelf and leave the place.

She and Lakota made their way out of the building and walked along Allegan Street. The full-length glass windows of the Farnum Building reflected their images. Lakota kept her eyes on the dog walking along beside her in the window's reflection.

"Come on girl." Kera grinned. "I know that pooch next to you is one beautiful specimen, but we need to hotfoot it over to the capitol. It's time for a meet-up with the senator."

De Graff's secretary had rattled off to her the meetings Jeffrey was supposed to be attending. She'd locate where they were being held when she got into the capitol, assuming the information would be on some daily events board or at an information desk. One way or another, she'd find out and catch him between meetings.

She was on a mission to find out how concerned De Graff was regarding his wife's past lesbian relationship. Assuming he knew, how threatened—both personally and professionally— did he feel? It might be difficult enough for him to take, being a heterosexual man, but politically, it was a scandal lurking in the cellar of his campaign. Its unearthing would be a media feast. And on top of that, the *pièce de résistance* of the story was that the senator's wife had not only been in a gay relationship, but had participated in a lesbian threesome. Kera shook her head. She almost felt sorry for the De Graffs.

Kera hopped up the steps of the capitol two at a time. She entered the door and showed Lakota's service dog certification to the security guard. Even though her dog had on a service vest, capitol staffers required a little more proof. After getting Lakota approved, the guard directed her to a place where she could find out what meetings were being held that day.

Never having been inside the building, Kera took in its elegant Victorian style, marked by a rotunda in the middle of the main room, where she was able to look clear up to the dome. It made her feel a little disoriented and dizzy. She had read, at one time or another, that much of what appeared to be marble was actually faux painted. The inside was certainly remarkable, a place of significance, a place where important people were making weighty decisions. Staid people's portraits hung on the walls, overwhelmingly men—most dead now. She was quite sure she wouldn't want—or have wanted—to have a beer and conversation with any of them.

Just as she was getting her bearings, Senator De Graff came down the staircase, dressed in the all-American political garb of a dark blue suit, white shirt and red and white striped tie with an American flag lapel pin. He carried a briefcase and was talking with a woman who was clad in the female version of a wrapped-in-the-flag politician. Their friendly manner suggested that they were political colleagues, seemingly in agreement. They moved in Kera's direction.

"Excuse me, Senator De Graff, may I have a word with you?"

He looked at her, smiled dismissively, and kept walking toward the door she'd just entered.

"Senator De Graff, it's very important that I talk to you. It won't take long," she called as she hurried after them.

The senator held open the door for the woman as they exited the building. Kera and Lakota followed.

The political duo walked out onto the portico, stopped and continued their conversation. Just down the steps, a reporter and crew were interviewing a person. Kera approached the senator, again, and got his attention.

"I just need a few minutes of your time, sir, if you'd be so—"

"If you'll give my secretary a call, I'm sure she will give you a time when we can meet." He turned back to the woman, obviously annoyed with her persistence.

"I'm not going to be in town for long, I need to speak to you today, now, if I could."

He ignored Kera, said goodbye to the woman and hustled down the steps to the sidewalk.

Kera caught up to him. "I need to talk to you about the murder of Stacey Hendriks," she yelled out. "I believe you know her, and I'm sure your wife does, if you don't."

Her tactic worked. The reporter had overheard her and stopped his interview to watch them. The senator saw the newsman's response as well. His face flushed, his jaws clenched.

"Why don't we go over under that tree?" He grabbed Kera by the arm.

"Keep your hands off me, De Graff. I don't react well to being manhandled, and my dog doesn't like it either." Kera ripped her arm out from his grip. She heard Lakota's deep growl, low pitch, crouched and ready to escalate…

De Graff had jerked back when Lakota snarled at him, prepared to attack. He seemed surprised, like he hadn't noticed the dog, or hadn't thought through the ramifications of grabbing the arm of the dog's owner.

"You better keep that damned dog away from me."

"And you better keep your fucking hands off me." She reached down to Lakota and stroked her. "It's okay, girl."

"Is everything all right here, Senator De Graff?" A security guard hustled up to them, glanced at the dog, over to Kera, then back to the senator.

"Ah, yes, I think so," De Graff responded. "We're going to go over by the tree and talk. I'm sure it will be okay." He turned to Kera. "It'll be fine, won't it?"

"As long as you can keep your hands to yourself."

The guard kept watching, evaluating.

"Thank you, sir," said De Graff as he nodded. "We'll be okay."

The guard went over by the steps that led to the portico, not taking his eyes off them as they walked over toward the tree. The reporter had lost interest in them and was back talking to his interviewee.

"Who are you? And, what's this about someone's murder?"

"Kera Van Brocklin and I'm a private investigator. And it's about the murder of Stacey Hendriks. You may know her, or not, but I know for sure that your wife is—was—well-acquainted with her." She showed her PI license to him while she talked. "Stacey was murdered a couple of weeks ago. Your wife came to her funeral service last Saturday. I'm sure she told you about that, right?" She could tell he was flipping back in his memory, trying to come up with last Saturday's activities. Or he was trying to come up with what he'd say next.

"Uh, no, I don't know anything about that woman or her funeral, but what's that got to do with me, or even my wife? Just because she knows the woman or goes to her funeral doesn't mean I know her." He cleared his throat.

"Are you absolutely sure your wife has never talked about her? For quite a long time, Stacey Hendriks was very important in your wife's life. I would have thought she'd have mentioned Stacey's name to you." Kera watched his face. He was showing her nothing. She suspected that, like most politicians, he could cover a multitude of sins with a placid smile glued to his face. And if he didn't know anything, why was his forehead popping out beads of sweat?

"I don't have to answer your questions. You're not the law." He swiped his forehead with the back of his hand. "But I will say, I've heard about her murder—everyone has, it's all over the news—but I don't have any personal connection to her, and I'm sure my wife doesn't either. You must be mistaken about Victoria being at the funeral. It had to have been somebody else who resembles her." He checked his watch. "I have nothing more to tell you and I have a meeting to get to—I'm already late for it." He hurried off.

Kera didn't see any reason to pursue him, and he was right, he didn't have to answer to her. But she saw how uncomfortable he'd been...

Who was lying, Jeffrey, or his wife?

If Victoria had lied about telling him, was it because she'd hoped Kera would just go away and not seek out her husband, since she'd told Kera that he knew about everything? Or did Jeffrey really not know? She felt herself leaning toward Victoria's story, after having witnessed the senator's discomfort and his refusal to discuss the matter. It just might be that Victoria's big secret had become his big secret.

As Kera got into the Jeep to go back to Lakeside City, a text came in from Brian asking her if she'd like to have breakfast tomorrow at the Big Ten Café in East Lansing. Interesting, when she'd emailed him earlier to ask if she could talk to him while she was there in Lansing, he'd said he was too busy to meet at any time, too many political meeting and obligations. Funny, now he suddenly wanted to have breakfast with her in the morning. He must have just heard from De Graff. No doubt the senator had put a boot in his butt to check out what Kera had on him. She'd wanted to get home for her Tuesday night television programs. She wondered if the Starlight Motel carried the Showtime network. Regardless, she had to stay. She couldn't pass up hearing what Brian had to say.

CHAPTER SEVENTEEN

This decision was harder than he'd thought it would be. On second thought, it really wasn't the decision that was difficult. He'd already made it. Now it was about the right time, the right place—the coming together of the *when* and *where* of it.

Ms. Mandy Bakker, J.D., would be having her political meeting this evening at the LGBT community center. He knew the meeting was ordinarily held on Tuesday nights but he wasn't certain when it would be finished. He'd confirmed the time by checking out LEAP's website. After the meeting would be a promising time for the *when and where*, combined with the *opportunity*, of course—and that seemed likely. Tonight there was a good chance for the confluence of those three factors.

A very good chance.

It was time to put an end to the lawyer. She was getting in the way. The woman would work way too hard to get Erin Duffy off. Furthermore, he'd observed her in action from the back of the room. She was the brains, inspiration, and glue that held the group together. Her death would cause the downfall of LEAP. Killing her would eliminate two birds with one stone. He chuckled to himself.

It'd started out that he only needed to get rid of Stacey, but he thought it interesting, curious, how once you opened the door to the forbidden, the unthinkable, you really don't ever close it, at least not tightly. A crack is left. The death card remains a possibility, a solution, a way to make things right.

He glanced around the waiting room. Some people were reading. A few folks talked quietly to each other, while others stared into space—all were waiting to be called. The two receptionists sat behind a half-wall/half-glass enclosure. He wondered if they realized they could be overheard in the waiting room, that the glass barrier didn't completely insulate. He often worried that his thoughts seeped through his head, like the voices through the glass barrier, exposing him—his past revealed, his future plans uncovered.

Paranoid thinking? Maybe. But, growing up, he'd known his mother could read his thoughts. She was always ahead of him, knowing what he was up to, shaking an accusing finger, berating him, humiliating him. He'd gotten a good lesson from her: women were bitches, good for only one thing. Once he was asked, more like forced, to see a counselor because he'd smacked a woman (who'd deserved it), the therapist had the nerve to suggest he was attracted to women who resembled his mother, so he could punish his mother through them. That made him so mad that he left counseling; that bitch didn't know anything. No woman he'd been involved with had any physical resemblance to his mother. The psychobabble bitch didn't know what she was talking about. She'd mumbled jumbled psychological shit, like displacement—what in hell did that mean?; delusional— hardly!; a psychopath—she was mad that day at something he'd said, so she slapped that one on him; misogynist—Jesus! Was she off on that one, he loved fucking women. He liked resistance from them, it was best when he had to fight for it. Resistance made his libido go crazy. Kinky, maybe. But, wasn't everybody a little twisted when it came to sex? Of course they were. That counselor must have gotten her psychology degree from a box of Crackerjack. He snickered to himself, or thought he had, until he saw several people look up at him.

He hadn't yet thought through how he'd dispose of the lawyer. In Stacey's case, she'd already been drugged and passed out. It made her pliable, easy to get in the van and haul to a burial spot. Really, she had it good; she never knew what had happened to her.

It was painless. It was humane. As deaths go, it was a good one.

However, that wouldn't be true for Bakker. He wouldn't have the opportunity to have her drugged up. So, he planned to take her to an isolated place, put her down, like he had his dog several years back when it was so sick that it could barely walk.

He'd taken the dog and his hunting rifle out to the country. When he saw a ditch filled high with water from the spring runoff, he pushed the animal out of the car and into the water, thinking it was too weak to survive. He'd watched it struggle and try to swim to the side. Finally, he put a bullet in its head.

It wouldn't be a quick or painless death for the lawyer. She needed to understand what he would do to her. He'd make her comprehend the error of her ways by dragging it out as long as possible. Didn't they call that a teaching opportunity? One that would feel like an eternity. Of course, the lesson would come too late, all in vain, at least for her. But others who might have considered taking up the queers' banner would be warned.

He'd have to think how he wanted it to go down. Maybe take it a step further, maybe throw in a little entertainment for himself. No, he wasn't like that. On second thought, he'd merely play with his victim. Come to think of it, he'd *played with* his prey before and enjoyed it—not with a person, but with his neighbor's cat. It had happened when he was a kid, about fourteen. The cat had it coming, though—same as Bakker. The fucker kept coming into the yard, shitting in his childhood sandbox. Of course, he was too old to play in the sandbox at that age, but his little cousin liked playing in it when she and her family came to visit, and they came quite often. When they showed up, his mother made him go out and clean up the cat shit every goddamned time. It was irritating.

Finally, he had fixed the problem. He'd taken care of the nasty cat by catching the feline intruder. He took it out into a field and whacked it over the head with a shovel. After the first blow, the cat staggered around. He thought it was amusing: the cat weaving around in circles like a drunk. He'd sat down on a rock and watched it as the cat tried to regain its equilibrium. He'd smoked a cigarette, then whacked it again. That did it.

His thoughts were disturbed by a woman who walked into the waiting room with two squalling kids in tow and a baby in her arms. She sat down across from him. The two older kids—one a boy about five, maybe older, and the other a girl, probably three—had blond curly hair and blue eyes. They were cute, like kids in a cereal commercial. The little boy held a gray plastic airplane with red, white and blue decals, that he swooped and soared through the air. The girl had a furry stuffed kitty. She'd diapered it with a multicolored scarf of some sort and cradled it in her arms, rocked and cuddled it, and brought it up to her lips and kissed it.

When the kids noticed him watching they stopped their play and stared at him. It felt like they could read his mind. He could feel himself start to sweat. He told himself to get a grip. Of course they couldn't know what was going on inside his head. He had to believe that. He wasn't schizo, crazy. Maybe a little nervous, but who wouldn't be in his situation? These were just kids. Their mother probably told them to beware of strangers, so they were being cautious, a little fearful. That's all.

He returned to his planning and decided on the place he'd take Bakker to kill her. The spot that came to mind—as he thought more about it—would be almost poetic justice. He wasn't really certain what that meant, but "poetic justice" sounded right and added some flare to his mission.

The little girl smiled at him.

He smiled back at her.

She hid her head in her mother's arm, and then peeked out at him playfully.

She must have decided he was okay. He winked at her, then went back to his planning, figuring a gun would probably be best when it came to Bakker.

The little girl walked over and stood in front of him, offering her kitty. He wasn't sure what he was supposed to do with it, but he took it. She asked him to toss the kitty in the air and catch it, like her daddy did. So he did. The little girl was delighted, and asked him to do it again. She giggled as he tossed her kitty up and caught it another time.

"Missy, don't bother the man, honey."

"But, he's a nice man, Mommy. He likes me. Don't you, mister?"

"It's okay. She's not bothering me…Cute little girl you have here."

The mother smiled and went back to tending her baby.

The little girl got up on his lap, put her soft furry kitty up to his cheek, and made kissing sounds. Then she offered the stuffed animal to him. He took it, put it to her face and made kissing sounds too.

The door that led out from the physician's examining rooms opened.

Erin walked out and over to him. "I'm sorry it took so long, Daniel. I hope I haven't made you late for your meeting."

CHAPTER EIGHTEEN

Mandy stashed the meeting's notes in her briefcase. She was tired from a long day but felt encouraged about how well the night had gone. Folks were excited about the mayor's decision to come out in favor of including LGBT rights in the city's civil rights ordinance—totally unexpected. His endorsement had pumped new energy into LEAP. Not that the mayor's announcement guaranteed a successful outcome, but it'd been a big boost to the group's morale. With the disclosure of the satanic symbols carved on Stacey's body and the fact that she was a lesbian, Mandy had feared that they'd lost the battle before it had begun. But then came the mayor's announcement. He'd given a speech on TV to explain that Wicca had nothing to do with devil worship, and neither one had anything to do with being gay. Mandy had done an eye roll on that one—only in Lakeside City, she'd thought. What did impress her was that he'd gone on about prejudice and hate being at the core of the misinformation the media was stirring up and spewing out. No one on the City Council responded. In fact, they seemed to have disappeared into dark cracks, unavailable to the media.

Out of town.

Can't be reached.

Unavailable for comment.

It was so rare to have a politician do the right thing, speak the truth, go against the grain of the constituency. She hoped the man had contingency plans, like a career change, and a secret way to get out of town. Or maybe he had a death wish.

But to the gay community, the mayor's bravery brought optimism, restored determination and rekindled courage. LEAP's new strategy: Come up with ways to educate the public about what Wiccan beliefs actually were and were not, as a way to counteract the false information currently whipping around the city and kicking up fear and hatred. She thought they'd come up with some pretty creative ideas.

Jessica had been the last person to leave the meeting. She'd hung around, trying to get Mandy's attention, but after Mandy gave her the cold shoulder, Jessica finally left. It felt like the woman had glommed on to her like gum on the bottom of her shoe.

Mandy wondered how Kera was doing on her trip to Lansing. Kera had said she wouldn't contact her unless it was important. Most likely Kera would text, so she wouldn't have to talk to her directly. A shooting pain in her foot reminded Mandy that she hadn't let Kera know about the attack on Sunday. She'd told Dee she would let her know but changed her mind, not wanting to take the chance that Kera might not even care anymore. But, she had to admit, Kera had sent a text to say that Daniel would come tonight to see her home. She didn't know how much stock to put in that. After all, Kera might be just seeing it as her professional responsibility in this case. She took in a deep breath and let it out.

She heard the door open and saw Daniel. That was a relief; everyone was gone. The Pink Door was actually in a pretty sketchy area, and given all that had happened, she wouldn't argue about having an escort home.

"Hi Mandy. How'd the meeting go?"

"Really well, thanks. People are ready to get back to work again. There's plenty of enthusiasm, thanks to the mayor's incredibly brave speech."

"Yeah, I heard that..." Daniel's voice trailed off.

"Did the doctor give Erin medicine to help her with her insomnia and nerves?" She picked up her pen and tossed it into her briefcase.

"Yeah, hopefully the meds will help her. Not sleeping has made her a mess." Daniel grabbed a chair, flipped it around, straddled it, and rested his arms on the back. His leg jiggled up and down, staccato.

"I know, when I talked to her yesterday, I couldn't make sense of what she was trying to tell me. Finally I figured it out, but it wasn't easy. She's lucky she has you, Daniel. You've been so good to her. And don't worry, we'll get her through this. One day you'll both look back on this time like it was a bad dream." She snapped her briefcase shut, then caught Daniel staring at her. His eyes pierced through her, cold and hard, like steel. His face was tense, motionless. Strange.

She bristled. His expression confused her. Surely she was picking up the wrong cues, misinterpreting them. Must be that all the spookiness of what was going on was getting to her.

If she didn't know better, she'd run.

But Daniel had come to her and Dee's rescue, and he was working to help his sister. He loved Erin, a lot. He was a good guy. Ah, it occurred to her. He couldn't be sleeping well either. Undoubtedly exhausted and having a hard time coping with it all. Certainly he had to be angry about what was happening to Erin. All this stress was wearing on him as well. Of course. That was it.

"How are you doing, Daniel?"

"I'm fine, really." His face softened, a bit.

"Are you upset? I mean, beyond what's going on with your sister?"

"No, I'm just preoccupied. There's a lot I have to do, that's all."

"I want to thank you, again, for rescuing us on the bike trail. If you hadn't come along I hate to guess what might have happened. I was scared to death. So was Dee."

"That's why Kera wanted my help. You just don't know who might be around the next corner, or who you can trust." His lips curled, as if he were holding back a smile. "I'm glad you'd told me what the two of you were doing on Sunday. When I got back to town from Erin's grocery shopping trip, I hightailed it over there. Luckily, I found you when I did."

"That's for sure. I haven't been able to get it off my mind. It really spooked me. I still get chills remembering that guy's face."

"By the way, how's your foot doing?" He pointed to the foot the man on the bike had rolled over with his bike tire. "You were hobbling on it, earlier." Daniel rotated his Boston Red Sox cap so the visor was in the back.

"It's still swollen, and it hurts." She'd had to wear heels today. The shoes were ordinarily too large for her, but she'd failed to return them to the store. "I'm thinking I should get it x-rayed. I should have done that sooner, but I haven't had time. Say, I reported the incident to the police but haven't heard any more from them. Did the police get a hold of you? I told them that you showed up, thank God, and they said they would contact you."

"Uh, no, but I got a message from them. I just haven't returned their call yet. I'll get to it." Daniel stood up, arched his back and groaned.

"Your back bothering you?"

"It's okay, I just lifted something too heavy." He sat back down and changed the subject. "How's Dee doing?"

"Like me, sore and frightened. You know, Daniel, I've been wondering if someone out there is trying to create an atmosphere of fear and hatred by using all this devil worship talk to scare people. And with the timing and all, I think it has to do with our renewed efforts of getting LGBT civil rights into the ordinance."

Daniel's eyebrows rose. "I don't know, maybe." He checked the time. "We need to get going, so I can get back and see how my sister is doing. Are you about ready?"

"Yes, for sure. It's been a long day." Mandy grabbed her purse.

"Oh, I forgot to tell you," said Daniel. "I drove my car here but I'm having problems with it. When I was driving, the damned engine kept stalling out on me. I was lucky to get here. In the parking lot, I shut it off and tried to start it again but couldn't get the motor to turn over." He shook his head. "My concern is, even if I can get it to run again, it might break down altogether. My plan had been to follow you home, but maybe that's not such a good idea. So I thought that if you'd give me a ride out to Kera's place in your car, I could pick up her old Buick, follow you back to your house, then later get a tow truck. I checked with Vinny before I came in, and he said it would be okay, and that you'd have Kera's house key, right?"

She nodded, wondering how long she'd have it. But she had it now.

"Good, and you know where she keeps the keys to the Buick?"

"Yes, I do. Let's go." She walked out to the parking lot with Daniel. When he noticed her limping, he took hold of her arm.

"Cute car you got here." He got in the passenger's side and pushed his seat back.

"She's old but she's done me proud, that's for sure." Mandy patted the dashboard. "This old dear has lots of miles on her, and a few dents, but she runs fine."

"Well, your car is working and mine isn't." Daniel glanced at the odometer. "And it's got," he calculated, "oh my god, close to one hundred thousand more miles on it than mine."

Mandy vaguely wondered why Vinny hadn't contacted her about Daniel taking the Buick. It wasn't like Vinny. Oh well, she thought, he was probably too busy, and it wasn't a big deal anyway.

"Has Kera come up with anything yet? My sister asked today and I didn't know what to say."

"No, she's working in Lansing today. I've not heard from her."

She didn't know how much Daniel knew about her and Kera's personal relationship, and though he was well aware that

Kera and she were working together professionally, he might not know about their relationship or problems. Well, their breakup was the more accurate way of putting it, although she didn't want to think that way.

"Yeah, I know she's in Lansing. Do you know why?"

For all Mandy knew, other than Dee, Ally, Kera and herself, no one else was aware of the Victoria-Stacey-Erin connection. Mandy didn't think Erin had told her brother about their relationship. She knew it would all come out eventually, but she wasn't going to be the one to let that fact out of the bag.

"Frankly, I don't know why she was going there. Most likely it was about another case she's been working on. Kera has several clients right now, and her work keeps her hopping." That wasn't true, but hopefully Mandy's explanation would make sense to him.

He didn't respond; he just kept staring straight ahead. His jaw clenched. He appeared deep in thought. Before he could ask anything more, she decided to redirect the conversation.

"Have you heard from Vinny? He's been tracking some person that Kera was concerned about."

"No, neither Kera nor Vinny tell me much about what's going on. I'm not really part of the team, but as you can imagine, I have a lot at stake in Erin's case. I mean, it's my sister that's in trouble."

"I understand. I really do. Being her brother can't be easy with what's happening."

"It isn't, not at all."

"Growing up, have you two always been close?"

"Uh, she's older than me, so it's not like we hung out, but yeah, I guess you'd say we were close."

"It's really nice that you two are so close. Some sibs aren't. When did she come out to you?"

"Couldn't say for sure but probably sometime when I was in my mid-teens. We were both eyeing the same girls." Daniel snickered.

His laugh was…odd. Mandy couldn't put her finger on it, why it sounded strange, out of place. Maybe he was thinking back to his awkward teenage years.

She turned down the dirt road that led to Kera's. She hated this stretch, no streetlights, no houses. Whenever she drove here at night, she worried that if her car broke down she'd have to walk the rest of the way and not be able to see much. Tonight, with the cloud cover, nothing was visible. The wind had picked up and was pushing against her car.

"I really don't understand," Daniel's voice broke through the darkness, "how the cops think my sister could have pulled off a murder like that."

"What do you mean?"

"Stacey was a big woman. I'm not saying she was fat, but she was good-sized. How could the cops possibly think Erin would have been capable of, you know, hauling her in and out of a vehicle and dragging her into the wetlands? Dead weight is even more difficult to carry than when someone is conscious, feels almost twice as heavy. I mean, Erin is strong, no fluff ball, but still…"

Erin looked strong and athletic to Mandy, so she'd understood how the police might think it was possible...But, had Stacey been hauled around by her killer while unconscious? She didn't think it had been established yet, or even talked about. Maybe it had been? Daniel had probably seen it in the paper. She hadn't read about the case in the last few days and didn't know what was being said about the murder. She needed to check into it.

"And those terrible carvings on her body, like bloody tattoos," Daniel continued. "I can't believe they'd think Erin would do that; she's not like that."

Mandy curved around the bend. The bright beacon in the lighthouse tower came into view. She was always grateful to finally see some light on this god-awful road. She supposed that she'd no longer be making this trip if Kera never came around to believing her about Jessica. Damn, her mind went to Kera so easily. It was like her default setting—regardless of what she was doing. Yesterday, in the middle of talking to a client, the person had made a remark that reminded her of Kera. That's all it took, the most innocent prompt, then off her thoughts went, hijacked, speeding off to Kera, distracting her, making her lose focus. When the client finished talking she'd had no idea what had just been said.

Something told her she needed to focus now, pick up the threads of what Daniel had said. Two words echoed in her head, making her feel uneasy.

"The carvings?" Mandy quickly glanced over at Daniel, then back as the car hit a pothole. She saw, in the glow of the dash lights, his eyes burning into her.

"Yeah, the reverse pentagrams," he said, "the ones that were carved on Stacey's breasts and on her belly." Daniel moved, straightening up in his seat.

"Yes, that was gruesome, wasn't it?" Mandy avoided thinking about that piece of Stacey's murder. It made her sick to her stomach. Whoever had done that had to be demented. Out of the corner of her eye, she caught a glimpse of Daniel, a smile on his face.

One of those smiles that offered no mirth. Maniacal.

He knows they're reverse pentagrams and where they were on Stacey's body.

The authorities hadn't announced, publicly, what the marking were—only that they were satanic—and even if he'd guessed it, he wouldn't know where they were carved on the body… Mandy could barely breathe, because whoever knew what the specific carvings were and, especially, where they were located was the person who'd killed Stacey.

Oh my God! Oh my God!

The killer was sitting right next to her.

He reached over, took her cell phone off the console, and tossed it out the window.

She had to think, stay composed, and find a way to get away from him. She could make a quick U-turn and head back out of this desolation. But what would he do? He'd probably kill her. Not a good idea. By the time she got to the lighthouse, her breathing had all but stopped. She had no idea what to do but to go along, at least for now, and hope to see an opportunity to flee.

"So, you must be wondering how I know about the markings on Stacey's body. Right?"

"Yes, but I think I know."

"Good, so we can go on from here; we both know our parts in all this," Daniel sneered.

She watched him as he put his hand in his jacket pocket and drew out a gun. He pointed it at her—no doubt the same gun that had saved her and Dee earlier.

"Get out of the car, bitch."

Her part in all this? He must have planned this all along. But why? For God's sake, her part was defending his sister… Why did he want to kill her? But he must have been planning it, otherwise, he wouldn't be telling her all this or bringing her here. This didn't make sense.

"I said, get out." Daniel yanked the keys from the ignition and waved the gun at her.

"Which one of your keys is to the door?" He pushed her in the direction of the lighthouse.

"It's on another key ring, in my purse." She gestured toward her car.

"Go get them." He pushed her to the VW and angrily tossed the key ring he'd held in his hand into the vehicle, then put the gun to her head. "Get Kera's house key. Wait, just in case you're in the habit of carrying a gun in your purse, I'll get them." With his gun hand resting on the steering wheel, he reached in and grabbed her purse and dumped the contents onto the driver's seat. He found another set of keys. "Which key is it?"

"That's not the right key ring." She pointed to the set of two keys for Kera's place that had fallen on the floor. "It's those, right there, by the gas pedal."

When Daniel bent over to get them, she saw her opportunity. He was leaning, off-balance. She pushed him, hard. He fell into the car, across the driver's seat, and his gun flew out of his hand.

She took off running, although she had no idea where to go or where she could hide. It would only take seconds before he'd be after her. She hoped she could draw him away from her car, then double back and get away.

Her left foot hurt like hell, and it was so dark. The high blinking light from the tower provided no help; it was meant to signal the ships coming in, not good for someone trying to make her way along the uneven ground, in pain and wearing heels. She kicked off her shoes and ran in the direction of a clump of trees, barely discernible. The ground was cold and sharp objects cut into the bottoms of her feet.

Her foot hit a hole, twisting her ankle, the one connected to her already painful foot. She tripped, fell, and smacked the ground. The air whooshed out of her, like a tire blowout. She couldn't catch her breath.

"Get the fuck up!" A cold gun barrel pushed against her temple.

* * *

A train wreck, she'd never been in one, but this must be how her body would feel. If that weren't enough, twine cut into her wrists and ankles. She sat on the floor, her ankles bound and her hands secured behind her back, leaning against the kitchen wall where he had shoved her.

Still unable to comprehend what was happening to her, she watched as Daniel opened the refrigerator, like it was his house, his fridge. He grabbed a beer, popped the cap and sat back in a chair at the kitchen table and threw up his feet on a nearby chair, took a swig of beer, and swiped his mouth with his sleeve.

"You must be wondering what this is all about. Right?" he scoffed.

"Yes. What the hell is going on?" The answer wouldn't save her life, but she wanted to know anyway. He'd already admitted to her that he'd killed Stacey, so she wasn't going to get out of this place alive, without divine intervention—or incredibly good luck.

"Let's start with I'm not crazy about your politics." Daniel stuck a cigarette in his mouth.

"My politics? You don't even know my—"

"I'm referring to your activities with that fag organization you're heading up." He took a drag, let out the smoke slowly, making it float upward in rings.

"LEAP?"

"You probably thought I was okay with Erin being queer. I didn't always care, one way or another, who screwed who—as long as it didn't interfere with my life—but I've been listening to a lot of smart people on TV and have come to see it in a new light. Now I get it, the dangers queers present. Educating my mind, if you will." He twisted his ball cap's brim back around and pulled it way down.

Yeah, educating your sick mind with garbage.

"Now I've always tried to do my part to straighten out sexually confused women." Daniel laughed. "Get it?" He slapped his leg and hooted.

She studied his face. Something about the way the brim of his hat, pulled down so far, seemed familiar, the square jawline...My God, was he the guy she'd seen in the back of the room at the LEAP meeting? At the time, his face had been a blur to her—not having had her glasses on—and he'd had the brim of his cap covering much of his face, too, and blue, like the one he wore now. Daniel certainly looked to be the right size, body-wise. And come to think of it, after she'd met him at Erin's house, she'd never seen the suspicious guy again at a meeting. Of course, she reflected, he wouldn't show up another time because he didn't want to risk being recognized. The more she thought about it, the more certain she became that it had been Daniel, watching her even before she'd gotten involved with Erin's case. My God, he'd been spying on her, even then. She realized she'd stopped breathing, again. She drew in air.

"Now, it's a cause, everyone needs one, don't you think?" Daniel taunted. "Something to give life purpose. But frankly, though I was determined to do whatever necessary to curtail your activist activities, what really rankled me and what prompted me to action so quickly was you taking Erin's case, before I could bring in my own lawyer. Then, I find out you'd teamed up with Van Brocklin. Jesus! I worked hard to get Stacey out of the picture. I couldn't have you and Kera fucking up my work."

Surely she'd fallen into a deep dark hole with a venomous-spewing snake. She felt frozen in place.

"Well, I actually, had a Plan A and a Plan B," he continued, "being the thorough genius that I am. Plan A was a compromise." He shook his head. "Not my personal favorite, but in this plan, Stacey's body would rot and not be found—by anything other than animals—so Erin would assume that Stacey had taken off, left her." Daniel strutted back and forth, expounding like a professor. "But the body was found, so my backup scheme went into effect. Plan B, my preference because it took care of a longstanding karma thing." He stopped in front of her. "See, I set it up so the authorities would suspect Erin, if Stacey were found. Cops always put the loved ones first on their suspect list, so I knew they'd be pointing Erin's way, but still, I wanted to be sure, so I pounded the last nail in her coffin, so to speak." He snickered. "God I'm good." He went back to his pacing. "I knew the cops and fine folks of this town would be more than happy to throw Wiccans into the same pot as the Satanists; see, it goes like this: Wiccan, witches, devil worship, Satanism—see how nice that connects? I did my research."

Good God! Just like Dee explained.

"I didn't want to leave things to chance, so I called radio talk programs and promoted my theory, and even wrote an editorial and the paper published it." He must have seen her incredulous expression. "I'm not kidding. My letter was in that opinion section." He pointed a finger at her. "It's gotten a lot of positive response, too, as did my comments on the radio…I set the ball in motion, and this town picked it up and kept it in play." His smile reeked of self-satisfaction.

Mandy shook her head, horrified by what he'd done and how he'd planned everything out, so strategic and detailed, like his mind was his private war room.

"Well, maybe you and Kera wouldn't buy it," he continued, "but more than enough people in this town are quick to find a route to witches and the devil's work. It's good to know your town, don't you think?"

His smile made her break out in a cold sweat.

"But back to you and what assured your presence here. You and your fucking PI sidekick were screwing my plan up, trying way too hard to get Erin off. I couldn't take a chance you'd succeed."

"But you and your sister are close, and you, I just assumed—"

"A lawyer should never assume, now should she?" Daniel stared at her, anger darting out from his eyes.

If Mandy wasn't already in so much pain, she'd pinch herself to see if she were stuck in a nightmare. She needed to get her wits about her and figure out what she could do to get out of this mess. To start with, she had to keep Daniel talking while she worked it out, if she had any chance to stay alive. Kera would show up soon, hopefully. But as she pictured Kera coming in, it became clear that she would be walking into a trap. Kera wouldn't have any reason to be suspicious when she drove up. She'd see Mandy's car there but that wouldn't make her wary and on guard for what was about to greet her. As far as Mandy knew, Kera didn't know about Daniel coming to get the Buick— he'd made that arrangement with Vinny—so the Buick still being here wouldn't set off any alarm for her. Even Lakota—if she got a whiff of Daniel's scent—wouldn't be suspicious. The dog knew him as a friendly person.

She'd read, somewhere, you're supposed to get the abductor to see your human side, relate to you as a person, making it more difficult for him to kill you. That strategy wasn't going to work here, unfortunately, because he already knew who she was and didn't like it. And, he'd confessed to her. But still, she might learn something that would help her out of this grim situation and maybe, by keeping him engaged with her, buy time.

"So, why did you set Erin up, surely not because she's gay?" Mandy tried to wiggle her body to get her muscles to move. She was cramping up; her feet were cold, and painful from the cuts and bruises she'd acquired in her attempted escape.

"No, that's not it, though now that I have a new slant on the gay thing, it won't hurt to get one more queer off the street."

"I don't get it," Mandy said. "Erin thought you were on her side in life, as did I, frankly."

"Well, my sister has to be crazy to think I'd care about her." Daniel came up close to her and glared, his face reddened, his voice tight. "Erin never cared what I was going through when we were growing up. She was my parents' little darling; she could do no wrong. Ever! I was the big mistake, the kid that needed to go to a shrink because 'something was wrong with me.'" He made air quotes as he sneered, spraying saliva toward her. "And she was little Ms. Perfect Pants, that's what I used to call her. It made her mad, but it was true." His expression had taken on the attribute of an angry little boy, a crazy, angry little boy.

She shuddered.

"But that was a long time ago," Mandy said. It didn't seem possible he'd still be so angry that he'd set up his sister to be a suspect in a murder, unless she was dealing with someone who was totally irrational.

"You bitch, you weren't there! She fucking enjoyed it. I know she did. Oh, she acted like she didn't, but she didn't fool me. She got off on being the favorite one and shoved it in my face by pretending to agree, be on my side…You have no idea! So shut your goddamned mouth!"

"But why now?"

"I'm a patient man, always have been." His demeanor changed to a haunting coolness. "I've been told I stockpile shit. I think that's a good thing, myself, letting things ferment, you know, until the time is right, then I take my revenge…And, I've got more than one stockpile."

Who else, Mandy wondered, was in line for Daniel's scheming revenge? It didn't really matter because right now she needed to focus on her plight, but how was she supposed to deal with someone so paranoid, so angry? And Daniel had had mental problems, early on… All she could think to do was to try and change the subject.

"Why did you come to my rescue on the bike trail?" She couldn't figure out why he'd even bother.

"I was still playing the role of protector. I didn't want to spoil my own plans for you." Daniel smirked. "Besides, that guy wouldn't have taken care of you the way I will. I wanted my time with you, alone." Daniel spotted a bag of trail mix on the counter. He tipped it to his mouth, letting the mixture flow over and spill on the floor. With the remote, he clicked on the television that sat on the counter, and began flipping through the channels.

He wasn't in any hurry to kill her. She wondered if he was waiting for Kera to get home so he could kill them both? He had certainly made it clear that he didn't like, well, had recently come to hate gay people. Then again, maybe he just wanted Kera to come home to discover her body. That would be hateful, but right up his alley.

The late news was on, and the local newscaster was reporting that there had been a new development in the Hendriks murder case. They'd found a weapon that may have been used in the murder of Stacey Hendriks. It was not known by the media when or where it was located.

"Aha!" Daniel gloated. "Life is finally going my way. Poor, poor Big Sister, I'm going to have to be so upset when they take her away."

A weapon? Mandy tried to figure out what that meant. Hadn't they decided she'd been strangled and/or drowned? Her head was foggy, what was she missing?...*Oh, they must have found the knife used in the carvings.*

"And how do you think you'll get away with what you're doing, Daniel?" The way she saw it, killing her and/or Kera would draw suspicion away from Erin.

"Easy. There are enough people who know that you and Kera are having a major falling out...and Kera has a short fuse. You know, that craziness our troops come back with—post-traumatic something or other. Anyway, I'll make this look like a fight to the death—a lover's quarrel, a shoot-out at the 'ole-gay' corral," Daniel sniggered. "When I get done, I'll have the whole community buying my staging efforts. They'll eat it up. They'll have their bellies full of all the LGBT shit, as well as their gay-friendly mayor. It won't take long for him to be run out of town."

His gallows laugh sent waves of shivers through her, but Mandy had to keep trying. Even if she couldn't get him to connect with her, she hoped she could get him to view the situation differently, like she would do with a jury. "Even if you get rid of us, there'll just be another lawyer and PI to fight for Erin. Killing us won't change her situation."

"Yes it will, because I'll see to it she gets a lawyer who's not as ambitious or invested as you and your cohort are, and not so convinced of Erin's innocence. And her new lawyer will be one who sits back and lets Detective Brown do his job." Daniel's upper lip curled up on one side in a snarl. "There are so many lawyers in this town who will be more than happy to let that happen to a dyke, trust me, but then I'm sure you are very aware of that, Ms. Lesbian Activist."

He was right, she realized. With Daniel in charge of his sister's defense lawyer, Erin wouldn't have a chance. The bastard had counted on hiring another lawyer for her. But when his plan was thwarted, he cleverly made himself available to Kera. Then she remembered, she was the one who had suggested to Kera that he help her out.

Oh God, Oh God, what did I do?

A film shot earlier was being rerun on the TV. A reporter interviewed people as they walked by, asking them what they thought about the mayor's address. Daniel reacted to each of their responses either by angrily yelling back at the people who agreed with the mayor's response, or cheering those that felt the mayor should be kicked out of office for supporting gay inclusion in the ordinance.

Mandy groaned. Her hands were icy and getting numb. The harsh cord ripped her skin from her continued efforts to get free.

"Trust me, Ms. Bakker, it is just going to get worse if you try to get your hands loose. And if you do succeed—which you won't—I'll have to kill you, which I'm planning to do anyway, sooner or later." He patted the gun he'd placed on the table. "But I know you want to hang on to your life as long as possible, hoping you'll get saved. Human nature, right?" His attention went back to the TV.

She wondered if Daniel knew about the threesome of Victoria, Erin and Stacey. Was that why he had killed Stacey?

Not suspecting Daniel at the time, there had been no reason for her to ask Ally if he knew.

"I don't understand why you killed Stacey." What the hell, she decided, might just as well ask, since she was going to die anyway. It was in her DNA, as well as in her legal training to try and figure things out, but usually she wasn't in the center of it all.

Daniel seemed to consider her question, but then he went back to the television, though he didn't appear to be attending to the content of the program.

"She took something from me," he finally said, his eyes narrowed. "Something I desperately wanted, and now I'll have a chance of getting it back."

"Get what back?"

"It's none of your goddamned business, bitch. Now shut the fuck up so I can watch my program." He took his now empty beer bottle and tossed it in the sink, shattering it. He got up and grabbed another.

Where are you, Kera?

CHAPTER NINETEEN

Mandy woke up, shivering. Daniel was still sleeping. She wondered how she could have been so stupid. Kera often accused her of being naïve. Well, this certainly proved Kera right. She should have checked with Vinny or Kera before swallowing Daniel's story about his car not working. Her body had gone from shivering to trembling; she couldn't stop, every cell prickled with fear.

She'd lost count of how many drinks Daniel had sloshed down, not that it really mattered. The fact was, he'd gotten drunk, dead drunk, on Kera's beer. He drained every last bottle she had in her refrigerator, then opened a bottle of wine and finished it off—the pinot noir Kera kept on hand for her. The drunker he became, the scarier he got.

After he'd gone on and on about his plans and how clever he was, he'd continued terrorizing her by going into great detail relating how he'd tormented animals. From there, he'd moved on to how he'd murdered Stacey. Her stomach had been empty, otherwise she would have vomited. Instead, bile had risen into her throat and burned its way back down.

Then, he'd started playing with his gun, like he was in an old-time western. He'd whip it out of his pants pocket, as though he were in some kind of shoot-out, and point it at her, snickering at the startled and fearful reaction he got.

Sometime in the night, he passed out, after coyly telling her how pleased some people or some person—she wasn't sure—would be because of what he was doing. After all of his antics, his head had fallen down on the table with a thud and lay there like a felled tree—it was still there.

He snored, loud, fitful, like a sputtering engine. Ever so often, his head would rise up a notch, and he'd check around through bloodshot eyes, then drop his head back down again. He was going to have some kind of headache. Maybe he'd be less attentive having to deal with his hangover, more careless, and provide a chance for her to escape. Or maybe he'd be more volatile.

The room smelled of stale beer, cigarettes, and the body odor that radiates from a night of drinking, along with the smell of his sweat. It oozed testosterone, hatred and spilt-over anger. He'd smoked so much, a haze still lingered in the air.

The morning sun glared through the window, aimed at her eyes. Her back hurt, her butt hurt. What didn't hurt? She couldn't understand how she'd slept at all. She'd mostly dozed in spurts—two hours, tops, all night, on the bare wooden kitchen floor. It hadn't been possible for her to stay awake, although she'd certainly tried. She was determined to keep an eye on him, not that she could have done anything, but she didn't want to be killed while she slept. At least that's how she felt about it through the night, but considering it in the light of morning, she found herself reevaluating. It would have been better to be killed in her sleep than to have to wait and wonder when and how it was going to happen.

She had to pee, the about-to-burst kind of need, but her desire to keep him asleep was greater—better she pee her pants.

His stupor bought time for her. A period of grace. Time for something to happen that might save her life, like in a movie where the Green Berets or Navy Seals come busting through the door—a flight of imagination from the naiveté of a ten-year-old. A hopeless hope. To get real, she had to come up with a plan, a plausible strategy, something adult, something that would offer her a grain of hope.

But first she needed to stop shaking.

In the night, she'd rolled over on her side so she could relieve the pressure on her butt from the hard floor. If she were going to be in a position to do anything, she would have to get back up to a sitting position. She kicked out and up on her legs to get her body to move upright, then scooted back closer to the wall and started wiggling and pulling on the twine that bound her wrists behind her.

Her hand scraped up against something, a few inches to her right. It felt like a nail protruding from the baseboard, about a quarter of an inch. If she'd rub the twine back and forth on the nail, maybe it would wear down and eventually break. The nail was smooth and wouldn't provide much friction, but then she didn't have any other great ideas. She wiggled, sideways, centered the nail to her wrists and began working to try and fray the twine. She'd have to quit when he looked her way, but for the time being, she could take advantage of the fact that he was still sleeping.

Daniel jerked awake and sat up.

She stilled her arms.

He yawned and ran his fingers through his thick hair, more stirring it up than combing it down. His hands went next to his face and pawed at his overnight stubble. He stood up and left the room. She could hear his footsteps going up the stairs, then a flushing toilet. When he returned, he sat down and rubbed his temples and took in a deep breath and let it out in a fit of coughing that scraped up phlegm. He got up from his chair and spat it in the sink.

She'd been feeling pangs of hunger, but not anymore. Only her bladder continued to cry out.

"I need to go to the bathroom too."

He stared at her, saying nothing. Was he going to keep her there, watch her burst her bladder?

"There's a bathroom off the kitchen, there." She motioned with her head in the direction of the adjoining half bath. "You wouldn't have to take me upstairs."

"Okay, but I'm going to have to go in with you."

"You wouldn't have to, just untie my legs, I think I can manage the rest. I'll only need help with my zipper." She was determined she'd get her pants up and down, someway, and not have to have him in the bathroom with her. It didn't matter how much her bladder was stretched, she wasn't sure she'd be able to pee with him in there, because her psyche would have to fight with the propriety of it all—not to speak of the creep factor. As it was, she had a hard time peeing in a public bathroom if someone was in the stall next to her—a shy bladder is what her doctor had called it.

"Uh, I don't know, maybe. Can you do it with your hands behind your back?" He didn't seem to be all that eager about being in the bathroom with her either.

"Yes, I think so."

Daniel cut the twine, freeing her feet, then yanked her up off the floor and jerked the zipper down.

"Don't be trying anything, and hurry it up."

He'd left the door to the bathroom open, a crack. She tugged on her pants from the back and around the sides as far as she could reach, working them down enough to sit on the toilet. She heard him close a cupboard door, grateful he wasn't hovering by the door.

There were times in her life when a good pee rivaled an orgasm; this was one of them.

She searched the bathroom with her eyes to try and find anything that could help free her hands. Something sharp, maybe scissors. She stood up, and pulled at her pants from the back, just enough to make her feel decent enough for him to finish the job. Her eyes fell on the metal wastebasket; a handle of a plastic disposable razor protruded through some wadded up tissues. She moved over to the wastebasket and turned around, then carefully squatted down in order for her hands to reach in. She was able to tip the basket and brace it against her back, then shuffle through the contents until she felt the razor. As she grabbed hold of it, the basket tipped over, clanking on the wooden floor.

Shit!

"What the fuck are you doing in there?"

Damn. He'd be there any second. She popped up with the razor in her hand as he came charging in.

"What the hell's going on?"

"I tipped that over trying to get my pants up." She held her pants level with her hips.

He looked around the room and down at the basket where used tissues had spilled out on the floor, then back at her. He must have believed her because he didn't challenge her story. He grabbed her pants on either side, glared down at her, his lips curled up on the sides in a way that sent cold streaks of terror screaming throughout her body. She couldn't breathe.

He yanked her slacks and underpants back down, grabbed around behind her, digging his fingers into her bare flesh, and yanked her close to him. "Nice ass, bitch!"

She screamed at him to stop, to get away from her, but he pulled her tighter until her face was pressed into his chest, allowing her teeth to find his flesh. She bit him through his shirt.

"You fucking bitch!" He shoved her down, the back of her head slammed on the floor. "I'll take care of you. And when I get done, I'll wring your neck like a fucking chicken."

She kicked at him with her two legs, now bound together by her lowered pants.

He grabbed her, pushed her legs down and held them on the floor. He leered at her, poised.

She closed her eyes and braced for what was to come.

The fire alarm screeched. Billowing smoke broke through the bathroom doorway, smelling like burning sausage.

"Goddamn fucking son of a bitch!" he growled. He coughed from the smoke and covered his mouth and nose with his hand, got up, and ran out the door.

She lay there, numb, stunned, unable to move, unable to think what to do—if she were even able to move. The smoke burned her eyes and irritated her throat. She began to cough.

He returned. She had no idea how long he'd been gone. He grabbed her, pulled her to a standing position, and with a jolt he jerked her pants up, then pushed her toward the door and took her back to her previous spot on the floor in the kitchen and shoved her down against the wall.

"Later, bitch, you fuckin' made me burn my sausage. After I get done eating, I'll get back to you and—"

His cell phone rang. He picked up his gun and pointed it at her, and then answered. "Hi, sis, what's up?" His voice calm, like nothing was happening. "I've been trying to get ahold of Mandy, but haven't been able to yet. But hang in there, I'll get a lawyer to you as soon as I can. See you later." He tossed his phone on the table.

Mandy cringed as he threw fresh sausages in the pan, and began whistling.

Oh God, if she didn't realized before, she understood now that she was the prisoner of a psychopath.

There was a Hell. And she was in it.

She felt herself begin to disconnect, mentally unable to stay with her nightmare. It was as though she were leaving her body, and for whatever was to happen, she wouldn't be in it. She was drifting to somewhere else, a place where she could endure. A place where her body felt no pain, like being packed in ice, numbed from the cold.

But, somewhere inside of her, way deep in, she heard a voice. It was faint, like a weak whisper where words slushed together, indistinguishable. But the vocal sound got louder, stronger, clearer, bringing her up to the surface of her life. It sounded like her mother's voice. The scrambled, fractured words separated and took shape, forming distinct sounds, a message repeated, over and over: *Don't do what I did, don't abandon yourself, keep fighting.*

She fought, pushed down, tried to get back to the frozen cube that insulated her. But the stern words became more adamant, and the pain found its way back into her body, pushing her to the surface.

Daniel sat at the table, eating. She watched as he got up and put his licked-clean plate in the sink with his busted beer bottles. She noticed her ankles had not been retied. Apparently, the burning sausage and phone call had distracted him. Maybe he wouldn't detect it, especially if she kept her feet together, as though they were bound.

In the bathroom, she'd hurriedly stashed the razor into her blouse sleeve, counting on her suit jacket to hide the bulge. He hadn't spotted it when he brought her back to her place on the kitchen floor. She struggled to retrieve the razor from her sleeve.

"Sorry for not offering you any breakfast." He stood over her, wiping his mouth with his shirtsleeve. "But I don't want to have to take you to the bathroom over and over. Besides," he smirked, "dead people don't require nourishment." He went to a window. "Where's your girlfriend? She should have been home last night. Hey, maybe she has someone new to spend the night with." He winked at her and laughed. "We'll fix her, won't we? We got a surprise waiting for her. Well, I'm not sure you'll be... uh, alive, so you won't be able to appreciate the shock on her face when she walks in." He stroked his chin. "I haven't decided, yet, whether or not to kill you both together, or individually— either scenario has its advantages."

His words fell flat. She was already so full of fear that it had spilled over a long time ago. He couldn't do or say any more to make her feel more terrified than she already was.

"I'm thirsty." He opened the refrigerator door. "Hmm, the beer's all gone, maybe I'll have to go down the road and get some." He stopped and looked over at her. "Oh, can't do that, can I? Your ex-girlfriend might show up in the meantime. Maybe I haven't searched everywhere. Could be she's got some stashed away." He opened and slammed shut cupboards. Not finding anything, he went into the pantry.

What if Kera had been with someone else last night? Would Kera do that out of spite for what she assumed Mandy had done? Mandy didn't want to think about her with someone else, unbearable. Her reality slammed through, *Good God! What is wrong with me? Why am I thinking about Kera with someone else right now? That's the least of my problems.*

"I saw these while I was searching for beer, and thought they might be useful if I have a need to keep you quiet." He held up gray duct tape and a white rag. "Sure wish I knew when your girlfriend was planning to show up today." He leered at her again. "I'd kind of hate to be…uh, how should I put this, having my way with you and have her walk through that door—not that I care about her seeing it, mind you. In fact, that would be one reason I'd keep you alive until she came back. It'd teach her how sex should go—between a man and a woman, in case you didn't get my drift. It's just that I can't have her catching me while I'm occupied with you. She'd have the jump on me."

When he wasn't watching, Mandy frantically worked to get the razor down from her sleeve. It had been a good place to stash and hold it, but the razor was proving difficult to retrieve.

He turned on the TV and told her he was searching for a local news show, but it was too late in the morning. "I guess I'll have to wait for the noon news." He flipped through all the channels, not giving up. His knee bounced up and down, nervously, like a paddleball.

Daniel peeked out the window to see if anyone was coming, then his eyes darted around the room and landed on her. *Oh God!* Was he considering raping her, getting back to where he'd left off, or was he thinking of killing her now, not waiting for Kera?

She would rather he kill her than rape her.

Her mind raced through her panic, grasping for a rock, something to hold her down, keep her calm enough to come up with a plan. *Something! Anything!* Even if she could free her hands, what would she do next? If she tried to get to her car, she'd still have to find her keys, tossed in the back—God knows where. If she couldn't find them right away, he'd catch her.

Running wouldn't work, even if she could run on a bad foot and ankle, she didn't know where she'd go.

Maybe, she considered, she could get his phone, call the cops—since there wasn't a landline in this place. But first she'd have to get a hold of his gun. She didn't like guns, had never even handled one before. Several times in the past, Kera had tried to get her to learn how to use one, just in case. Kera had even offered to take her out to a firing range and teach her, but Mandy didn't want anything to do with a gun, didn't like them and didn't see the need. Well, she chided herself, that decision had come back to bite her in the butt. As it was, she wouldn't even know how to hold the damned gun. She'd seen shows on TV where they used both hands, one supporting the other. They would hold it shoulder-high, not down to the side, like in the old western cowboy movies. But did you cock them anymore? No idea. If she got a hold of his gun, she was going to have to fake it. *Appearing confident is everything*, she hoped.

He was back watching TV. She struggled to get the razor's blade in a place where she could rub it against the twine. But even when the razor connected, it was difficult to put enough pressure on it to do much good, if any at all. Damn Kera, she never bought anything that wasn't super strength this or super strength that—in this case, super strong twine, probably made to hold back a charging bulldog. At the rate Mandy was progressing, she wouldn't cut through this stuff until Christmas, if then.

A commercial came on. Daniel said to her, "Guess this isn't what you were planning for today, was it?" He snickered, then picked a piece of food out of his teeth, and rubbed it on his pants.

"No, it certainly isn't. People will be missing me, and I assure you they'll come looking."

Daniel had an incredulous expression on his face.

"My secretary is expecting me in the office today to do some paperwork to get ready for a trial. She'll be worried when I don't show up. Knowing her, she'll be calling all around and if she can't find me, she'll contact the authorities." She could see that Daniel wasn't buying it. "It happened once before and that's what she did," Mandy added.

The fact was, she wouldn't be missed at Legal Aid, not today or tomorrow. She had taken two days off to work in her private practice, catching up on phone calls and contacting some new clients. No one would miss her—telling him about her secretary having called the authorities on another occasion was a desperate lie. In fact, she'd told friends that she was thinking of taking one of the days to drive to Saugatuck to do some shopping to distract herself from her problem with Kera.

"Well, I have to say, Ms. Bakker, I'm not too worried about them searching out here, given everyone knows about you and Kera." He laughed. The commercial ended and he went back to the television program. "Oh, while you slept, I got a call from Vinny. Seems they can't find you anywhere, apparently he's worried you won't be around and Erin will need your services. To make it short, I told him I couldn't get to Erin because I was on my way up to Traverse City to talk to my boss, who's calling me back to work. He bought the whole story, so Erin will be all on her own."

That creepy smile, again, flashed her way. He was already planning his next move. He'd have his new lawyer in place even before he killed her. It was as though she were already dead and watching the next phase of Erin's saga. Her stomach felt raw, sandpapered.

She tried to watch the TV to divert her fear and feeling of hopelessness, as she struggled to weaken the twine. But she couldn't follow the program. It was like a slush of voices and blurred pictures, not making any sense to her. She was exhausted. What little sleep she'd gotten last night had been shallow and sporadic. Her eyelids drooped and her chin migrated toward her chest. She fought to stay awake, but lost the battle.

* * *

Mandy opened her eyes to the afternoon sun shining through a window. Daniel held the remote browsing through

TV channels. Had he been doing that all morning as she slept? There was a clip on the screen of Erin in a blue and white jogging suit, being escorted out of her home with a terrified expression across her face. Then she was stuffed into the backseat of a police vehicle. That's where the film stopped, abruptly, and took up again at the point of her being removed from the cop car and led into the police station by Detective Brown, who held a coat over her head, as if trying to keep the press from seeing her face. That surprised Mandy. She wouldn't have expected him to shield her like that. Maybe there was an ounce of decency in him after all.

"Yahoo! I bet they found it!" Daniel threw his arms in the air, like signaling a touchdown. He flipped through the channels to catch other broadcasts of the same event, one after another.

"Found what?"

He heard her question and glimpsed her way. "It's for me to know and you to find out," he sang in a childlike voice.

What was there for the police to find, she wondered, that had convinced them to take Erin in? She wished Daniel would turn up the volume, but she knew not to ask. He'd enjoy not doing something she wanted. From what she could discern from the TV coverage, the police weren't responding to reporters' questions.

"Okay, okay, I'll tell you," he said in his singsong voice, as though she'd kept begging him for more information. "No one else will ever know, and you'll be dead, and, well, someone should be able to appreciate how clever I am. I planted my *carving knife* in Erin's house for the cops to find. I wore gloves but carefully made sure not to clean the blade off," he said proudly. "The lab will verify Stacey's DNA."

They must have searched Erin's home sometime this morning, Mandy thought. The blood on the knife along with Erin being the beneficiary of Stacey's insurance policy… and then it occurred to her, "And I suppose you tipped off the police regarding the insurance policies, too."

"Bingo!" Daniel was strutting around the kitchen like a banty rooster.

The local news finally signed off the Erin spectacle, but not before the anchor promised to return with any new developments. Daniel picked up the remote. "I wonder if this is being carried on any of the major news networks." He flicked through the channels until he came to CNN. A woman was talking about the presidential election, then flashed on a picture of one of the right-wing presidential candidates for the Republican Party. "Now there's my man. Mark my words," Daniel said, as he pointed at the TV, "he will knock Obama off his throne and back to Hawaii." He paused. "Or I should say, Kenya." He took his gun off the counter and started twirling it around his finger. "Oh dear, I'm so sorry you won't be around to see him become president." He threw his head back and laughed maniacally.

Mandy didn't think she could take it much longer, and she could barely hold her head up; it wobbled on her neck. Whatever sleep she'd just gotten didn't seem to have lessened her fatigue, and she was tired of the fight to stay strong. Why didn't he just kill her? The sooner the better.

She wanted an end to it all.

Her vision blurred as she regarded him. Then, he seemed to move about unnaturally: *His head bounced around, as though it were detached and left on its own without the neck for an anchor. His eyes, quizzical, or maybe concerned because his head bobbed around untethered. The gun was now free of his hand, dancing alongside his head, but always pointed at her...*

Her mind raced out of control, she couldn't keep up with it; her thoughts sank down into dark holes that led to weird and scary places. She couldn't muster up enough of whatever it took to try to stop her descent.

The head and gun followed her.

CHAPTER TWENTY

A bell on the door jingled as Kera entered The Big Ten Café in East Lansing and was met with the morning smells of breakfast. The flags from the universities making up the Big Ten Conference hung on the walls encircling the room. She found a table in the corner and ordered coffee.

Sitting by the windows gave her a view of the street and alley. She tapped her fingers on the table, waiting, watching people, bikes and cars going by. A three-wheeled vehicle came up the alley driven by a woman about her age. The bike had a cargo trailer attached with Go Green Trikes written on the side. The rider quickly got off, grabbed a couple of boxes and hauled them into the restaurant's kitchen. On her way out, she came over to Kera and asked if she could give the dog a treat. The woman had light brown hair squirting out from her bike helmet, sparkly eyes, and a beautiful smile that said more than just that she loved dogs. Kera wished she felt like following up on that smile, but her heart wasn't into it. She wasn't over Kelly, she wasn't over Mandy, she wasn't over loss. Period. She sighed, checked the time. Brian should have been here by now.

She was tired of being away from home and wanted to get back to check on things. She wondered if Vinny had anything new on Clark. Probably not or he'd have let her know. She needed to check with Daniel to make sure Mandy got home safely last night. She must have, otherwise he'd have called.

The bell on the door announced Brian's arrival. He was taller than she'd remembered, six foot, maybe more. He had one of those great bodies that clothes were made for, buff, like a male model stepping out of a fashion magazine.

"Thanks for seeing me." She stood up and shook his hand.

"Hey, sorry I'm late—"

"No problem." It was a problem for her. She hated waiting for people but she needed his cooperation and didn't want him to feel defensive, at least not right off.

"I love this café. I hope you will too. Great food." Brian picked up his menu.

"So, how is it going in the world of politics these days?" Kera had made her selection and set the menu aside.

"It's a little rough out there, as you can imagine." He loosened his necktie. "But, that's not what you want to know about, is it?"

"Not really."

"How are things going with you and Mandy?"

"Could be better, but as you say, we're not here to talk about that, either, are we?" Kera took a sip of her coffee. "As you are no doubt aware, I'm investigating the murder of Stacey Hendriks—"

"I understand that and I'll answer your questions as best I can, but I don't really know how I can help you." His political smile said to her, *I'll tell you whatever I want you to hear.*

"I appreciate your willingness to speak with me. I just need to clear up a few things you might know something about, like how Victoria has dealt with the death of Stacey. How did that go for her?" Kera halted the conversation as the waitress took their order.

"She took it hard, real hard," Brain replied after the waitress left.

"That makes sense then, why she came to the service, though it was incredibly unwise. But I'm really curious as to why you'd chance taking her there. If either of you'd gotten caught that day, it would have been curtains for the senator's career. Don't you think?"

"Yeah, you're right about that. And I didn't want her to go, but she was determined—I couldn't stop her. She told me that this time she'd say goodbye—since last time she'd just up and walked away. Taking her there was nerve-wracking, to say the least, but either I helped her or stay away and worry she wasn't being careful and would get caught. At least by getting her there and back, I felt I had some control over the situation."

His explanation squared with what Victoria had said. Her question about the funeral was an easy one that he knew he couldn't deny. It was the question that she'd hoped would put him at ease. Now, having gotten through that without a problem, she would hit him with the most important question.

"Did the senator know about Victoria's relationship to Stacey or Erin? I mean to say, their past relationship?"

"Uh-huh."

"How do you know that?"

"Victoria told me."

"How long ago did she tell Jeffrey?"

"Not sure, but a while back, in the past year, maybe. Frankly, I really can't remember."

She leaned in and lowered her voice. "Wasn't the senator concerned about it getting out to the public and ruining his career?"

"He really doesn't talk to me about personal issues. He trusts me, to a point, but not with something like that—"

"But his wife trusts you?"

"Yeah, we're pretty close. We've known each other from way back, and we've been each other's confidants—" Brian caught himself and stopped cold.

Kera let it drop. She sensed that trying to push him down that road wouldn't be wise, not right now. But what were the secrets that bound them? She waited to see what he'd say next.

"Let's just say that we've become close, we worked together, coordinated stuff. When you spend that much time with each other, you share things." He stopped when the waitress brought their breakfasts. When she left, he continued. "Not that big of a deal, nothing important, really."

"Do you know where the senator was, say five or six in the evening on Tuesday, March thirteenth?"

"Not offhand." Brian appeared taken aback by her question but recovered quickly. "But let me see if I can find out for you." He put down his fork, reached for his iPhone, and tapped on it until he got to his calendar. "Let's see now…okay, here it is. I can tell you where he was, actually, where Victoria and I were too. We were all at the Republican headquarters in Lansing. It was an all-day affair and went on into the evening, late. Well, let me check, here it is. Jeffrey had a meeting in the early morning, but he came around one o'clock. It broke up around eleven or so, that night."

"None of you left there for any reason at all, like even to have dinner?"

"No, because Victoria and I got there about noon that day and no one had to go out for eats because food was constantly being brought in—I ate way too much." He rubbed his stomach, as if remembering his discomfort. "Anyway, we all just kept working and eating pastries, pizza, and other shit that was bad for us. That was pretty much it."

"What was going on there?"

"It was a big Republican state organization deal. You know, lots of campaign planning, some workshops, and generally attending to some of the details of upcoming events, stuff like that. A very tiring day, but we got a lot of—"

"So, you're telling me that after you and the De Graffs got there, none of you left, even for a while?"

"Now that you mention it…" Brain scrolled around on his calendar again. "Oh, that's right, it wouldn't be recorded in here, but now I remember. Jeffrey had to go to another meeting around dinnertime. I didn't know about it—a last-minute thing—but he'd told me about it after he got there, around three o'clock or thereabouts. So that's why I don't have it in here."

"Do you know where he was going, and when he got back?"

"Hmm, let me think." He poured cream in his coffee.

She wondered if he was trying to remember what De Graff was doing, or trying to come up with a good cover. Whichever it was, he'd found an answer.

"Oh, I know, he was going to see some big-time contributor; meeting with and making campaign contributors happy takes precedence, of course, over just about anything else that's going on in the life of a politician. I'm sure he can tell you who it was. He keeps a record of all that. I can find out for you, if you'd like."

"I'd appreciate you getting back to me on that…Did he ever come back to the headquarters that night?"

"It's not on here but I know he came back, about the time they were closing down. I heard it was about eleven or eleven thirty before everyone was out of there."

"You *heard* it was eleven or eleven thirty? So you didn't stay that long? You weren't there at the time?"

"No. As I said, we'd eaten shit all day and it wasn't sitting well with me. I don't have a good stomach and I shouldn't do that to myself. Anyway, that's why I left."

"What time was that?"

"I don't know for sure, maybe five or six."

"I thought you said you stayed all day."

"Sorry," he said, obviously annoyed. "I'm doing my best to figure this all out. It's not like I remember every move I make. In this business, one days blurs into another, so I'm trying to reconstruct it, as best I can." He kept scrolling.

"Did anyone see you after that?"

"I was home. I live alone. I didn't go out after that. Are you trying to imply I had something to do with Stacey's death?" He slapped his napkin on the table and got up from his chair. His face flushed.

"Sit down," Kera ordered, in her mother's don't-mess-with-me tone. "Cool it, Brian."

Brian was clearly startled by her demand, and when he noticed people from other tables staring at him, he sat back down. He glared at her. "Do you think I killed her?" He lowered his voice to a whisper. "Is that what you're saying?"

"I'm investigating a case and I'm asking questions of everyone who knew Stacey," Kera said evenly. "If you had nothing to do with it, you have nothing to worry about. Right?"

"Right, but, why are you asking about that night? They don't know—from what I've read—when exactly she died. Do they?"

"That's an important timeframe because a man was seen at her motel room around dinnertime on Tuesday. A few of the tests are back and they believe she died sometime Tuesday night or early Wednesday morning. The man that was seen at the motel was likely to have been involved with her death."

"Did they get a description of him?" Brian's eyebrows rose.

"Yes, to some extent, but I'm not at liberty to talk about that." She had no such restriction but wanted him to think she did. If he or Jeffery had anything to do with Stacey's death, she wanted them worried. Worried people made mistakes.

"If you think," he began, his voice stern, "Jeffrey could ever have—" Brian swallowed, hard. "Believe me, he'll be able to account for that time. He'll have proof of where he was. I'm certain of it."

"I'm sure he will," she replied incredulously. He'd find an alibi, all right. The De Graff family had enough money to buy a truckload of alibis, if they needed them.

"Kera, I'm afraid you're trekking through the wrong neck of the woods. I get where you're going with all this. You think Jeff might get worried about his wife's past and get rid of Stacey so it wouldn't come out to the public. Right?"

"Sure sounds like a motive to me." Kera picked up her napkin and wiped her mouth.

"He's not that way. He wouldn't do that." Brian looked hard into her eyes. "Kera, he didn't kill Stacey."

"How would you know for sure?"

"First," he said, exasperation in his face, "he wouldn't have the time, even if he were so inclined. Second, as I said, that's just not something he'd do. Third—" He held up three fingers. "He was with someone all day long on that day, and I'm sure that would be pretty much the case on any day that you'd want to know about."

"Okay, so he has an alibi for every day that might be in question, but given his position, wouldn't he get someone else to do his dirty work for him?"

"Are you trying to stir up a scandal to help the Democratic candidate get Jeffrey's job?" Brian glared as though he were about to do bodily harm to her, right there, right then. "Because if you are, I guarantee it won't work. We won't hesitate to sue your ass for slander. I promise you that."

"I have to tell you, Brian," Kera offered, her voice level. "There's something else that concerns me." Kera watched closely. She wanted to be able to study his expression when she dropped her next question into his lap. "How deep into Satanism are you?"

Brian's eyes popped wide, and his jaw dropped.

* * *

Kera was on her way home, still a little hungry. Grilling Brian hadn't left much opportunity to eat her food. She'd had the waitress give her a coffee to go to help her stay awake. She was suffering from a serious lack of sleep; a deficit of sleep led to frayed nerves; her frayed nerves led to edginess; edginess led to bad decisions—and sometimes a visit to the psych ward. Humiliating. Even having one hand on Lakota, her agitation wasn't mitigated one iota. If she were a dog, she'd probably bite someone.

She took in a deep breath, then a few more, in and out, in and out. Maybe a little better, but not much. She was almost to Lakeside City. Perhaps she'd scrap going to see Ally at the bar and go home instead. There she could light up her pipe and relax a bit. She could always talk to Ally later.

Lakota began acting like she did when she needed a patch of grass. "Hold on for a few minutes more, we'll be to a roadside stop in a few minutes." Kera stepped on it.

She parked close to the dog run area. Lakota's tail showed her appreciation. She opened the door and let the dog out.

Lakota quickly peed and ran toward a white labradoodle, who welcomed a friend to play with. Kera decided she could wait a bit longer and give the dogs a few minutes of playtime.

Leaning against the front of the Jeep, she watched as Lakota romped with the other dog. The labradoodle apparently belonged to two women. They sat on a bench, holding hands as the dogs played. The scene brought to mind the many times she, Mandy and Lakota had been on road trips and stopped at rest areas. She drummed her fist against the fender, biting her lip. She got back into the Jeep and got out her pipe. She took a few hits and let her head fall back against the headrest.

Out of the corner of her eye, she noticed a state trooper drive into the parking space next to her. She quickly snuffed out the pipe, burning her fingers in the process; she stashed the pipe under her seat. She turned her head away from the cop and exhaled the smoke.

The officer got out of his car and briefly glanced her way before he made his way to the building with the bathrooms.

Damn, that was close, but I'd better get the fuck out of here. She called Lakota back to the Jeep and took off.

Ten minutes after she got back on the highway, she saw a police car in her side view mirror. Was it the officer from the rest stop? The cop car was in the left lane, moving up. When the police vehicle drew near, it tucked in behind her. Kera checked her speed. She was seven miles per hour over the limit. That shouldn't get her stopped, but she let up on the gas pedal anyway. The cop stayed with her. At the exit for Lakeside City, she drove off. The cop followed.

Flashing lights came on.

Shit!

Kera pulled over and waited for the cop to come up to her vehicle, but he remained in his cruiser, probably on his computer checking out her license plate. She wished she could've tossed the weed out the window instead of stashing it under her seat— not a good hiding place. But the cop had been too close, and most likely would have noticed her doing that, putting her in a worse situation. She'd never hidden her stash; she always kept it in the console, so she didn't really have a hiding place for it. She opened the windows, trying to air the vehicle out, then grabbed a mint and popped it in her mouth. That was about all she could do. She felt trapped like a snared animal. She watched, hopeful that it wasn't the cop from the rest stop, but the rearview mirror indicated otherwise.

Fuck, fuck, fuck!

* * *

Kera tapped her fingers on the steering wheel as the cop walked up to her window. Aggravated. Wanting to bolt.

"Are you in hurry, miss?" The officer bent over and peered in at her.

"Not really, I wasn't going that fast…a little over but—"

Lakota growled.

The cop jerked back. "Is that dog under control?"

"She'll be okay." Kera fantasized sending Lakota through the window and into his face.

"I'll need to see your driver's license, registration and proof of insurance, miss. What's that I smell?" the cop asked.

"I don't know what you're talking about." She was certain, now, that he'd smelled the weed when he'd walked by her parked vehicle.

"Oh, I think you do. Smells like pot to me."

"No, but I might have been around someone who did." She knew that was a dumb thing to say. He undoubtedly heard that excuse every time.

"Do you mind if I search your vehicle?"

"Why don't you just give me my speeding ticket and be on your way." She could lose her PI license over this. Her livelihood.

"I'll ask again, do you have a problem with me searching your vehicle?"

She knew if she didn't let him, he could impound her Jeep and get a warrant to search it, but damn, she was tired and in no mood for all this. The bastard should be looking for more important shit than someone who'd smoked weed. She pounded her hands against the steering wheel.

"Miss, you need to get out of your vehicle, right now." The cop called for backup.

She knew she could take him. Of course, it'd land her in jail. But with her license revoked, what did it matter? What did anything matter, anymore? All her resolve to move on—forget Kelly, forget Mandy, forget trying so fucking hard—was coming untied. Might just as well go out fighting. Her hands clenched into fists.

"Get out! And put your hands behind you." The cop opened her door, cuffs in hand.

Just then a Lakeside City cop car came screaming up and stopped behind the first cop's car. Kera and the state trooper watched as a uniformed female got out and walked toward them.

Holy fuck, it's Casey!

CHAPTER TWENTY-ONE

The slam of a door jarred Mandy awake, somewhat, a fissure opening to consciousness, a narrow stream of light. Her body felt lifeless, as though she existed without form. But as the crack widened, pain showed up, blowing in like a sudden storm, ushering her from one nightmare into another. She'd had a dream: She'd stood on the gallows, waiting to be hanged, the noose dangling before her, while the hangman lowered a black hood over her head. She couldn't recall why she'd met this fate, what she had done to deserve to die.

"Well there, sleeping beauty." Daniel came into the room carrying a beer. "You finally woke up. You kept conking out on me this afternoon." He smiled, like someone who really cared.

Creepy!

"I was beginning to wonder if you were ever going to be able to keep your eyes open. You know it can get lonely around here without anyone to talk to, and you fell asleep when I was telling you good stuff about the bigger picture. But oh well, you snooze, you lose. I had to go outside and have a chat with the damned birds." He drained the bottle and slapped it on the table alongside the other empties.

She'd tried to stay awake, but her eyes wouldn't cooperate. Just as well, she'd had enough of his crowing. She wondered what time it was. Given the light in the room and where it was coming from, it had to be early evening. She was thirsty, like crossing the desert and running out of water kind of thirsty.

"I'm getting a little disgusted with your ex-girlfriend. We've been waiting all day around here and she hasn't come home yet. Hell, in a little while, it's going to get dark." He glanced out the window. "Her tardiness is irritating me. Besides—" He stopped, and seemed to be considering something. "I need to get going. Got people to see, business to get done."

Mandy scooted up tighter against the wall to support her back, trying to get into a position to help relieve the pain. That's when she realized her ankles had been retied while she'd slept.

"I'm hungry. How about some dinner, then we'll wrap it up here. Shit, I'll even share my food this time." He grabbed a pan out of the sink and put it on the stove. "Unfortunately for you, you won't be able to name what you want for your last meal. Sorry." He flashed his eerie I-give-a-shit-about-you smile again.

She was hungry too. She realized she hadn't had any dinner last night, and had hurriedly grabbed a package of nuts, trying to get to the meeting on time.

"Pancakes, how about we have some pancakes for dinner? There's not much else left around here, like I said, not a great menu for your final meal. But it looks like there's enough pancake mix to feed us both. Let me see, is there anything we can put in them, like blueberries?" He opened the refrigerator and then rustled through the cupboards. "My sister used to make pancakes at dinnertime for us when my parents were going out with friends. It was her specialty. Say, let's have some coffee too." He talked to her like she was a willing participant in this whole affair. "Pancakes won't be the same without some steaming hot coffee. Besides, I need to be alert, in case Kera happens to show up before I'm done here. But no way am I staying a second night. Besides, I have an early dental appointment in the morning." He put down the pancake mix to make the coffee.

She flashed on the last time she'd had pancakes, right here in this house. On occasions when she'd stayed overnight, Kera would get up and make her breakfast. Before she could even raise her head off the pillow, hot coffee would greet her. Soon breakfast would follow with a wildflower on the tray—and when out of season, purple silk flowers. It now all seemed so ironic, bizarre. She wondered how her brain could go to a place like that, now, when she was living in a nightmare.

"Ah, here's a can of peaches. That'll work. You like peaches, don't you?" He peered around the cupboard as though he really wanted to know.

Besides evil, he's got to be delusional.

She didn't respond. The smell of food and coffee made her both hungry and nauseous.

For her to eat, he was going to have to untie her hands, or else he'd have to spoon-feed her. She was sure he wouldn't; he'd sooner untie her hands. A chance to get away. Eating the pancakes would help her up her energy level. Maybe there was a chance for her, the first real spark of hope she'd had since she'd gotten into this mess.

Maybe this *wasn't* her last meal.

"Dinner's ready." He put his plate of pancakes on the table and set hers down on the floor. "Guess you won't need a fork?" He laughed, obviously delighted.

The bastard intended for her to eat the pancakes off the plate, like an animal. How humiliating. But what did she expect, that's what it was all about for him: degradation. She stared at her pancakes. He hadn't even cut them up for her. There was a big slab of butter slowly melting under the syrup he'd dumped over the stack, drowning it in the sticky sweet stuff. It would take some doing to get herself in a position to be able to eat them. He regarded her like a cat watching a mouse.

"Oh dear, I'm sorry, so rude of me." He jumped up, went over to the coffeepot, poured a cup and brought it over to her, and set it down next to her syrupy mess. He went back to his seat, picked up a fork, and stabbed at his food. He shoveled it in, grinning, with his mouth full, too full.

"You're an asshole." Her throat was so dry the words came out raspy and low, but he heard them.

"Now, now, is that being appreciative?" He clicked his tongue at her. "All the work I've gone to this evening to give you a fine meal, your last meal. You don't want me to take your food away for having a smart-ass mouth, do you?"

She didn't respond. It would only entertain him, feed his love of torturing her.

He went back gobbling his pancakes. "Yum. I outdid myself on these. The peaches were a good addition. Come on, try 'em."

The smell of the pancakes made her ravenous. There was no way she could have food next to her and not eat it—even if her eating like a dog would entertain the bastard. She had to, somehow, get herself in position to roll onto her side and lay down by the plate—not on it—so she could be in position to get to the food. There would be no way she could ever drink the coffee out of that mug without spilling it. That made her think of Mr. Moxin and his water glass, never spilling a drop. Unfortunately she was no Moxin. *Oh my God, I hope Moxin's okay.*

"Your food's getting cold, Mandy."

Ignore him, ignore him.

"Come on now." He snickered.

I will not rise to his bait. I will not!

She rolled over and down. Her face hit the side of the plate, tipping it, syrup running down toward her face.

"Good show." He clapped.

Ignore him, ignore him.

She couldn't see him. At least she didn't have to look at his face, knowing the delight that would be painted all over it.

She rolled her face over further, squarely onto the plate and stuck out her tongue, grabbing onto the sticky sweetness, lapping the maple syrup into her mouth. It was hard to force the thick substance down her dry, cracked throat.

"Good, isn't it?" He chuckled. "Nothing like sweet maple syrup." He kept talking though his full mouth. "Did you know Michigan produces a lot of maple syrup? It's not just those eastern states. They think they are the only ones that make it."

Her tongue reached for more, then with her lips she got hold of a pancake. She snagged it with her teeth; she shook it, ripped off a piece, and coaxed it into her mouth, barely chewing it before swallowing. The first bite tasted like the best food she'd ever had. She began devouring it, like a starving, wild creature, fearing the arrival of a larger hungry animal.

"Bravo, Bravo!"

His mocking didn't matter to her. Survival had taken over.

"My, my, my, you almost have that plate cleaned up."

She licked the dish, getting the last crumbs and what was left of the syrup.

"I used to make my sister really mad by telling her that girls who clean their plates don't grow up to be models." He laughed. "But I suppose you don't have to worry about that, hardly any meat on your bones, is there? Come to think of it, that's how they like models, skinny. Did Kera like you that way? Huh? Not going to answer me, eh? Myself, I prefer my women with a little padding. But I guess I can't have it all, at least not in your case."

She heard him put his mug down on the table. The legs of his chair scraped on the wooden floor. He must be getting up…

Oh God, oh God…he's coming for me now. Why doesn't he just kill me, get it over with! Where is Kera? Damn it. Where is she?

She struggled and got herself in an upright sitting position, not that it would do her any good if he planned on doing what she feared. But somehow it felt better to be sitting, more in control—an illusion, she knew.

He took off his belt.

Please God, please!

"Son of a bitch, Mandy, I've put this off, all this while, worried Kera was about to come home and catch me off guard. But frankly, I'm tired of waiting around. Shouldn't take long. I know it won't take long." He licked his lips.

She wanted to plead with him, but she'd be damned if she'd beg. It wouldn't do any good and, worst of all, he'd get off on seeing her groveling. At least she wouldn't give him that pleasure.

He had one of Kera's kitchen knives in his hand. "I guess I'm going to need to cut your feet loose, it would be a bit hard on me if I didn't." He severed the twine that bound her feet and stood over her, smacking the doubled-up belt against his hand. He bent down, his face an inch from hers. "You didn't need to sit back up like that, you're just going back down." He pulled back his hand with the leather strap in it, ready to strike.

Before his hand could make it to her face, she pulled up her legs and thrust them forward, punching her feet into his gut.

He let out a gasp of air, but recovered, and righted himself, his eyes glaring. He took the belt, wrapped it around her throat, pulling it tight. "You bitch! You're going to pay for that."

CHAPTER TWENTY-TWO

It'd taken Kera a while to convince Casey that she'd calmed down and didn't need medical attention. At first, Kera was pissed at Dee for telling Casey about her PTSD and her past trips to the hospital, but after Casey had pulled the state cop aside and convinced him to let her handle the situation, Kera was grateful. Otherwise, she'd be in jail.

It was after three o'clock when she parked in front of the Out-and-About. She decided to stop and talk to Ally instead of waiting. Besides, she needed a drink.

"Hey, Ally, how's it go?"

"Kera, where have you been?" The distress in Ally's voice was startling.

"In Lansing. Why, what's the matter?"

"God, I'm so glad to see you. Did you hear about Erin?"

"No, what about her?"

"They arrested her this morning!"

"What? You're kidding. Why didn't someone call me?"

"Vinny tried to, but your phone kept going to your messages. I'm sure if you check them, you'll find he's called several times... Want a pint?"

"Yeah, sure could use a drink." Kera checked her cell. "It's dead, no wonder I didn't get his message. I didn't have my car charger with me, and last night I forgot to plug it in, but I didn't realize my phone was totally out of juice." Kera tossed it on the bar.

"It was horrible. I watched them take her in. It was on TV." Ally came out from behind the bar with a glass of water and Kera's beer and sat down. "Erin must be terrified. And what's been really weird, beside the fact that no one could find you, we haven't been able to locate Mandy either."

"Really? I wonder where she is." Kera tapped her fingers on the bar, trying to think where Mandy could be.

"Yeah, and that's left Erin without a lawyer, or a brother."

"What do you mean without a brother?"

"Vinny said that Daniel had gone up north, something about being called back to work."

"Geez, Ally, it's not like Mandy to be out of communication with people, especially given the kind of job she has. I know in the past, when we took some time off and went out of town together, she still checked her messages and made phone calls back to people, and damn, she knew the shit Erin was in."

"I agree with you." Ally shook her head. "Fortunately, Daniel quickly made some phone calls and found a lawyer who could fill in for her at the jail, at least for now."

"Glad he did that," Kera said. "But I don't understand Mandy not answering her phone. I think I'll call Dee and see if she's heard anything from her." Kera held up her phone. "Can I borrow yours? Remember? Out of juice."

"Sure, I got it right here."

"Hi Dee, I don't have much time, but I'm calling to find out if you've heard from Mandy?"

"The last time I saw her was on Sunday. She and I went for a bike ride together. That reminds me, did Daniel tell you about what happened when we were out on the Riverside bike trail? It was horrible, but—"

"What was horrible?"

"A man and woman came along when we were resting by the trail. He recognized Mandy; he must have seen pictures of her in the paper or on TV, not sure, but he knew she was Erin's lawyer and he attacked us and we—"

"Goddamn, were either of you hurt?" This was the kind of incident she'd worried about. "How come you didn't call me? I would have come back immediately."

"Well, at the time, I didn't think we should worry you since Mandy and I were okay. There was nothing more you could do, anyway. Besides, Daniel said he would call and tell you. In fact, he was the one who came to our rescue. He drew a gun on the jerk and—"

"He didn't call me." Kera couldn't understand why he wouldn't, but then wondered, since he'd taken care of it, maybe he hadn't wanted to bother her. But Vinny hadn't let her know about the attack either. "Do you think the attack on the trail has anything to do with why I can't reach Mandy now? Like did she get scared, take off for a few days, you know, get away?"

"No. She would have told me, if she were that upset. And besides, she heard Daniel put the fear of God in the guy and told the jerk he was Mandy's security guard."

"Hmm, I can't figure out what's going on with Mandy. And it's not just me who can't get a hold of her, no one can."

"Really?"

"I'll give Vinny a ring, see if he's heard anything yet. I need to check in with him anyway."

Kera found out from her phone call to Vinny that Daniel was on his way up north, something about him getting called back to work. Daniel told Vinny he thought Mandy was out of town due to her job. Strangely, Daniel never mentioned anything about the attack on her sister and Mandy—probably preoccupied with getting his job back. Vinny had been busy following Ralph Clark around, still not coming up with anything solid to report. He said he'd leave Clark and check Mandy's house, but Kera decided she wanted do that herself.

* * *

She didn't see Mandy's car anywhere, not in the driveway, not out on the street, not in the garage, nowhere. Then it occurred to her, maybe Mandy had taken the car in to have the brakes checked. Kera had driven the VW several weeks ago and suggested that she get them checked.

Leaving Lakota in the car, she went up to the door and rang the bell.

Nothing.

She waited, thinking Mandy could be in the shower. She knocked. With no response, she banged on the door.

Still no Mandy.

She went over to a window and peeked in. Nothing, no movement.

Mandy's mailbox was full to overflowing; a few days' worth of mail had gathered there. Mail piling up was an open invitation for a home invasion, as well as letting her know Mandy hadn't been there for a while. Mandy might just not have brought it in, but that wouldn't be like her.

Kera searched her key ring to find the house key. She hadn't gotten around to giving it back to her, and for that matter, Mandy hadn't returned her key to the lighthouse either. Kera winced thinking about that little ritual. It was going to hurt like hell, the giving-back, the official end of the relationship.

Divorce, gay style.

She opened the door. Mr. Moxin came tearing over to her, whining as he wrapped himself around her leg.

"Hey, Moxin, where's your mama?" Kera reached down, petted him, and then went into the kitchen. "Mandy...Mandy, are you home?"

No response, other than Moxin hanging around her, crying, demanding more of her attention. As she reached down and picked him up, she noticed his empty dish. It usually had food in it. Moxin ate when he pleased; he was more of a grazer than a big meal eater. Moxin's water glass had tipped over—amazingly, it hadn't broken. If there had been any water in it, it had been lapped up. The poor cat had to be really upset to knock his glass over. She kissed his head, ran her hand over his fur. "Moxin, what's going on here? Where's your mother?" She put him down, got his dish, and poured in some dry cat food. "I know you prefer the canned stuff, but how about this for now?" Moxin was grabbing food out of the dish before she could set it on the mat. She picked up his water glass and filled it.

"Okay, kitty, I'll leave you to eat. I need to look around." The scene didn't feel good to her. Mandy loved her cat and would never let his dish or glass stand empty.

Kera searched the house, but found nothing out of place, nothing suspicious. She went back up to the kitchen. Moxin was at his glass, trying to drink. The water level had gone down to where he was now dipping his paw in and bringing water back up and licking it. Since she'd just filled it, it had to have been a long time since he had had any water. She picked up his glass and topped it off.

Watching Moxin, she realized she hadn't checked out the utility room where the cat's litter box was kept. Actually, the smell of the box found her before she entered the room. Moxin's box had not been changed for several days. She knew Mandy cleaned his litter box every evening, come rain or shine. Kera quickly took care of it.

Something was definitely wrong.

Unless, maybe, Mandy had gone out of town on a case. It had happened a few times in the past, and one time it had been a spur-of-the-moment kind of thing. Possibly she'd hired someone to watch after Moxin and the house, and that someone hadn't shown up. That was the only other explanation she could think of as to why Moxin had been neglected.

She was stumped about where to go to find Mandy, but for now, she decided to go home, feed Lakota dinner, and figure out what to do next. As she sped along, a picture of a dead female body in the wetlands haunted her but it wasn't Stacey's, it was Mandy's. The scene flashed in her head, over and over, to the pulse of her racing heart.

She needed to get to her computer to find Jessica's address and phone number. The last thing she wanted to do was to talk to that bitch, but she might know where Mandy was. She didn't want to think about them together, but...

Shit! Goddamn it!

Jessica no doubt knew where Mandy was. With her! They'd secluded themselves, not getting out of bed—Jessica's goddamned bed or at least some bed with Jessica in it. Why didn't she think of it sooner? But then, why would she want to go there in her head? It wasn't something she wanted to consider...Fuck, fuck, fuck..."

Okay, move beyond, get control, breathe...Think!

The two of them were probably out of town, not at Jessica's place. Probably somewhere like Saugatuck, at some lesbian B & B, something like that.

Goddamn Mandy for not answering her phone.

Mandy certainly wasn't that irresponsible. Back when she and Mandy had holed up at a resort in Traverse City for two weeks, Mandy continually checked her messages—interrupting their love nest. Kera figured Jessica surely must have more going for her than she did. Of course Jessica did, she'd stolen Mandy away from her.

"Damn her, damn her, damn her!" She wondered if she needed her pipe to get calmed down...*No, no, I can't.* Even though her work was intermingling with her private life, she had to view this as work, not risk getting stoned because that's what she felt like doing.

Lakota stretched her body across the Jeep's console, squeezing her head between Kera and the steering wheel.

"It's okay, Lakota. I'm just having a bit of a meltdown right now. Nothing you have to be concerned about." She took a couple of deep breaths. "I'll get over it, I will, but probably not in this lifetime." She scratched Lakota's ears. "Not to worry, I'm in control. Now, let's get home."

As Kera turned down the road leading to the lighthouse, she saw the tower protruding into the darkening sky. The rest of the structure and the house were silhouetted against the last of rays of the setting sun shooting up from below the horizon, casting a background edged with a purple-pink glow that stretched into the sky and reflected onto the lake.

Kera pressed the brakes. "Look, Lakota, isn't that beautiful? Keep your eye on it, girl, because it doesn't last long and will be gone in a flash—like most of the women in my life." *Goddamn it, I can't keep crap out of my mind any better than the sky can hold onto a sunset. I need a drink.* She stepped on the gas.

When she was almost to the lighthouse she heard a dog barking, then saw the golden retriever, Mayday—Lakota's beach friend—running up alongside the Jeep. Lakota jumped up and stuck her head out the window. Her tail flipped back and forth, like a windshield wiper, slapping Kera in the face. She put her hand up to protect herself. Lakota barked and whined at the same time. Her tail was starting to do damage to Kera's head, in spite of her defensive efforts. She grabbed it, keeping it away from her. "If you want to play with Mayday, go for it. Come home when you get hungry." She opened the passenger door and Lakota leapt out to the excited dog, panting, slobbering and bouncing up and down. They charged off, Lakota chasing after Mayday.

Kera was puzzled when she noticed a parked car at the lighthouse. She knew she'd put the Buick behind the shed, and besides, it was definitely smaller than the Buick. As she got closer she realized it was a VW, but it was still too far away given the dim light of dusk to be able to make out the color. Was it Mandy's VW? Her heart started to beat faster. It could be. It had to be. She pulled up behind it, stopped and got out. It was Mandy's, all right. But why would she be here? Surely she hadn't been here the whole time that people hadn't been able to get a hold of her. Even if she had, she'd have her phone with her. Kera peered through the VW's window and noticed Mandy's purse, the contents spilled out and scattered all over the driver's seat and on the floor.

What the fuck?

Her body—every cell of it—jumped to alert, like in Iraq when something bad was going down.

She peeked around the VW and checked out the house. There was a light in the upstairs bathroom, a faint glow in the living room, and a flickering light, dim and erratic, in the kitchen area—most likely the TV making those sporadic flashes. Why on earth would Mandy be there? Was someone else with her? The whole thing didn't make sense and raised her hackles. She hoped her headlights hadn't been seen when she'd driven up behind the car; it didn't appear to have stirred any motion in the house. With little cover, there was no way she could sneak up to the windows and peek in without being seen. Even if she knew who was in there, and where or how many, she wouldn't be able to quietly slip in. Opening the front door would make too much noise with its squeaky hinges and creaky, weathered wood, and she never did own a key to the outside door to the connecting room. Windows wouldn't work; she kept them latched. Not wanting to risk an ambush, there was only one way in: the rope to the tower.

To get there, she'd have to sneak over behind the shed, hold close to the ground. From the shed, some large bushes would provide cover as she made her way to the tower. Then, she'd use her rope to climb up to the galley rail and onto the deck where she could gain entry to the lantern room. From there, she'd make her way down to the connecting room and into the kitchen where she'd seen the flickering light.

Something stirred ahead of her. She stopped and dropped flat to the ground. A flash of lightning from an approaching storm helped her survey the area, but nothing moved. It must have been a raccoon or some other animal.

Kera hurried over to the tower to the climbing rope and untied it. At the bottom of the tower she'd be able to use her feet and push up and out against the wall, but as she got higher, the wall wouldn't be available anymore. The rope was attached to the gallery rail that stuck out from and surrounded the lantern room. So, she would soon be hanging out there with nothing to push off from with her feet. It would be all arm strength. Of course, that was why she set this up in the first place, to keep her arms strong, but it was a tough climb, she'd already had a long day and was tired.

A scream!

At least she thought it was a scream, but reconsidered, it had to be a gull. They made those screechy noises, like a human's scream. Or it could easily be a catfight, with all the feral cats that hung around the grounds. She'd heard their piercing screams plenty of times, especially at night.

She grabbed the rope.

The wind came in from the lake, fast, vicious. The storm was here, full blast. Below her, white-capped waves crashed on the shore. Rain blasted against her body, pushing her sideways toward the tower. She lost her grip and slipped down, but squeezed, tight, stopping the descent. Now her hands burned like fire.

Exhausted and out of gas, she stopped to rest. Her shoulder had begun to ache from an old wound. She'd felt pain the last time she'd done this climb, but it was worse now. She regarded the last third of her climb. To be able to make it up, she'd have to approach it the same way she'd been taught, when it'd seemed impossible: hand over hand, one grip at a time—like her military instructor had hammered into her brain, "You don't have to make it all the way, just the next pull."

Just the next one…just the next one…just the next one…

Finally, she reached the gallery, drew herself up to the rail and climbed over. Out of breath, she stood there a moment and then opened the door to the lantern room. As she stepped in, the heavy door smashed into her back, thrusting her forward, as it slammed shut. *Shit!* She'd tried to bring it in slowly but the strong wind had other ideas. She could only hope that no one downstairs had heard the slam.

She lifted the hatch to the watch room and descended the ladder, then slowly started creeping down the iron staircase. There were over two hundred steps with several landings. In spite of the windows at every landing, the overcast night offered no light in the cave-dark tower. On tiptoes, she hugged the wall and held onto the rail. In daytime she'd be able to gauge where she was on her way down by looking down through the small holes in the metal stairs. But in the dark, she had to count her steps to keep track of how far she had yet to go.

When she made it to the connecting room, the door to the kitchen was closed—she always kept it open. She put her ear to the door and heard the canned laughter and voices of a TV sitcom. She reached back and pulled her gun from her waistband. Gently, she pushed the door open, slightly, and peeked around, opened the door a few inches more, holding her gun, barrel up, head high, ready.

Still, nothing but TV noises.

Maybe Mandy and/or whoever had been in there had left or moved to another room.

She opened the door just enough to push her gun and head through.

"We were wondering when you'd finally get down here," a male voice said. It took her a moment to realize it was Daniel standing there, his gun aimed at her. "Come on in, Kera. Make yourself at home."

She and Daniel stood there, like two cowboys in the middle of a dusty main street, guns pointed at each other. A standoff.

But then, Daniel turned his gun on Mandy.

Kera hadn't seen her on the floor propped up against the wall, tied up with duct tape over her mouth. Terror screamed from Mandy's eyes as she shifted her gaze back and forth between Kera and Daniel.

"I think you'd better drop your gun," Daniel snarled, "or I'll blow your ex-girlfriend's fucking head off. I assume you still have feelings for her."

That broke the standoff.

She didn't know if he could shoot Mandy before she would be able to disable him, but she wasn't going to take that chance. She dropped the gun.

"Kick it over here," he ordered.

She pushed it toward him with her foot.

"Good girl." He picked it up, removed the magazine, and tossed the gun on the counter. "Thought I'd get rid of the ammo, keep you from doing something stupid, like trying to go for your gun." His lip curled up in a sneer.

What in hell had she walked into? Her slinking around, climbing up that damned rope hadn't accomplished anything—she might just as well have walked through the goddamned door with her hands up. There she was, dripping water like a drowned rat. Her heart thumped, like it could blow out of her chest.

"Well, now that we've got the gun issue settled." Daniel waved the barrel of his revolver, gesturing for her to move on into the room. "How about you take a seat at the table." He looked down by her feet. "You're getting water all over the place." He clicked his tongue and shook his head.

She ignored his remark and sat down, trying to evaluate the situation. Mandy's clothes were disheveled, her blond hair a mess, red marks on her face.

"What the hell is going on here, Daniel?"

"Well, you have just joined us for Mandy's final hour, that's what's happening here. And, since you showed up, I've made arrangements for you to be a part of it. In other words, this is going to be your last stand as well."

"What do you mean?" This whole scene made no sense to her. "What the fuck's going—"

"It means I'm going to kill you both." Daniel's voice was level, emotionless, chilling.

"Why?"

"It's simple, really. I need you both to stop trying to prove my sister is innocent. And besides that, I'm not that crazy about women sleeping with women. That's why." His tone remained indifferent but his face was now flushed, as if anger had crept up and broken through. "My sister deserves what she's getting and Stacey deserved it too."

"You killed Stacey?"

"That's right."

"And carved that shit on her body?"

"An artist I'm not, but—"

"Shut up, Daniel, that's sickening! Disgusting!" Kera wiped her forehead where water had dripped down into her eyes. "You did that to Stacey just because you don't like lesbians?" This was all feeling surreal to her.

There had to be some other reason. Kera knew Lakeside City wasn't short on its supply of radicals and people with twisted minds, but goddamn, this was incomprehensible. Was she looking at a demented serial killer, focused on killing lesbians? And now he had his sights on her and Mandy?

"Now, now, Kera. You are in no position to tell me to shut up and—"

"What difference does it make? You're a disgusting piece of shit and you're planning to kill us anyway. Right?" Rage ran through her like a bolt of lightning. She knew she needed to control herself, think clearly, and not go off half-cocked.

"That's right, but you could hasten your demise by talking shit to me. I'm sure you want to buy as much time as possible, hoping to get out of this." Daniel moved away from Mandy, waving the barrel of his gun like a pointing stick. "How about you move over next to your girlfriend there, so I can keep a better eye on the both of you. Careful now, don't try anything or it will be the last thing you ever try."

She did as he asked.

"Sit down," Daniel snapped.

"I'd rather stand." Sitting would definitely be to her disadvantage.

"I'd rather you sit down, bitch." Daniel stood a few feet from the connecting room door she'd just come through, gun pointed in their direction. "Now! I'm not a patient person."

Kera sat down. She touched Mandy on the leg, wishing she could somehow reassure her that she would get her out of this mess, but she couldn't. This might be it: the end for both of them.

"I love you," Kera whispered. She didn't know where that had come from. It just popped out of her. Actually, she did know. It came from her heart. What difference did it make now? This was no time for petty mind games. Mandy's eyes seemed be telling her that she loved her too. But maybe it was only because that's what she wanted to believe, so that's what she saw in Mandy's gaze.

Daniel watched them intently, as though they were lab mice in an experiment. Had he heard Kera tell Mandy that she loved her? Didn't matter. But she hated being his entertainment. His face said he was enjoying this a great deal. She had to come up with something, fast, but her mind raced too quickly to land on anything long enough to figure out what to do. She worked on slowing her breathing, in and out, in and out. She forced her fingers to remember what it felt like when they ran over the dog's silky coat…Her heartbeat slowed down, decelerating her mind as well…

Okay, what are my options?

If she could get to him, she was certain he could be disarmed and she would be able to best him in a fight. Her only hope was to catch him off guard.

"Oh, what the hell, ladies, we'll let Mandy talk now, that is, if she wants to. You two might like to have a few last words. I can go along with that. I'm not a monster. And it could be interesting. But I warn you, if I'm not amused, I'll put an end to this scene, fast. Make it good because I don't handle boredom well." He moved toward them. "I really hated putting this tape on your girlfriend, but your bitch here wouldn't stop screaming like a wild banshee, damned bloodcurdling screams." He shook his head. "I had to slap this over her mouth." Daniel grabbed the end of the duct tape and ripped it off.

Mandy let out a groan.

"What in the hell have you done to her?" Kera snarled. She felt her face get hot, her hands curling into a fist.

"Tell her, Mandy, tell her that I've been pretty damned good to you, haven't I? I provided a last meal for her. Pancakes, my new specialty." His lips curled up, his eyes wide in a glassy stare.

"Yeah…right, Daniel." Mandy's weak voice was barely audible.

"I've been debating, all afternoon, whether to fuck your girlfriend before you made it in here, or wait to let you watch—I decided on *both*!" He laughed.

Kera had heard that kind of crazy laugh from holding rooms in a psych ward.

"You know how men are." Daniel's eyes went to Mandy. "We can't control our urges. I sort of wondered, at one point, if the flash of light was you coming home, but I decided it was lightning. But when I heard something slam up there," he said as he pointed his gun to the ceiling, "well, you don't need all the details, do you? Enough now, you're here, so let's get the show on the road. Mandy, what do you say, you don't mind if I let Kera watch us, do you?" He didn't wait for a response. "Surely you wouldn't want to deny her the pleasure…"

That was it. That was all Kera could take, no matter what the consequences. She jumped up and charged at Daniel. At the same time she heard a loud sound coming from the connecting room, and then saw Lakota blasting through the doorway.

Distracted by the noise behind him, Daniel turned toward the door just as Lakota came flying in. He fired his gun but it didn't stop the dog's assault. Lakota leapt at him, knocking the pistol out of his hand and smashing him to the floor.

Kera scrambled for his gun. But by the time she got it, he'd managed to escape out the door, and Lakota lay flat on the floor, bleeding.

"Oh, god, Lakota, you got hit!" She grabbed a dishtowel and pressed it over the bullet wound. She searched the dog's body to see if there was any more damage. She found it on the other side.

"Is she okay?" Mandy asked.

"Yeah, I think she's going to be all right, if I can stop the bleeding. She seems to be breathing okay. But the blood is pouring out from two places, where the bullet entered and where it apparently exited. "Can you get me another rag?"

"Uh-huh. But first you need to untie me."

In her distress over Lakota, she'd forgotten Mandy's wrists were tied. She cut the twine and helped Mandy up. Mandy wobbled, barely able to stand.

"Are you okay…can you do this?"

Mandy nodded, unconvincingly. Kera helped her to a kitchen chair, then rushed back to Lakota, ripped her rag in two and put pressure on the wounds. The dog was whimpering. "It's going to be okay, girl."

"How are you doing?" Kera asked Mandy.

"I need to get some water." Mandy's voice was raspy. She was rubbing her wrists, and stretching her arms and legs. She started to stand up, but slumped back down.

"Don't push it, Mandy. Give yourself some time. I'll get your water." Kera got up.

"No, no, I can do it." Mandy held up her hand. "I need to get my legs under me and move. First, I'm going to lock the door, just in case he decides to return." Mandy wobbled to the outside door, reaching out to steady herself on whatever was available.

"He won't come back," Kera said. "He doesn't have a gun."

After Mandy secured the door, she poured herself a glass of water and drained it, then refilled it. "This is the best water I've ever had…if you give me that other towel, I'll hold it for you."

"I can handle this, you need to rest."

"No, I want to help with Lakota."

Mandy sat down next to her. She explained to Kera how Daniel had tricked her and his plan to make it all appear like a lover's quarrel, as well as details—as many as came to mind—that she'd learned from Daniel during her long ordeal.

"Oh my god, Mandy, I did this to you. I asked him to keep an eye on you, to see you home that night. I wanted you to be safe but I set you up for all this, instead. I'm so—"

"How could you have possibly known?" Mandy placed her hand on Kera's back. "It's not your fault."

"Yeah, right," Kera muttered. She didn't think she'd ever forgive herself. Somehow she should have known, should have seen it. "I didn't check him out before I let him—"

"I should have too, but I didn't. Why would we have even thought he had a part in Stacey's death? For God's sake, he was supposed to be helping his sister."

Kera moved Lakota so Mandy could get a better angle to hold the cloth against the wound, then asked, "Did that fucking bastard rape you?"

"No, but he was about to, yesterday, then again, just before you…" Her words trailed off, faltered, then stopped while she composed herself enough to go on, "The first time, he got distracted…But today, if you hadn't come when you did…" Mandy's voice trembled. She took a deep breath, coughed, flinched and grabbed her side and held it, but went on. "If you hadn't shown up when you did—" She closed her eyes, her lips pressed together, tight. She opened her mouth to say more, but it was as though her words had clogged up in her throat, unable to come out. Her face blanched, frozen.

"You don't have to say any more. What's wrong, there?" Kera pointed to Mandy's rib area, where she'd grabbed it when she coughed.

"It's okay, really, just been sitting too long, probably cramping or indigestion or something."

"He hurt you!" Kera doubted it was a cramp, more like a sharp pain, given the expression on her face.

"I don't want to talk about it now. I'll be all right, don't worry. It's better now."

"Okay." It wasn't okay with Kera, but she could see Mandy didn't want to say any more, and she'd dropped her hand from her side, as though it were better now, but Kera didn't believe the indigestion story. "We need to get you to a doctor."

"I'm all right, Kera, really. Lakota's the one that needs medical attention."

She and Mandy sat on the floor, together, not mentioning anything about their relationship, tending Lakota's wounds. Kera didn't know what to say, so she said nothing, but she felt the pile of agony that sat between them, too hot to touch.

"See here," Mandy finally spoke. "I think this one's starting to clot." She showed Kera Lakota's wound.

"I do want to hear about what happened to you, Mandy, but only when you feel you can talk about it." It was clear to her that Mandy had gone through Hell.

Mandy, teary-eyed, looked away.

Kera changed the subject. "The bleeding is slowing down. I think we almost got it stopped." She kissed the dog's head.

"How about I get you to a doctor?" she said to Mandy. "And Lakota to the vet. Then I need to see if I can track down that bastard."

"No," Mandy replied, "I'm okay." She paused, her brows furrowed. "I've been thinking—unfortunately, I've had lots of time for that—I don't believe this is all just Daniel's doing. I believe someone else is involved."

"Why do you say that?"

"At one point he mentioned Stacey had something he wanted and he was going to get it back."

"What do you think that was?"

"I have no idea, but I saw his face when he said it. Angry, like he could kill. Well, I guess he did, didn't he?" Mandy grimaced.

"You said that you believe someone else is involved or knows about it? Why do you think that?"

"When I was coming out of sleep, I heard him talking on his cell phone. It sounded like he was speaking to someone he knew pretty well. I can't be sure of it and I can't tell you why I thought that. I was so drowsy, but he was talking about me. I'm pretty sure the person on the other end knew what he was doing here. When I opened my eyes, he was staring directly at me and told whomever he was talking to that, 'she's waking up,' so he had to go."

"Maybe, but it could also be that he was making someone think he was at Erin's house, and it was his sister who was waking up?" Kera put down the towel she was using as a compress, the bleeding under control.

"I don't think so."

"Someone he knew, huh?" Kera rolled that information around in her brain, seeking a connection. Having just seen Brian this morning, and the expression on his face when she'd popped the Satanism question on him, she wondered if Brian happened to be the guy Daniel had been talking to on the phone, which led to her earlier speculation that Brian might be protecting De Graff by shutting Stacey up, permanently. Maybe Daniel had been given the job of carrying out the dirty work. Was that how it all went down?

"Try to remember, Mandy. What was it you heard that made you believe Daniel and the person on the other end of the call were friends—or knew each other—and knew about what he was doing to you?"

"Let me think." Mandy rubbed her forehead. "Gosh, maybe he said something that made me realize it at the time, but I'm sorry, I'm not remembering anything specific. Like I said, I was in a haze, to put it mildly. It sounded like it had to do with me. That's all I can come up with right now."

For now, she needed to put her speculation aside. It was Daniel she had to focus on and hunt down. She checked Lakota's breathing. The dog seemed okay to her, and the bleeding in both wounds had slowed to a trickle, and then only when Lakota moved.

"Do you really think you could get Lakota to the vet for me?" Kera could see Mandy's face was getting some color back, and she seemed to have gained some strength. "I mean, are you feeling well enough to drive now? You were pretty shaky on your feet. I wouldn't ask you to do this, but—"

"I'm doing better, really. You showing up has done wonders for me."

"I'm glad." Kera smiled. "And I think Lakota's going to be okay, doesn't look like the bullet got near any of her organs—though I'm worried about it, right here." Kera pointed to the dog's left upper foreleg where the bullet had exited. The wound gaped open there. "See the bone."

"Uh-huh."

"We'll get you back to your old self," Kera held Lakota's head in her hands and gazed into the dog's eyes. "I promise."

Lakota licked her hand.

"Mandy, I want to get out of here and go after Daniel. Are you sure you feel strong enough to drive Lakota to the vet? I want to go after Daniel but I won't if you're not okay."

"Quit your worrying, Kera. I can do it. I've been infused with a little energy, something I didn't think I'd ever have again."

"Well, okay, if you're sure. I'll get her into your car. Once you get there, the vet can move her inside. I don't want you to even try lifting her. You're hurting and should go to the ER as soon as you drop Lakota off."

"He probably took my car; the keys were in it." Mandy peeked out the window. "No, he didn't, that's strange…I can't see behind the shed, maybe he took the Buick, since your Jeep is still there…But the Buick keys are here on the hook."

"That is odd he didn't take your car. He wouldn't have taken my Jeep because I always lock it. Maybe he hotwired the Buick…Or, he's still around? She hadn't heard a car leaving, but under the circumstances, she most likely wouldn't have.

Lakota struggled to get to her feet, but when she tried to put weight on her left front side she slipped back down.

"Okay, girl, stay down. I'll carry you out to the car, but first I have to look outside and make sure Daniel isn't around." She patted Lakota on her behind as she got up and asked Mandy, "Would you make sure she doesn't try to get up again?"

Kera walked out behind the shed. The Buick was still there. And there was no sign of Daniel, anywhere. He didn't have his gun—she had it—so she wasn't overly worried but was baffled as to why he hadn't taken a vehicle. In her search, she came across Mandy's shoes. Coming back in, she assured Mandy he wasn't in the area and handed her the shoes. "These were outside. How'd they get there?"

"That's another story I'll tell you sometime." Mandy tried to put her shoes on. "I can't get my feet into these. I'll have to go barefoot."

Kera got Mandy a pair of her slippers. They'd be too big, but would work for now. Then she found a blanket and gently rolled Lakota onto it and carried her out to the VW. All the while she kept scanning the area for Daniel in case she'd somehow missed him.

"You barely fit back here, big girl." Kera struggled getting the dog in the VW's backseat.

Mandy picked up the scattered contents of her purse and found her car keys, then held them up for Kera to see. "Here they are."

"He probably thought I'd be tearing out the door, hot after him. Guess he didn't figure I'd take care of you and my dog." Kera closed the back door of the VW. She watched as Mandy put the last of her stuff back into her purse, snapped it shut, and then slipped into the driver's seat.

Mandy rolled down the window. "Really, Kera, don't you think you should call the police? Or I could? Though I'd have to wait till I get to the vet. Daniel threw my phone out."

"Don't worry, I'll call." Kera hustled over to her Jeep and got in, mumbling to herself. "After I catch the bastard." She didn't trust the cops. She'd do this job herself, and call later. Luckily, her phone was out of juice, so she had a good excuse for not calling them.

Kera waved Mandy on ahead, but Mandy drove up alongside of her and called out, "You still take Lakota to Dr. Terry Lipinski, right? Her office is on Maple, isn't it?"

"Right, she lives there too, but go to the office part and ring the night bell. Terry will answer it."

"Okay. Be careful, Kera!"

Kera didn't know what *careful* meant in a situation like this. She would do what she needed to do and hope it turned out well for her.

"I mean it, Kera." Mandy pulled ahead a few feet, stopped and yelled back to her, "He's a dangerous, sadistic killer."

"I know."

"Don't forget, he knows that we know he killed Stacey. He won't hesitate to—"

"I'll be *careful*, don't worry, Mandy." She shook her head. "Geez," she muttered to herself, "I'm not out trying to kill myself." Daniel wasn't out to die today either, but for one of them, it could be their last day.

Mandy pulled ahead a few more feet, stuck her head out of the window, and looked back at her. "I love you too, Kera," she shouted, then drove off.

Kera wanted to jump out of the Jeep, stop her, put her arms around her, kiss her, hold her. But then, Kera began to doubt the words she'd just heard, like those were the words she'd wanted to hear, but did Mandy actually say them? Even if she did, it might easily have been a spur-of-the-moment feeling of gratitude. Understandable, but no doubt Mandy would end up regretting having said them. So, she wouldn't count on it and would be better off keeping her pessimism. It would protect her from more pain, but she couldn't push back down a surge of hope that had shown up with those three words. She stepped on the gas, determined, no one would get away with doing what that bastard had done to Mandy…

No one.

CHAPTER TWENTY-THREE

After Mandy left to take Lakota to the veterinary hospital, Kera took off down the road, then stopped, realizing she had no idea where she was going.

It was only eight thirty p.m. but she was beat. Fatigue was her enemy, likely to produce a panic attack, a flashback, a bad decision—or all three. She needed a strategy to keep herself from doing something stupid.

What she knew wasn't much, other than that Daniel must have taken off on foot. What else? Her thoughts raced so fast she couldn't stop on an idea long enough to evaluate it. Automatically, her hand reached out for Lakota, but the dog wasn't there. Her heart pounded like it could break loose and fly out of her chest. She got her pipe from the console, lit it and took a few hits, just enough to calm her down, help her think. Her spinning thoughts slowed and landed on footprints, Daniel's. She wondered if she might be able to find his tracks. The front that had come in earlier had produced rain and would have washed out old prints, leaving his, hers and Mandy's. The rain, though fast and furious, hadn't lasted long. She wheeled the Jeep around.

Her flashlight picked up Daniel's prints coming out the door. She followed them toward a field, on a diagonal, going northeast. It made sense he hadn't tried to descend the bluff to the beach—too tricky for most folks during the day, let alone at night. If he stayed on the northeast trajectory, he'd be headed toward the woods, then most likely to the paved road. But maybe he'd stay in the wooded area, where he'd not easily be seen—though it would be difficult trekking through the underbrush—and continue going north, paralleling the lake and road. The problem with following his trail toward the woods was she'd quickly lose his prints in the soft sand before she even reached the trees.

She calculated he had about three-quarters of an hour on her, so she needed to get on it. She jammed the Jeep in drive and traveled to the main road, and pushed north.

The area was heavily forested and in the dark of night she wasn't able to see much, except for what the headlights could pick up. Maybe Daniel had put out his thumb and had already caught a ride. If that were true, she was wasting her time, but she couldn't play every eventuality she might come up with. She drove on for a while then made a decision to head on down a dirt road that led further into the trees toward the lake. There was public access to the water at the end of the road; maybe he was thinking of grabbing a boat. There were a couple old fishing boats someone had abandoned there that might be usable. Maybe he knew that too.

She bumped along on the single-track road, scraping the sides of the Jeep against encroaching tree branches and bushes. Her lights picked up several sets of glowing eyes, none of the human variety. Probably raccoons. A deer shot out in front of her and stopped in the middle of the car's path. It stood there like a statue, eyes glowing in the headlights. Kera rolled up, slowly, close to the stunned creature and turned off her headlights, breaking the animal's spell. It ran off into the trees. She drove on, glancing from side to side until she got to the lake. The two boats were still there, no signs he'd been out this way.

She drove back to the main road. Up on the left, she spotted the convenience store/gas station that she'd stopped at several times in the past, mostly for coffee, soda, or roller food. Daniel could have made it to that store by now. She pulled in, grabbed the gun, tucked it into her waistband and covered it with her jacket. Before going in, she circled the building…Nothing, no sign of him.

Opening the door, she noticed a young guy with straggly long hair behind the counter. She couldn't see if there was anyone else in the place, so she wandered through the aisles.

"Hey, if I can help you find anything, just give a holler."

"Thanks, I will." Kera moved up and down the rows, but didn't hear or see anyone else in the place. She was hungry and thirsty, so she took a couple of power bars and a bottle of cold water to the checkout counter.

"Did you find everything you wanted?" The guy rang up her purchases.

"Ah, yeah, but I was supposed to meet a friend of mine. The problem is, I got a late start. We planned on meeting here fifteen or twenty minutes ago. Has a man come in lately?" Kera took out her wallet to pay.

"What does he look like?" The clerk counted out her change.

"He's about six foot, in his thirties, and—"

"Reddish hair?"

"Yeah. How long ago was he here?"

"Let me think." The clerk rubbed his chin. "I'd say it was, maybe five, ten minutes ago. He bought a couple of candy bars, a pop and trail mix. He seemed in a big hurry. In fact, he got upset when I told him I didn't have enough quarters in my till, and I needed to go to the back and get some. I told him it would only take me a minute, but when I came back he was gone."

"Geez, I wonder why he didn't wait for me. Maybe we miscommunicated about our meet-up time. He probably thought I wasn't coming."

"Were you his ride? I know he didn't drive up in a car."

"A mutual friend of ours dropped him off. Maybe he panicked when he thought I wasn't coming and decided to thumb a ride before it got too late." Her ability to embellish a story—come up with a lie on a dime—had served her well. It was a talent she'd developed when she was a closeted dyke. She tried to keep that skill out of her personal life now, but when it came to the investigation business, she found it was an essential skill in her toolbox.

"Hope he got a ride because it's supposed to rain again soon, and it's gonna get pretty cold tonight." The guy handed her the bag with the bars and water. "Not the best night to be out there on foot. That's for sure."

"Yeah, he'd do that sort of thing. But damn, I really wanted to get together with him. He's an old school friend I haven't seen in a long time, and I was hoping to catch up on our lives and mutual friends. You didn't happen to see what direction he was going, did you? If he's still on foot, maybe I can catch up with him."

"As a matter of fact, I did." The storekeeper came out from behind the counter and walked over to the glass door. "I saw him head down that dirt road." He pointed toward the lake. "Back there, where all those beautiful beach homes are."

"Hmm, maybe he knows someone who lives there." Kera opened the door. "Thanks a lot, you've been a big help."

"No problem."

She drove toward the lake. The houses the clerk had mentioned were mansions really, lining the lakeside bluff. She hadn't ever been down this particular road, not that she could remember, anyway. But when she was out on the lake in a boat or jogging on the beach, she'd seen them.

Why would he be going back there? She doubted he knew anyone, but maybe he wanted to get off the main road, find a place to hide for a while. Not all, but some of the homes were summer places for the rich, euphemistically referred to as *cottages*—as though they were fairy-tale small and cute, like the one Little Red Riding Hood's grandmother lived in. Most of them would be vacant at this time of year. Perhaps Daniel planned on breaking in to one of them to hole up for a time, to wait for the cops to give up, thinking he'd taken off and was out of the area.

She reached for her cell phone, then remembered it was out of juice. *Damn*, how was she going to keep in touch with Mandy? She tossed her phone on the floor and kept driving, slowly, scanning back and forth, searching both sides of the road. She guessed Daniel would be vigilant, spooked by vehicles coming his way. He would probably hold close to the side of the road where walking would be easier than in the thick underbrush, but stay in a position to jump and dash undercover if necessary. She considered shutting off the headlights but it was way too dark.

She decided to speed up; otherwise, he'd likely interpret a slow-moving vehicle as searching for something. Moving faster would give her less opportunity to see anything, but—

Her lights flashed on something, but it slipped into the woods. Slowing down, she came up to where she'd seen the movement. Whatever was there had disappeared into the trees. She thought she'd seen a flash of color: red.

Daniel was wearing a red shirt.

Damn. It had to be Daniel. Either that, or it was her imagination willing it to be him.

No, she decided, it was a flicker of red she'd caught with her lights. She needed to trust that, at least for now. She drove around a bend in the road and pulled off at a narrow road leading into the state park. She left her vehicle by some trees, well out of sight. Now, she'd double back on foot through the woods where she'd seen the flash of red. She patted the gun in her waistband, reassuring herself.

She was getting sopping wet trudging through the spring thaw. Her leather shoes sank into the muck with each step; raising her foot out made a sucking sound and stepping down, it slushed. She soon realized sneaking up on him would be impossible, but then, he would be having the same noise problem slogging through this crap. That gave her an idea. He would be heading her way. If she stopped, stayed right where she was, she could wait for him to come to her.

A little light from the stars shone through a break in the clouds and trickled down through the leafless trees. This was the lull between the two fronts that had been forecast. The next storm was predicted to bring a lot of rain with it, so there'd be little or no light for her to see. She moved carefully around stumps, downed trees and other protrusions in the soppy earth, designed to trip up intruders. She searched for a tree that would work for what she had in mind. One that was climbable and had a solid branch to sit on, and high enough that Daniel wouldn't see her, yet low enough to jump down without killing herself. Now, the sounds of plodding through the muck would be to her advantage. And, he didn't have a gun. She did. She had no qualms about killing him if it came to that. No misgivings whatsoever.

Kera tramped around until she found the right tree for her purpose and scaled it. The limb she perched on hung about seven or eight feet up off the ground. Her hands burned from the rope and now from the tree bark. From her vantage point, she was able to see out to the road through a small opening in the trees—a spot she'd chosen in case he decided to leave the muddy trail and go to the firmer ground of the road.

Except for the scurrying noises of small critters running through the brush, it was incredibly quiet and peaceful. Her mind rehashed the scene in which Mandy had stopped her vehicle and yelled back to her: *I love you*. Hopefully, she wasn't wishing it so much that she'd made it up, like a child's imagination, or a false memory created by yearning. She worried that painful memories and desire for different outcomes might be fucking with her reality. It wouldn't be the first time it'd happened to her.

She hated waiting, dead time made her call up memories she'd rather not revisit, like being tricked by Daniel. The more she stewed about what had happened, the more pissed she felt. Her agitation was swelling. She was familiar with this kind of anger, the kind that came from not being able to control events. She was damp all over, not just from her wet pant legs but from the ooze of nervous sweat meeting the chilly night. Her heart pounded so hard that it drummed in her ears. Her breathing, now almost panting, was accompanied by her body shaking, like an engine not bolted firmly to the frame of the car.

She felt like a bomb ready to explode.

To be able to keep functioning she knew she'd have to get control of herself, fast, or she'd detonate.

It was as simple as that and as hard as that.

She held her breath, then took in air, more slowly in measured breaths. She needed something more, like weed, but she couldn't go back to the Jeep to get any, not at a time like this. If not weed, what? Words from her shaman came to her. She needed to be like the creatures of the woods who quieted themselves when their prey neared. That's what this was all about for her.

Now, sitting here, she was the predator, not the prey.

She told herself, *become one with everything, part of the eco-system, a piece of the whole.* That's what Moran would tell her, and that's what she'd do. *Become my power animal, Owl, embody its essence. Owl sits on the limb at night, becomes part of it, patient, watchful, knowing when to strike.*

She let her mind wander until it met with Owl; she became one with it, on a mission, without emotion, a case of survival.

She'd gotten to stillness. She'd be the eater, not the eaten.

She heard something slushing through the mud. She kept vigil, listening.

Not near enough yet.

The sound moved closer.

She slipped the gun out, waited, mulled over whether she should shoot the bastard or try to take him in and let the law have its way with him.

She'd just as soon shoot him.

Owl was patient, in control, and when the time came, Owl reacted from the head, not from the gut—the key to a successful mission, to a successful kill.

The slushing neared.

He had to be close but she still couldn't see him. Any starlight she'd had earlier had disappeared into the storm clouds that had arrived in the last few minutes. The wind intensified, bending the smaller branches and threatening to push her out of the tree. She gripped her branch firmly with one hand and held her weapon with the other.

The rain suddenly hit hard, sheets of it, smacking her in the face. She thought she heard him but there was too much rain belting her, still she was sure he was close. Not that she could see anything but she could feel his presence.

A flash of light, a loud cracking sound lit up the sky like day, followed by a deafening boom of thunder.

She fell, hit the ground, air knocked out of her, something sticking into her back.

Pain, everywhere.

Flashes of light, an enemy attack, back in Iraq:

Bombs exploding, gunshots…
Screams, crying…
Stomping, fleeing.
Body parts flew all around her, a head—a male's or female's? Couldn't tell. Feet, legs, and flesh separated from its whole, unidentifiable.
A blast of blood against her face, drenching her body in bright red.
Kelly's head, wide-eyed, not blinking, empty…
No body attached.
Stuff inside of her rose up, spewed out. Erupting like a geyser, projectile. She couldn't stop puking, retching. Taste of metal, melting into liquid.
Spitting out blood. Spitting out all that mattered.
She ran, going, going, going. Somewhere off this planet, out of this life.

Rain pelted her face and pulled her out of Iraq.

She tried to get up, steady herself, but a blow from behind slammed into her head, pushed her back down, burying her face in the mud.

"Get up…now!" A male voice: Daniel's.

The barrel of a gun poked into her head. She pushed up on her knees, but collapsed.

"I said, get the fuck up." A foot kicked her in the ribs. "Or you'll never get up again."

Kera struggled to her hands and knees, then slowly stood. Everything was spinning. She reached out and steadied herself on a tree trunk. She wiped her face with her mud-soaked shirtsleeve.

"Well now, it seems I have the gun. My gun," he emphasized. "Funny how life can change in a flash, eh?"

To stay on her feet, she needed to get the world to stop spiraling. The wave of thunder and lightning had moved off, along with some of the cloud cover, leaving faint light. She fixed her gaze past Daniel, using the silhouette of a tree behind him as a visual steadying-post. If she could get the tree to stop moving, she hoped the rest of her visual field might at least slow down or pause.

Daniel was talking, threatening, going on about something, but she could barely hear him. Her ears were ringing, the wind was blowing, strong and relentless.

Daniel stood about four feet from her, undoubtedly ready to fire. It was too dark for her to get a good view of his gun, but she knew it would be in his right hand and she had no doubt about where it was pointed. Any second now he would shoot, and leave her dead or dying. Weird inconsequential memories popped into her head, bits of minutiae strung together like beads on a necklace. She saw her mother cooking in the kitchen, Dee swinging in their yard, her dad sitting at his desk at City Hall.

She forced her mind back. She needed to get her bearings.

"Any last wishes?" he asked.

So, he wanted to play with her, make her squirm, see to it that her last minutes on earth were terrifying. Good, she figured it would work for her, give her time to get herself together. She'd play his sick game to her advantage.

"Why did you do it, Daniel? Why did you really kill Stacey?"

She tried to move a little, stretch out her muscles so she could get her body working again. Nothing seemed broken, though even slight movement was painful. However, she was beginning to feel more stable, more grounded, like her legs wouldn't crumble.

"I said, your last wishes, I didn't say I was up for twenty questions."

"That is my last wish, and it is only one question."

Just then a flash of lightning, off to the west, signaled another wave of the storm coming inland. The light gave her a read on where he was standing. She needed that, so she could get the right angle to attack, without getting shot.

When the darkness returned, she charged with her right leg targeted for the hand that held his gun. The impact knocked him on the ground, and the momentum took her with him. Another lightning strike provided enough illumination for her to see his gun fly off a few feet behind him and to his left where he couldn't have seen it land. Daniel got up and came at her. Not to her feet yet, she grabbed his foot and rotated it, causing him to twist to the ground. As she tried to get up, his fist smacked her on the jaw and sent her back down. Her face next to the gun. She grabbed it. Daniel took off. She fired twice, but the trees provided him cover. One of her shoes had come off in the scuffle. She scraped the mud out of it, put it on, and trudged her way to the road…

She couldn't see him.

Shit!

* * *

Kera cranked up the heat in the Jeep. She cleaned off her face, but there wasn't much she could do about the muddy, wet clothes. She drove off toward the lake, guessing that Daniel was still headed that way, and would look for a place to break into and hide out. Since he knew she was on his tail, he'd probably find the first vacant—

Fuck!

Why hadn't she remembered this before? The De Graffs had their Lakeside City home out this way. They kept it open all year round, going back and forth between Lakeside City and Lansing.

The goddamned senator has to be involved in all this.

Daniel had been heading toward his place, all along. She thought she could get to the De Graff home in less than five minutes, ahead of Daniel who had most likely taken the trail through the state park.

She spotted the De Graff cottage. She'd only seen their place from the lake side when she was on the beach, but the distinctive Cape Cod with its weathered cedar siding gave it away, along with the Michigan and US flags that flew on high poles, both in the front and back of the place.

She scanned the area for a place to park her Jeep out of sight. Two houses down from the senator's, a driveway ran alongside another cottage, appearing to coil around to the back. No cars were there, that she could see, and the house was dark. Newspapers lay soaked on the sidewalk, and fliers were stuffed in the door handle.

She pulled into the driveway and followed its curve around behind some evergreen trees. It was perfect. No one would be able to see the Jeep there.

Staying close to the neighboring homes, she crept over to the De Graff's. The senator's house was a two-story with large windows that wrapped around, giving its inhabitants a great view of the lake and wooded area. Lights were on in the house, and it smelled like the fireplace was in use.

A copse of evergreens on the side of the house would be her spot; it'd provide both cover and a decent view of the front, back, and one side of the home. Several old-fashioned lanterns stationed around the house cast a faint glow over the premises. A large window, probably a family room or maybe an office, could be seen clearly from where she stood. Somebody walked by the window—the curtains hadn't been drawn—then moved on into the adjoining room, turned on the lights, and a moment later went back to the first room. It appeared to be Jeffrey De Graff, or someone about his size, but from Kera's vantage point, she couldn't be certain.

Though she huddled close to a large spruce, the icy wind from the west still found its way through the branches and into her bones. A rock, close to the tree, was big enough to sit on and keep her off the miserable wet ground.

When was Daniel going to get here? It shouldn't be taking this long. She'd been there probably ten minutes. Then, out of the corner of her eye, she thought she spotted movement in the wooded area across the road, down about twenty yards. She watched. Nothing. Maybe an animal. The gun was muddy from being on the ground when it fell. She used the edge of her jacket to clean it off.

Now a man was at the window peering out: De Graff. A woman came up from behind and wrapped her arms around him. When she moved to his side, Kera saw Victoria.

They seemed to be watching the storm coming in; its huge white-capped waves slammed onto the shore. A lake storm never ceased to captivate Kera. Undoubtedly, the De Graffs felt the same. But they were inside and she was not. The rain ran down her face. She kept wiping it away with her sleeve to keep it from dripping into her eyes.

Kera glanced back up at the window. Victoria had left the room and was now walking through the house, lights coming on, one after another, leaving a trail of illumination. The senator sat in a chair with his back to the window, reading a newspaper.

She heard movement in the tall undergrowth near the road, almost directly across from the De Graff's front door.

It had to be Daniel.

Come on you bastard. Show yourself.

She moved off the rock and onto her knees, bending a branch back so she could get a better view.

A shadowy figure emerged from the brush and glanced around the area. Daniel! Apparently satisfied, he hustled across the road and ran up onto the porch. He pushed the doorbell, and then tightly wrapped his arms around himself, and jiggling up and down. Maybe the bell wasn't working because he then knocked…

Still not getting any response, he pounded on the door.

De Graff was in the back part of the house, near the lake, and Victoria was up on the second floor. She doubted they could hear his knocking from there.

He kept pounding.

Come on, Senator, go to the door, your psycho killer needs refuge, and his money.

Finally, De Graff got out of his chair and went to the door. After a moment, he let Daniel in. Kera followed them through the series of windows as the two men made their way through the house back to the room where the senator had been. She snuck up closer, hoping to get a better view. Maybe she'd even hear something.

Pressed up against the outside of the house, she peeked in the window. A prominent Republican was being interviewed on the television. De Graff's attention appeared to be split between Daniel and the TV. Luckily, both of them had their backs to her so she was able to watch them, but she couldn't hear what they were saying. She needed to get into the house. Hopefully, the door had been left unlocked.

She kept low as she hustled around to the front door and carefully pushed it open. If she were an invited guest, she'd have taken off her dirty shoes, but it wouldn't matter. Daniel had already left a trail of mud. Kera crept through the front living room area and down a hallway, following the mess from Daniel's shoes, until she got to the door that opened into the room where De Graff and Daniel stood. The door was more than half open, and strangely, it opened out into the hallway, not back into the room. *Thank you to the dumbass who doesn't know how to put on a door correctly.* She positioned herself in the hallway behind the door, bringing it in toward her as close as possible; that way, if Victoria came down the hall toward that room or if the men left, she wouldn't be seen.

Now, even though she couldn't see them, she'd be able to listen. The volume of the television was on a bit too loud. It made it difficult for her to distinguish the voices in the room from those on the TV. Apparently someone else—most likely the senator—felt that way too. Just then, the sound lowered.

"You knew about this project, right?" Daniel said in a stressed voice.

"Like I said, I have no idea about a campaign project, you'll have to check..."

"I know you don't want to dirty your hands in all this, but—" Daniel's voice got louder.

"I don't know who you are or why you're here or what you are talking about. I'm afraid you're going to have to leave. And if you don't go right now—"

"I thought I heard someone else down here." Victoria walked by the door Kera hid behind and into the room where Daniel and De Graff were talking. Kera got a glimpse, through the crack, of Victoria and her large dangly earrings. Goddamn, she hadn't even heard Victoria coming. It was probably because she was concentrating on Daniel and De Graff's conversation, along with the TV noise, but shit, a lapse like that could have blown her cover.

"All I had to do was follow this muddy trail on the floor," Victoria said angrily. "What's going on Jeff?...Daniel, what are you doing here? My goodness, you look like you've been rolling in—"

"You know him?"

"Well, uh, yes, honey—"

"You'd look like this too," Daniel snapped, "if you'd been out running around in the rain and mud."

"What the hell's going on here, Victoria?"

"Jeffrey, honey, I'm sorry about this. Of course you don't know Daniel, but he's been helping with one of our projects for the campaign. We're going door-to-door, polling folks to find out how they feel about issues, as well as let them know where you stand. You know, educating people. I'm sorry, I guess I failed to tell you about this particular venture. It's really going well," she added quickly. "And as you can see, Daniel is very dedicated, being out in this horrible weather."

It was hard for Kera to believe Daniel would support a moderate Republican, or do anything for one; but on second thought, it would make sense if De Graff had surrendered to the right wing of his party. He wouldn't be the only politician to make that move. Kera tried to put it together, to make sense of what she was observing: Daniel was working for Victoria on a door-to-door project, and Victoria thought that's why he was out this way tonight. Or, Daniel was doing De Graff's dirty work and it'd gotten messy, out of control, so he headed over here to get the senator to help him. Perhaps De Graff really didn't know Daniel. Maybe Daniel had been hired by someone else in the campaign, like Brian, to kill Stacey. That way, the senator could keep his hands clean—or at least appear clean.

"Well, I'm sorry Daniel," De Graff said. "I didn't know about all your efforts. I think you've gone way beyond the call of duty being out on this horrible night. I'm sorry I didn't realize who you were and what you were doing for me. Sometimes, I feel like I'm losing touch with my own campaign. I don't know who's working for me or who's doing what. Is there something I can help you—?"

"I'm sure it's nothing for you to worry about, honey," Victoria butted in. "Whatever it is, I'll take care of it. That's why I've taken such a big role in your campaign this time around. You've got enough on your plate, having to stay up with the politics of everything, all your meetings, obligations, fundraisers. I'll handle this. You go back to your program, dear. You've been waiting to watch it all day and I know it's important to you."

"Okay, thanks sweetie."

Kera saw Victoria through the crack coming toward the door with Daniel in tow, but then she turned back to her husband.

"I forgot to tell you, Brian called today—when you were out—about some project you and he had in the works. Anyway, he asked for you to call him back."

"When did he call?"

"Early afternoon, don't remember exactly." Kera watched as Victoria and Daniel passed by the door.

"Oh God, what's wrong now?" De Graff mumbled.

Kera adjusted the door just enough so she could see the senator through the crack. Scowling, he paced back and forth, periodically glancing at the television.

Kera waited for Daniel and Victoria to disappear from sight, then crept over to the staircase. She couldn't wait to hear why Daniel thought he could come here tonight. She paused at the bottom of the stairs and waited to hear a door close before heading up. She found them at the end of the hall and put her ear to the door.

"Damn it, Daniel, what are you doing at my house? I told you never to come here. If you need to talk, you—"

"There's been a complication, Tori."

He called her "Tori?"

"What do you mean 'a complication'?"

"There are two other people, now, who know what happened to Stacey."

"What do you mean, two other people know?"

"Uh, well—"

"Come on, Daniel, who are the other people?"

"Mandy Bakker and Kera Van Brocklin."

"For God's sake, Daniel, how did they find out? Don't just stand there like a pathetic stray dog. Tell me."

"It's complicated, like I said, it's too long for me to go into, but the short version of it is…well, I don't know how Mandy found out about me killing Stacey but she did. She threatened to go to the cops, so the only solution was to kill her. But then Kera came onto the scene, so I was going to have to kill her too, but—"

Holy fuck! Kera could feel her mouth drop open. *Victoria knows Daniel killed Stacey…She's a part of it.*

"I think you know how Mandy found out you killed Stacey. You're lying to me, Daniel."

He sure is. Kera wondered how Daniel thought he could get Victoria to buy that explanation. It was silent in there. Daniel must be trying to conjure up another story, another lie.

"Okay, I told her."

"What? You told Mandy? Why, for God's sake, would you do that?"

"Well…she asked me, and I was about to kill her anyway. I didn't think it would matter."

"You were going to kill Mandy?" Victoria's voice rose, but quickly lowered into almost a whisper. "Why on earth would you do that? That wasn't part of our plan."

"I…okay, let me explain."

"Tell me everything and make it the truth this time. No more lies."

"As you know, Mandy and Kera were on this big crusade to get my sister off. And if they were able to do that, it would put us in jeopardy."

"I know, you told me that on the phone, but you said you'd solved that problem. You were going to convince Mandy that

Erin had confessed to you that she'd killed Stacey, then Mandy would give up on Erin's innocence. And, that you planned to go the cops and tell them that Erin owned up to Stacey's murder. You didn't say anything about killing Mandy or Kera."

"I know what I said but I decided it wasn't going to work. Mandy and Kera wouldn't buy the confession strategy. They're relentless. They would never give up trying to prove Erin was innocent."

"For Christ's sake, Daniel, I can't believe you did this. You've screwed everything up. You've gone too far…and I don't believe for one second that you've told me the whole truth about any of this."

"Goddamn it, Victoria, we had this plan all set up and they were out to ruin it for us. And when that happened, the cops would start focusing on other people, people close to her. I'd be a sitting duck. They always suspect family, believe me, and it would have led to you too. I told Mandy I killed Stacey only because, like I said, I was going to kill her anyway. But then Kera came and all hell broke loose. I had to get out of there."

"So, you're saying that neither Mandy nor Kera is dead…Is that right?"

"No, Tori, they're not dead. I had to run, get away. That's why I'm here. Kera and that damned dog charged me and—"

"Oh my God, Daniel, you sure have fucked this up."

"It wasn't my fault. Things went to shit on me. I didn't know what to do next. I was hoping you could help me."

As Kera imagined the scene in that room, an image flashed in her mind of a silver three-hooped earring—not the one hooped pair she'd seen on Victoria's ears through the crack in the door—but the one that she'd found at the motel room in Lansing. Now, Kera realized she'd seen the identical, single three-hooped earring when Victoria opened her purse to get a tissue out when they were in the country club parking lot. That earring had been folded in a tissue and jammed into her Kleenex packet. Victoria had taken it out to get a tissue, and it had fallen on the floor. Kera had seen it, momentarily, before Victoria retrieved it, but at the time she hadn't made the connection.

Goddamn it. That earring had been right out there, inviting her to make the association with the one she'd found in Stacey's motel room—and she'd missed it! Victoria had to have been in that motel room sometime prior to Stacey's death. One of the earrings must have accidently fallen off, and sometime later, Victoria realized she'd lost one, so she'd removed it, wrapped it in the tissue, and put it in her Kleenex packet for safe keeping.

Victoria didn't just get Daniel to do it; she had to have had a part in the killing.

"My God…let me think, let me think," Victoria said in a panicky voice. "You're sure Mandy and Kera both know that you killed Stacey, right?"

"Yeah."

"And they're both still alive?"

"Yeah."

"Does anyone else know?"

"No."

"Do Mandy and Kera know any more about all this, like about me…what I did?"

"I don't think so. No, I didn't tell them…Tori, I have to get out of here, away from Lakeside City. Kera is after me and soon the cops will be too. I need a place to go, some wheels, and you've got to help me. You owe me that. I did it for you… for us."

"There is no 'us,' Daniel. There hasn't been an 'us,' not for a long time. You can't let go of that fact, can you?"

Victoria and Daniel? "Us?" Jesus!

"Daniel, I don't owe you a thing, you fucked up big-time. I'm sorry but I can't help you. But I've come up with a solution to my problem…"

Kera heard a desk drawer opening.

"What the hell are you doing, Tori?"

"Help! Help! Help! Don't do it! Stop hurting me! Daniel, stop, don't…"

"Tori, no, no. What are you—?"

A gunshot.

"What's going on up there?" De Graff yelled. "Victoria, Victoria, what's wrong, was that a gunshot?" He sounded breathless.

Kera heard his footsteps on the stairs and ducked into a nearby bedroom.

"What the hell? Oh my God, Victoria, what happened here? Are you okay?"

Kera eased out of the bedroom and peeked into what appeared to be a home office. She saw Daniel on the floor, bleeding on the white carpet. Victoria still had the gun in her hand and De Graff stood there, alternately staring down at Daniel and then up at Victoria. Neither one was in a position to notice her, so she stayed, watched.

"Oh my God." He pulled his wife to him, held her and said, "Victoria, my poor sweetheart, what happened?"

"He came at me...he, I can't..." She let the gun slip out of her hand and drop to the floor.

"Victoria, tell me, what did he do to you?"

"Daniel came at me. I, I grabbed my gun out of the drawer and told him to stop, but he still kept coming. Oh Jeff, I was so frightened, but I just meant to scare him, keep him from attacking me, but he didn't stop. He said things, nasty horrible things to me. Oh God, I had no idea he was like that. I don't understand...I don't understand at all. And now I've killed a person. I can't believe it." She put her head into his chest, sobbing.

"Honey, I'm so sorry. I can't believe that bastard would think he could get away with that, right here in our home—and with me home. What the hell was he thinking! But you did what you needed to do, dear. I'm proud of you for having the courage to use the gun. I know it had to be hard for you...I'll call the police."

Kera stepped into the room with her gun pointed at them both.

"I'm sorry, Senator, but your wife is not the little innocent female she's making herself out to be."

"Who the hell are you?" De Graff's chin dropped. Then a look of recognition spread across his face. "I remember, you were at the capitol the other day, bothering me about someone getting murdered…What the hell are you doing here?"

"Well, Senator, it's about Stacey Hendriks's murder, remember? I tried to talk to you about it but you weren't interested. But maybe you will be now. However, that's not what I what to discuss this time. We need to talk about what I've witnessed tonight."

Panic flashed across Victoria's face, but she quickly recovered her composure. "Well, well, good, then you must have heard this man threatened to rape me, didn't you?"

"No, not at all, Victoria." Kera kicked Victoria's gun under the wooden desk where it would be hard to get to. "He's evil, all right, but he didn't do that. What I heard was that you and Daniel were both in on the killing of Stacey Hendriks." Kera knelt down beside Daniel, who hadn't moved, keeping her gun on Victoria and De Graff. She felt for his pulse. He was still alive. She stood back up, glared down at him. Anger bubbled in her, like scalding water. She pointed the gun at his head, thinking about what Daniel had done to Mandy, torturing her, and how the bastard had wounded her beloved Lakota.

She needed, needed bad, to put another bullet into Daniel, finish off the piece of slime.

The world would be better off without him.

Michigan didn't have a death penalty. Usually she was in agreement with that, but right now, it felt different. Stacey would never take another breath; Erin would never have her partner back or a teaching job. Mandy would never forget the nightmare he'd put her through, and Lakota would be in pain for a long time, and she didn't know what else the bullet might have done to her.

Her anger swelled, no controls in sight…

She was becoming light-headed, hot, sweating. She looked toward Victoria and De Graff. They seemed stunned, didn't move.

Kera felt strange, detached—observing, wondering what was going to occur, believing she had no say in the matter. Her trigger finger was independent, the judge and jury, in control, ready to pronounce a death sentence.

An explosion...then another.
Ground shaking...smoke billowing,
Sand flying in her face...can't see, can't see. Shouting, screaming...
Shrapnel flying...hitting. Blood everywhere on everyone...
An arm landed at her feet.
Her hand covered her mouth, trying not to puke.
An enemy soldier on the ground, wounded...
She rolled him over with her foot, gun in hand...
Pointing, ready to fire.
Then, Wolf appeared, standing over Daniel. Its eyes imploring...
Don't shoot.

Kera felt herself being poured back into her body, like plaster into a mold. Her fog dissipated, her mind began to clear. Her gun was still pointed at Daniel's head. Her other hand was in her pocket, grasping her fetishes. The senator and his wife stood, still frozen in place, and stared at her with confused, scared expressions.

She raised the barrel of the gun, and aimed it at them, and then went over to Victoria's desk. "I hope you don't mind if I use your phone, Mrs. De Graff...I have to call the police."

CHAPTER TWENTY-FOUR

Days Later

"Hey Ally, would you hold the door open for me?" Kera was trying to get Lakota in through the door.

"Sure, be right there." Ally put down her tray.

Kera pulled a wagon, Lakota in it, through the opened door. She didn't know what she'd do without the wheels to haul Lakota around in, but it was cumbersome, heavy, and a pain in the butt getting it in and out of a vehicle.

"I've heard about Lakota and her fancy rig. How long will you have to be toting that big lug around?"

"The vet didn't know exactly. She said Lakota would let me know when she was ready. As it is, she can walk short distances without it, she gets tired quick."

"I have to say," Ally said as she squatted down by the dog, "Vinny sure did one hell of a fast job with that wagon, scrounging around for parts to make something big enough for her. Did Lakota pick the red color or was that your choice?" She chuckled.

"It was all Vinny's doing. He wanted to jazz it up and the fire-engine red was appropriate given how she'd come to my rescue. Did you see what he named this contraption?" Kera pointed along the side where black hand-painted letters spelled out *Lakotamobile.*

"Aww, that's cute." Ally popped up and went around the bar and got Lakota some dog cookies. "Do you think she knew what she was doing when she attacked Daniel?"

"I think so. She's never done anything like that before. She'll growl to get someone to back off, and would attack if I cued her, but I didn't do that. In fact, I didn't even see her at first, I was completely focused on Daniel. But before I got to him, she came flying in, like a tornado. All I can think is that she'd heard the hostility in Daniel's voice as she came through the doggie door."

"Remarkable." Ally went back behind the bar. "Have you heard anymore from the police?"

"No, not much from them, directly, but Casey keeps me well informed. Really, it's best I stay clear of Brown."

"How about I buy you a drink, on the house?" Ally asked. "You can celebrate not having to deal with him anymore."

"Thanks, I'll take you up on that."

Ally filled a mug and set it on the bar in front of her. "Erin's life in Lakeside City has been ruined. The school system doesn't want her back. They claim it's because they have to lay off teachers due to the economy and has nothing to do with Stacey's death or that she was a suspect in the case. But of course, it is about that, along with her being Wiccan and gay. Then the fact that she had a 'relationship' with both Stacey and Victoria sure didn't help."

"Yeah, it's all too much for this little town to take. Folks here will be munching on this well into the next century. Hell, it would make a big uproar in most any city, but here, it's over the top. Way over." Kera took a swig of her ale.

"Erin told me she's going to have to move. She doesn't believe she can get another teaching job, anywhere, since she won't get a decent recommendation."

"What's she going to do?"

"She's going to Alaska. She has a cousin there who's offered to have her come and stay with her. Fairbanks, or was it Anchorage? I can't remember exactly."

"When Dee and I were little and our parents pissed us off, we used to say we were going to run away and thumb a ride to Alaska." Kera couldn't help smiling, thinking of their childhood plans for escape. "I hope it goes well for her there. Hell, maybe I'll go see her someday. I'll see if Dee wants to thumb her way there with me." Kera snickered.

"That's a hoot. I can just see you two as kids, hitchhiking all the way up there, with your bandanas filled and hooked onto the end of a stick."

"Now, I'd have to scrap the thumb for my Jeep." Kera pictured her and Dee driving to Alaska. The fantasy felt good but highly unlikely.

"Do you know how Daniel's doing?" Ally asked.

"He's off the critical list. If Victoria was aiming for his heart, she missed, but not by very much. According to Dee—she hears the scuttlebutt at the hospital—it was touch and go for a while."

"It's too bad he didn't die and save the taxpayers some money." Ally left to wait on a customer.

Kera thought back to the moment she'd almost pulled the trigger on Daniel. She'd wanted to finish him off, right there, right then. But if she had, she wouldn't be sitting and having a drink. She probably wouldn't be in jail, but more likely, on the lam. Jail time was something she couldn't do. She'd rather be dead.

Ally came back. "Daniel's and Victoria's faces have been splashed all over the media. Boy, she sure must have had him on some kind of hook to get him to do what he did."

"A hook is a good word for it." Kera lowered her voice. "There's more to it. I'll tell you—it's not public, at least not yet, and I'm sure Erin doesn't know this either."

"Got ya." Ally pantomimed zipping her mouth shut.

"Victoria has been involved with Daniel, romantically, sexually, whatever the fuck it was—no pun intended—on and off for years, even when she was with Stacey and Erin. Guess it wasn't just a threesome. Come to think of it, more like a threesome plus a side dish. Apparently neither Stacey nor Erin had any knowledge of Daniel's dipping at the trough."

"Oh my god." Ally looked incredulous. "Really?"

"Yeah, Victoria had a stable full of sexual partners—even before De Graff came into the picture."

"Crazy shit. I'm sure Stacey and Erin didn't have a clue. At least I know Erin didn't. She would've gone berserk if she'd found out her brother was involved with the same woman she was—I'm sure she still doesn't know, or she'd have told me. Seems kinky or incestuous. Definitely not cool."

"It doesn't stop there." Kera sipped her drink. "A few months after Victoria left Stacey and Erin to be with Jeffrey, Stacey approached Victoria, wanting to continue their relationship, and they did—unbeknownst to Erin, of course."

"Holy shit!" Ally exclaimed. "So, Daniel found out about Stacey and Victoria and became jealous, and that's why he killed her?"

"Sort of, but not exactly. Casey told me that Victoria stopped the affair with Daniel sometime after she and the senator got married. Daniel never accepted it and hoped he'd get her back. However, Victoria continued her on-the-side relationship with Stacey. At some point, Daniel found out that Victoria was still involved with her, and that, as you can imagine, didn't sit well with him—he'd been kicked out of Victoria's sex life, but Stacey was in."

"Wow, Kera, good soap opera material. But trying to follow and understand it all is almost above my pay grade."

"A real Peyton Place."

"But if Daniel didn't kill Stacey because he was upset with her relationship with Victoria, why did he kill her?"

"Well, I'm sure Daniel was more than happy to erase Stacey from the picture—hoping he'd take her place, but the reason he killed Stacey was because Victoria wanted her dead."

"You're shitting me. Why?"

"Stacey had become too demanding for Victoria, wanted more time than Victoria was willing to give her. Victoria tried to break it off, but Stacey threatened to expose their relationship to her husband and the press. Unfortunately for Stacey, that threat was the kiss of death for her."

"Erin once told me that Tori could be ruthless when she wanted something, but this?" Ally shook her head. "I guess she didn't want to do the dirty work, so she asked Daniel to kill Stacey?"

"Well, to help her do it."

"She was involved in the actual killing. Really?"

"Yeah, Victoria promised Stacey she would continue their relationship so that she could buy time to figure out a way to shut her up and get her out of her life. And that's where Daniel came in. I'm sure it wasn't difficult to convince Daniel to kill Stacey. He was obsessed with Victoria and viewed it as a way to get back in with her, but Victoria was just leading him on and had no intention of starting back up with him. Anyway, the plan they'd concocted involved Victoria meeting Stacey at her room at the Starlight Motel in Lansing. All Victoria had to do was slip her enough drugs to put her out cold. That's when Daniel would come in and kill her, and then get rid of the body. Victoria would then take Stacey's car and dump it. That's what they did, except Daniel brought her here to kill her, instead of Lansing. I don't know why."

"Yuck." Ally grimaced. "That's the last time I'll meet up with anyone in a motel. This whole deal has been surreal…so Chicago…I wonder why she came to Stacey's service? That's really weird. She had Stacey killed, even participated in it, then went to the funeral. Grisly." Ally shuddered.

"In my opinion, she was like a pyromaniac who wants to view the aftermath of her work—and who knows, maybe she did have feelings for Stacey still. It's all really sick, but sick minds travel their own path." Kera paused. "I asked Dee, being a social worker, what she thought of Victoria—and Daniel as well. She went into this long psychological mumbo jumbo about various mental pathologies until I was sorry I'd asked her."

Ally shook her head as if she couldn't absorb it all. "Did her husband know anything about this?"

"So far, it doesn't appear that he did. And from what I observed that night at their house, I'm convinced he was clueless." Kera chuckled. "Speaking of sickos, you know how Daniel tells people his job in law enforcement caused his divorce?"

"Yeah."

"Well, Daniel got into some trouble and lost his job, and apparently his wife in the process. But what it was all about, I don't know yet. I'm sure it wasn't pretty, but stay tuned."

"Wow, how little you know about some people. I don't make a practice of drinking on the job, but I'm going to have a beer." Ally grabbed a mug. "God, it reminds me of the old Nancy Drew mysteries my mother passed down to me, but they didn't have sex, drugs, gruesomeness and sickos." She laughed. "Well, I guess it really isn't much like Nancy Drew's adventures at all."

"No, Nancy Drew was pretty tame reading, next to this. Unfortunately, this city produces way more than its share of wackos with twisted minds...Daniel, Victoria, Stacey...shit, pretty much the whole town is twisted, in one way or another, if you ask me." Kera shook her head.

"Had you suspected any of this?"

"I'm sorry to say I was pretty much in the dark. Maybe with time, I would have figured it all out. Maybe not."

"You would have gotten there, Kera. You were in the ballpark."

"Yeah, in the dugout...or maybe out in left field, somewhere." Kera laughed.

"Did Brian have any part in it?"

"A little. He lied when it came to Victoria's alibi for the night of Stacey's death."

"What was her alibi?"

"Brian backed up Victoria's story that she'd spent the whole day at the Republican headquarters in Lansing. That wasn't true. She was there for a while but left to go to Stacey's motel, then returned to the headquarters. He told me, recently, that the reason he covered for her was because Victoria threatened him, said she'd tell her husband—and the world—that he's transgender if he didn't help her."

"What a bitch! Is Brian in trouble for lying about that?"

"He only lied to me, not to the authorities. I won't say anything; I don't see the point. Besides, it's not a crime to tell me a lie, as long as he didn't lie to the cops."

"We must look like sin city to the rest of the state, to the whole nation, for that matter. Our asshole city fathers have to be having heart palpitations, suffering from severe cases of AFib over all this shit."

Kera laughed. "That's the only good to come out of all this, upsetting those old farts. But I feel bad for Mandy. It kills her hopes for changing our city's civil rights ordinance. This whole affair makes LGBT people appear even more perverted than the way many people in this town already viewed us. Even the mayor admitted that the gay inclusion issue would have to be tabled indefinitely. Mandy had her hopes up, and this was her second go at it. And that's another thing," Kera paused and cleared her throat, "I didn't support Mandy in her efforts around the ordinance. I wish I had, even though I didn't think it had a chance. But she deserved my support. It was important to her."

"You know, Kera, soon this whole issue is going to be irrelevant."

"What do you mean?"

"It's 2012, and the way the LGBT movement is going nationwide, communities like ours will be left in the dust. Attitudes are changing all over, big-time. So Lakeside City will have to come around, not because it wants to, but because it'll be known as a backward place stuck in the nineteen hundreds. And if that doesn't bother them, it won't matter because the state or national laws will supersede the city's laws."

"I like that scenario," Kera said. "I hope you're right."

"Speaking of Mandy, when does she get out of the hospital?"

"Tomorrow, with pain pills in hand." Kera felt her eyes watering. She turned away, hoping Ally couldn't see them.

She'd gone to the hospital to see Mandy every day. But the visits had been strange: They'd mostly talked about how Mandy was doing and the progress of the police's case, new information the cops were gleaning from their interrogations of both Victoria and Daniel. Neither one of them had mentioned the *I love you* they'd spoken to each other. Kera kept the visits brief because she worried that Mandy would retract her words of love. After all, Mandy had plenty of time in the hospital to realize it was Kera's fault that she was in there.

"This has been hard on you too, Kera."

"I failed her. I didn't protect her, in fact, I brought Daniel right to her." Kera wiped a tear that rolled down her face.

"Hey, you got to her in time. She's alive. She's going to be all right. You can't blame yourself for anything. No one knew who Daniel was or what he was capable of. No one."

"Well, she's better now, I'm grateful for that, but it will be Jessica that will be there for her now."

She had run into Jessica at the hospital, once coming out of Mandy's room and the other time leaving the hospital parking lot. Mandy never mentioned anything about Jessica's visits. At first Kera was excited that Mandy had asked her to take her home, but then concluded it was because Jessica had to work.

"Kera, believe me, Jessica never was in the picture. That woman was fixated on Mandy—probably still is, from what I've heard—but Mandy didn't and still doesn't want anything to do with her. Mandy talked to me about her, both before and when I visited her in the hospital a couple days ago. And, as for what it looked like that night, there were others there who saw what went down between the two of them, and have a totally different interpretation. They saw Mandy trying to dump Jessica, but Jessica kept pushing herself onto Mandy…Geez, I'm surprised you and Mandy haven't talked about that?"

Kera shook off Ally's words, hearsay interpretation. Believing what Ally said would set her up for disappointment.

She'd seen Jessica visiting Mandy.

* * *

Kera pulled in under the hospital's portico. She'd driven the Buick, with Lakota in the backseat. Given the shape Mandy's body was in, especially her broken rib, she'd need a smoother ride than the Jeep could offer. Mandy, in a wheelchair, and a nurse's aide were already outside, waiting for her.

Mandy didn't talk much on their ride home and Kera didn't know what to say. When they arrived, Kera steadied her into the house, though Mandy insisted she was doing fine and didn't need the wheelchair coming out of the hospital, saying it was merely precautionary on the part of the hospital.

"Before I came to get you, I went to the grocery store and picked up a few things I know you like to eat. If you need anything else, I'll be happy to go back for you or take you there. I know you aren't supposed to drive until your dizziness is completely gone."

"Thanks, I appreciate it." Mandy sat down on the sofa.

A second later, Mr. Moxin made his appearance. He jumped on her lap and demanded attention, then went over to Lakota and rubbed noses with her. After their initial greeting, Lakota lay down, undoubtedly tired from her trip into the house without her wagon. The cat walked around Lakota several times but soon situated himself next to her and snuggled up by Lakota's belly and closed his eyes.

"I'd say they're happy to be back together," Mandy said.

"They've missed each other." Kera felt her eyes water again. *Damn it.*

"It had to be hard on them," Mandy remarked, "not being able to be together, like they're used to…I know they love each other." Mandy patted the sofa for Kera to join her. "Sit down, let Lakota and Moxin have some time together."

"Yeah, sure." Kera could barely breathe. Mandy was so close to her. She smelled her scent, not just in her imagination like at Stacey's memorial; she was right there next her. So close, but still not touching. She wanted to grab her and hold her near, not let go, but why would Mandy ever forgive her for what happened with Daniel? She couldn't even hope that Mandy still loved her. She'd better leave, get out of there, before she made a fool of herself. "Well, I think I should go—"

"I don't think they're the only ones in this room who love each other and want to be together." Mandy reached out for Kera's hand.

"Well, no." Kera's eyes sank into Mandy's; she couldn't pull them away. "But how could you ever forgive me for sending Daniel to you? That was my fault."

"My God, Kera, there's nothing to forgive you for. You were there for me, even when you were angry and convinced I had cheated on you with Jessica. How could I ever blame you for caring about me?"

"Aren't you still with Jessica?"

"I never have been with her. She was a pest who kept trying to put her arm around me at the bar. After she did it a second time, I left the bar to get away from her, but she followed me around all that night, making her way into conversations I was having with others. That's why some people thought we were together, but I assure you I'm not and never have been interested in her."

"But she's been visiting you at the hospital. I saw her."

"I know and I didn't appreciate her coming, and told her not to come back, twice! Finally when I refused to speak to her the third time, she stopped."

"Really...I'm sorry. You know I love you, but, well, it's just that I realize I don't give you everything you want, and I can't do the living together thing, and I thought you wanted to move on, find someone—"

"Stop. Stop right there!" Mandy put her hand over Kera's mouth. "You've come a long way since your return from Iraq. Probably further than most people who've been through what you have. And there are soldiers who have PTSD that never get better at all. Look, in the past three years you've gotten your PI license, have your own detective agency, and even an employee. And there was a time, not that long ago, when you wouldn't have even listened to me or believed me if you thought I'd cheated on you."

"I didn't when you told me about it at the bar."

"I know, but you are now. You didn't walk away this time. That's big for you. You and I are on a good path, and even though you're not ready for, as you say, 'the living together thing.' I love you. That's all that matters to me, and if it never happens, I'll be okay with it." Mandy took her hand and walked her upstairs toward her bedroom.

A wave of joy washed over and sank into every cell of her being. She believed Mandy. She loved Mandy, and Mandy loved her.

"We've got lots to talk about, lots of life ahead of us, but right now, I think it's time for makeup sex," Mandy said with a sly smile.

"Hey, you just got out of the hospital. You aren't in any shape for what you're up to. We don't need to do this, I'm just happy—"

"You talk too much, Kera."

"But you're weak and hurting all over. I don't want to do anything that—"

"Not a problem." Mandy held up her bottle of prescription pain meds. "I won't feel the pain, and we'll be lying down."

Bella Books, Inc.

Women. Books. Even Better Together.

P.O. Box 10543
Tallahassee, FL 32302

Phone: 800-729-4992
www.bellabooks.com